The
PROMETHEUS
OPERATION

Also by Mark Elder

Jedcrow
Wolf Hunt

The PROMETHEUS OPERATION

Mark Elder

McGraw-Hill Book Company

New York
St. Louis
San Francisco
Toronto
Düsseldorf
Mexico

1 2 3 4 5 6 7 8 9 BPBP 8 7 6 5 4 3 2 1 0

LIBRARY OF CONGRESS CATALOGING IN PUBLICATION DATA

Elder, Mark.
The Prometheus operation.
I.   Title.
PZ4.E357Pr   [PS3555.L33]   813'.54 80-14577
ISBN 0-07-019191-3

Book design by Roberta Rezk

For Wanda

Prologue

STEFAN ROEBLING had been awake for almost an hour when he heard the motorcycle. He still was not sleeping well. His left
leg began hurting by five o'clock each morning and did not
ease off until he had been up and about for an hour or
more. Often he had to take one of the little white tablets
the doctors had given him before the pain went away, but
he always tried to work out the cramps without resorting
to the tablets. The problem was mostly circulation—so the
doctors said—and the tablets only masked that problem,
not helped it.

The motorcycle kept coming up the hill, and he recognized the familiar note of a dispatch rider's machine. It was
definitely heading for the house. He turned to look at
Gretchen. She was still asleep, lying on her side, emitting
small sighs from partly open lips. Even in the dim morning
light, her face devoid of makeup, her fine blond hair a mass
of tangles, she was still a desirable woman.

How long had it been? Only two months? *Mein Gott.*
How could so little—and so much—time have passed since
he had first seen her in the Berlin hospital? She had been a
reluctant volunteer, hating the sight of the broken bodies
but under constant pressure by her family, her friends, to
do something useful, re-enter life after the mourning pe-

riod for her husband. He had also needed something, someone, during those long, pain-filled hours when the nightmares came and the doctors talked quietly about the possibility they might have to remove the leg.

Later, when he was well enough to be allowed short furloughs, he did not go home to the family estate in Mühlhausen. Instead, he spent the time with her in her flat near the Leutzow Platz. They made love to the limits of his strength, then talked for hours, the topics not nearly so important as the closeness, the sound of each other's voice, the constant touch, reassurance, of intertwined fingers. Finally, he had been discharged from the hospital and they had come here, to his family's Bavarian retreat. Now he wondered if the world, the war, had found him again.

The motorcycle stopped outside the house, and he heard a heavy knock on the front door. Although he was sure that the *Haushälterin,* Frau Krueger, would answer, he slipped quietly out of bed and reached for his robe. Gretchen stirred but did not waken. The knock sounded again, louder and more insistent. He heard Frau Krueger moving across the main room downstairs and then the door opening.

A male voice, more accustomed to battlefields than to quiet houses, boomed out a request as Roebling sat down on a chair and pulled on his slippers. He managed the door, the needles in his left leg telling him that he should be using his cane, by the time Frau Krueger finished climbing the stairs.

She told him that a soldier was asking for him. He limped heavily to the railing of the balcony and waved the man up. The corporal took the stairs two at a time, saluted smartly, then handed Roebling a sealed envelope. Roebling signed the man's receipt book and held up the envelope. It was unmarked, except for his name.

"Are you to wait for a reply?"

"No, Herr Hauptmann."

"Then would you like some food before riding all the way back to Berlin?"

The corporal hesitated. Roebling nodded to Frau Krueger.

"Get this man some food."

"We do not have enough to feed every soldier who—"
She bit off the words as Roebling frowned.

"Come along, *junger Mann.* And try not to muddy the
floors any more than you already have!"

Roebling took the envelope back into the bedroom and
read its contents by the light from the east window. When
he had finished, he put the envelope on the small bureau,
took off his robe and slipped back into bed. Gretchen
roused, murmured his name sleepily and settled back. He
lay on his back, staring at the ceiling, waiting for the heavy
bedclothes to rewarm his feet. The ache in his left leg was a
steady throb, but he tried to ignore it. The message had
been terse, without any accompanying explanation. It was
an order.

Gretchen moved toward him sleepily, her breasts
brushing his arm. Suddenly, he did not want to leave these
mountains, the quiet forest, to go back into a world that
was a little more insane, a little more deadly, each day.
Gretchen moved again, slipping an arm across his chest.

"Stefan?" The husky voice was not as sleepy as he expected.

"I am here, *Liebchen.* Go back to sleep."

"Stefan, I am cold. Hold me."

He turned on his side and took her in his arms. She
snuggled against him, warm against his chest, his stomach,
his thighs. He lay still. Finally, she lifted her head to look
at his face.

"Liebling, what is wrong?"

He kissed her lightly. "Nothing. Nothing is wrong."

"Then make love to me, darling. I need you."

Roebling kissed her again, more deeply this time, and
began to stroke her back.

The
PROMETHEUS
OPERATION

1 A STAFF CAR met Roebling at the Berlin railway station and drove him directly to Abwehr—the German Secret Service— headquarters. The October air was unseasonably cool, and overcast skies gave everything a gray, somber appearance. It would probably rain again tonight. He was surprised by the new destruction inflicted by the American and British bombers while he was away. Some areas were nothing but piles of rubble; others held buildings that were only fire-gutted shells, their deserted hulks starkly contrasting with happier times when he had shopped along these streets, ate *sauerbraten* in small *gaststätten* and drank dark beer in local *biergärten*.

The people had changed, too. They hurried along the streets now, their eyes downcast, their faces intent on conducting their business and getting home. The respite given by the weather was only temporary. When it cleared, the bombs would fall again from the B-17s by day and the Lancasters by night.

The war was not going well for the Fatherland—despite the barrage of propaganda from Herr Reichsminister Goebbels' presses. The string of victories for the Wehrmacht had been broken by the British at El Alamein in

1942 and by the Russians at Stalingrad in the spring of this year. On July 9, a combined British and American force had invaded Sicily and was now attacking up the Italian peninsula. Mussolini's government had collapsed, but the Wehrmacht units under Feldmarschall Kesselring were holding the Gustav line at Monte Casino. However, not even Kesselring could hold such a line forever without help, and the units available—those now occupying France—could not be moved because of the feared invasion across the English Channel. No, the war was not going well at all for the Fatherland.

The staff car stopped on the Tirpitz Ufer, a stone quay alongside the Landwehrkanal, and Roebling got out. This section of Berlin had received almost no bomb damage thus far. To his right were the headquarters buildings of the various military branches. The main Defense Military building at the corner of the quay and Bendlerstrasse was untouched, as was the Wehrmacht General Staff headquarters farther down the street. He thought longingly of the Tiergarten—the zoological gardens a few blocks north, where he had spent many happy hours in the early war years—then put it out of his mind. Even if he found time for a visit, his leg would never stand the walk.

Roebling started up the walk beside a narrow side canal, leaning on his cane, the driver following with his small bag. A row of elegant townhouses faced the black waters of this side canal, seemingly nothing more than the residences of upper-class burghers. Roebling knew better. He stopped in front of 72–76 Tirpitz Ufer and looked up at the five-story graystone building. This had been his home base for two years. It was the headquarters of the Abwehr, known among the agents as the Foxes' Lair.

The guard inside the door read his orders, then called a burly security Unteroffizier, Sergeant Krause. Krause compared Roebling's face with the picture on his identification papers and told the guard to take care of his bag. Roebling followed Krause down the hall to a small elevator. They rose two flights, then walked along the corridor to an office near the end. Roebling was left in a small anteroom with a secretary he did not recognize. He took off his overcoat, and she raised an eyebrow at the Panzer insignia on his collar. He waited exactly five minutes, then was told to enter the inner office. A stocky man with a broad, peasant face and a baggy gray suit rose from behind the desk.

"Hallo, Stefan."

Roebling didn't try to conceal his surprise. "Jost?"

Heinrich Jost smiled. "It is good to see that you have not forgotten old friends."

Friends? They had been anything but that. Roebling looked around the room. The desk was plain but highly polished. The walls contained several good paintings but of varying styles and periods. The rug was genuine Persian but matched neither the desk nor the paintings. Jost had obviously improved his position but not his tastes.

"Just why have I been ordered here, Heinrich?"

Jost ignored the question, watching the way Roebling leaned on the cane.

"Sit down. Sit down. Would you like a glass of Schnapps?"

Roebling hesitated, then accepted. Jost would insist on all the formalities before revealing anything. He delighted in irritating the "aristocrats" by using their own customs against them. Jost poured two glasses, handed one to Roebling, then held his up in a toast.

"To the Führer!"

Roebling lifted his glass slightly. Jost drank deeply of the liquor. Roebling tasted his, studying Jost over the glass. Jost seemed to be in a very jovial mood.

"Now will you tell me why I am here?"

Jost smiled again. "You are still impatient, Stefan. Unfortunately, that is no longer a virtue. By the way, how is Frau Jahnke?"

Roebling took another sip of the liquor to cover his second surprise.

"She is fine. Do you know her?"

Jost's smile changed, taking on a suggestive quality. "Quite well."

"Oh?"

"Yes."

"She has never mentioned you."

The smile changed only slightly. Jost was much better at concealing his emotions now.

"I admire a discreet woman."

"I will pass along your compliment," Roebling said. "I still would like to know why I have been ordered here."

Jost feigned a sigh. "If we must." He took another swallow of the Schnapps and set the glass down. Roebling tried to quell his irritation. His leg was aching again. Jost took out a package of cigarettes, offered Roebling one, then lit his. Roebling noticed that the cigarettes were American—Lucky Strike—and that the package was now red. The last time he had seen "Luckies," the package was green. Jost inhaled deeply, holding the cigarette between his thumb and forefinger in the European manner.

"An assignment has come up requiring an agent with certain qualifications and experiences, Stefan. I—"

"I am not interested," Roebling said quickly.

"You are uniquely qualified for—"

"I said I am not interested."

"You have not heard me out."

"It will not make any difference. I am no longer an agent. I am a soldier."

"Are you?" Jost asked. "I doubt that your leg will allow—"

"Panzer commanders ride, not walk," Roebling said, his patience at an end. "And they ignore the yapping of bureaucratic lap dogs, Heinie."

For a moment, Jost lost a good portion of his control. And in that moment, Roebling caught a glimpse of an intense hatred that startled him. He had not thought their animosity went that deep, especially after four years.

"No one has called me by that nickname in a very long time, Stefan," Jost said harshly. "Shall I tell you what happened to the last man who did?"

Jost's tone was that of a man who had killed and had ordered killing. Roebling knew immediately that he had made a mistake by reminding Jost. He had coined the nickname for Jost during their training at Quenz Lake, and it was in widespread use before Jost discovered that in American slang the word meant "ass." He had intended only to repay Jost for his pomposity; he had not expected so strong a reaction. Roebling planted his cane solidly on the floor and rose.

"I have reported as ordered, Heinrich. Now you will tell me why I am here or I will leave."

Jost recovered his composure. He even recovered part of his smile.

"You are here, Stefan, because you have been transferred back to the Abwehr."

"What?"

Jost's smile widened. He was enjoying the moment. "As of now, you are a member of this section—*my* section."

"I have not received any such order."

Jost reached into his inside pocket and handed a single sheet of paper to Roebling. Roebling unfolded it. The letterhead was that of the Oberkommando der Wehrmacht. The order contained only one entry—the transfer of Captain Stefan Roebling from the Wehrmacht to the Abwehr immediately. Roebling read it a second time, his stomach sinking.

"How long do I have before I must report?"

"You have already reported," Jost said. "You will be taken by car to Quenz Lake as soon as we have finished."

"Quenz Lake?"

"I expect you will need refresher courses in several subjects, as well as the special instruction I have planned."

"And what is that?"

"You will be told when I think it is necessary."

Roebling hesitated. He needed time to think, to contact Uncle Max and a few friends, see if the transfer could be rescinded.

"I have very little with me. I must get the rest of my clothes from—"

"We will provide everything you need."

"I would like to go anyway," Roebling said. "To explain to Gretchen—"

"I will express your apologies to her personally," Jost said, smiling again. "From this time forward, you are not to contact anyone—*anyone*—without direct approval from me. Do you understand?"

Roebling flushed with anger at Jost's tone. "Are there any other restrictions I should know about?"

"Yes, but I will let the instructors inform you of those."

Jost abruptly crossed to the desk and pushed down a button on the intercom.

"Has the driver arrived yet?"

"Yes, sir. He is waiting."

"Good. Jost released the button and turned back to Roebling. "Your car is waiting, Hauptmann. You are excused."

Roebling started to respond, then realized that any outburst would only add to Jost's pleasure. He started for the door. Jost waited until Roebling had his hand on the knob.

"There is one other thing, Stefan."

Roebling looked back.

"I am now *Major* Jost. In all future conversations, I trust you will remember that and act accordingly."

Roebling nodded. "I will try, *Heinrich.*"

2 FIRST LIEUTENANT CHARLES OATES came up out of the Gorky Street metro station and walked a half block back toward Gruzinsky Val before stopping to watch. As far as he could tell, he was not being followed. Still, he would take a roundabout route to the apartment. The Russians were a very suspicious people, even of their allies, and usually had one or more members of the NKGB follow Embassy personnel around the Moscow area.

The NKGB, or Narodny Komitet Gosudarstvennoy Bezopasnosti—People's Committee of State Security—had only recently become independent of the Narodny Kommissariat Vnutrenniky Del—People's Commissariat of Internal Affairs—the dreaded NKVD which carried out Premier Stalin's political purges and ran the forced labor camps. But the separation of the two organizations had not lessened the NKGB's determination to eliminate all threats, real or imagined, to their masters.

The wind drove a blast of snow into Oates' face, and he pulled the overcoat tighter, hurrying down the narrow, crooked side street between the gloomy, irregular apartment buildings. He stopped twice more and took one side trip down a narrow alley before reaching the two-story

wooden building that was his destination. He had met a
number of workingmen hurrying home in the early-eve-
ning darkness, but none had paid him the slightest attention. If the NKGB was aware of his visits to the apartment,
he should have seen at least one of those rather obvious
men in the rumpled overcoats and unshined shoes.

Once inside the building, Oates went quickly up the
stairs and down the hall to the back. He glanced up and
down the hallway one last time, then inserted his key into
the lock and let himself in. The shades were drawn, and
one lamp in the far corner illuminated the room dimly. He
noticed Anna's coat lying on the back of a chair and stood a
moment, listening. She was in the small kitchen alcove,
humming an unrecognizable tune.

He took off the overcoat and hung it and his hat on the
wall rack near the door. The apartment seemed warm after
the street, but he doubted that it was much above fifty-five
degrees. All fuel supplies were scarce, and the Russians
were much more acclimated to the cold weather than the
Americans. Visitors to the Embassy—especially high Russian officials—usually found a way to remark about how
warm the Americans kept the entire building and how
wasteful of fuel they were.

Oates shrugged off his suit coat and laid it on the back
of the chair as he passed. At the entrance to the alcove, he
stopped. Anna was standing in a large enameled basin—
stark naked and busily sponging soap suds off her breasts.
She looked up and smiled.

"You are too soon, darling."

He smiled, admiring her composure as well as her body.

"I'll try to come early every time after this."

She made a face at him and knelt to resoak her sponge
in the pan of water.

"The building has hot water for the first time this week
and I could not pass the opportunity for a bath."

He picked up the towel and waited for her to finish
rinsing off the soap. When she reached for the towel, he
took it to her and began drying her. She snuggled against
him, shivering.

"Ohhh! I am cold. Make me warm again!"

He quit attempting to dry her and took her in his arms, feeling spots of dampness penetrate his shirt. She lifted her head for a kiss. His hands forgot the towel and began to stroke her back. She shivered again, gooseflesh rising on her skin.

"Darling, love me now."

He carried her to the narrow bed and put her down gently. She burrowed under the heavy bedclothes. By the time he had completed undressing, she had quit shivering and was waiting, ready to slip into his arms.

He tried to go slowly, to prolong their pleasure—although he had been ready to make love to her since he first saw her in the washbasin—but she would not let him. Even as he began to kiss her, stroke her breasts, she was already pulling him onto her, guiding him between her legs. Before he had fully penetrated her, she was rocking her hips, pulling him deep, then pushing him back. He could only match his movements to hers, trying to hold himself, to wait until she arched her back in the beginning spasm before giving himself up to the moment. Finally, they lay quietly, legs intertwined, exhuasted. He tried to speak, but she put a finger on his lips and snuggled deep against his chest. He drifted slowly into sleep.

Two hours later, Oates stirred and checked his watch on the bedside table. It was almost ten. If he did not leave soon, he would miss the last train back to the Embassy. He turned over and Anna awakened, holding onto him sleepily.

"Do not go yet."

"No. Not yet. We have to talk."

She shook her head slowly. "I do not want to talk. I want to love."

Oates laughed. "You're insatiable."

"What is that? I do not know that word."

"It means you're beautiful."

She laughed and hugged him. "Do you tell the truth?"

"I tell the truth."

She hugged him tighter. "Then love me again."

A sound reached his ears, and he put a finger to his lips, listening. She tensed, listening with him. Outside, the early-winter storm was blowing tiny pellets of sleet against the roof, the windows of the building. He held his breath, trying to separate the sounds. In a lull of the wind, he heard the footsteps again, coming down the corridor. He hesitated, trying to decide whether to reach for his clothes. The steps passed the door and continued on to the bathroom at the end of the hall. Anna relaxed.

"It is only Comrade Lubinsky. He has the bowel trouble."

Oates smiled in relief. "I thought it might be Comrade Chernov coming to call."

Anna snorted, sending a small puff of air through the hair on his chest.

"That pig! He would not dare come here! I would tell his fat wife! You know she is Comrade Voroshilov's niece!"

He knew. That was the reason why Grigori Chernov had become a section chief under Kliment Voroshilov, the Politburo member closest to Premier Stalin. Otherwise, the old fox would have never allowed such a borderline incompetent to remain in a position of trust. He had alienated most of the members of his own section, providing Oates with the opportunity to penetrate the security curtain surrounding the top Soviet leaders.

But even with an incompetent heading Anna's section, Oates was playing a dangerous game. The Russians technically were allies since Hitler had broken his secret nonaggression pact with Stalin. But only technically. If the Soviets had truly cooperated with the Allied intelligence services, then Oates would not be here, masquerading as a junior military attaché to the American Ambassador.

"Speaking of Comrade Chernov," Oates said, "what has been happening in your section? Have you received any more agent reports?"

"I have seen only three. Two were from the agents I told you about—the ones in Germany. One report was a list of German field commanders seen in Berlin and the dates. The other contained ship arrivals and departures at Bremen. Do you want me to get a copy of those for you?"

He thought a moment. That would give him something to send to Baltimore in the diplomatic pouch, but he doubted that the information would be of any real value.

"No. What about the third report?"

She frowned. "It was odd. I have not seen one like it before."

"Who was it from?"

"I do not know. I did not recognize the code name."

"Do you know where it originated?"

She hesitated. "I do not think it was from one of our agents. The decoded message was in English. A translation had been added, but it was not very well done. I think it may have been something that the radio monitoring section intercepted."

Oates' curiosity grew. If the Russians were intercepting and decoding American messages, then Baltimore would be very interested in knowing.

"What did it say—in English?"

She took a moment to recall. "It said that the Prometheus Operation was on schedule and to continue as planned."

"Was that all?"

"I cannot remember any more."

"Do you know what this Prometheus Operation is?"

She shook her head quickly. "Do you?"

"No," he admitted. "Are you sure you can't remember any more of the message?"

She concentrated again. "Capricorn. The message was from someone called Capricorn. I am sorry, but that is all I can remember."

"I'd like to have a copy of the full message. Can you get one for me?"

"That would not be easy. It was taken to the classified file room, and no one is allowed in there without a permit signed by Comrade Chernov or Comrade Voroshilov."

"That's too bad," he said, withdrawing a little. "I really would like to know what this Prometheus Operation is all about."

She caught the subtle movement and snuggled closer to him.

"You know I would get it for you if I could, darling, but I do not know how."

"Perhaps you could forge a pass," Oates suggested. "You said you could sign Chernov's signature almost as well as he can."

She pulled back to look at him. "But that is only for receipts and things, to make the office smooth. I could never sign something as important as a file pass. What if someone should check?"

He smiled. "You're right, of course. Forget I asked."

"You are not mad at me?"

"No." He leaned back to check his watch.

"You are certain?"

"Yes. I've got to go now."

"Can you not wait a little longer? There is a little time yet."

"I can't afford to miss my train."

Oates swung his legs out and sat up on the side of the bed. The room was very cold now. He shivered. Anna came quickly across the bed and put her arms around him.

"Please."

Oates reached for his pants. She held onto him. "I will try to get the information for you, darling. I promise I will. Stay with me tonight. I need you."

Oates looked back at her, feeling a surge of triumph intermingled with shame. Finally, he tossed the pants back on the chair and slipped back into bed. Anna locked her arms tightly around him, holding onto the one anchor she had left in this world.

3 ROGER STOREY roused, became still, then roused again as the knocking resumed.

"All right. All right! What's so bloody important that a man can't get some sleep, anyway?"

The banging ceased. Storey ran a hand over his grainy eyes, the stubble on his cheeks. His mouth was dry and his tongue felt swollen. He squinted one eye, then the other, at the light pouring through the undraped windows. It must be around noon. He tentatively stuck one foot from under the blankets and shivered. Bloody landlord had turned the furnace way down again. Just because most of the tenants worked in the mills during the day was no reason to let the rest freeze in their beds.

The knocking started again.

"Blast you! I'm up already! I'm coming!"

Storey slipped out of bed and found his pants and robe. He couldn't find his slippers, so he settled for a pair of dirty socks. The flat looked worse—much worse—in the daylight, empty gin bottles sitting on the table, dirty dishes piled high along the counter, clothes strewn across the furniture. One overloaded ashtray had been upset on the rug in front of the couch. All he needed now was for the caller to be Simpson. The old bastard had already warned him twice about maintaining the flat properly, cutting down on the noise and keeping the tarts out of the place. Storey looked around, rubbing his eyes. He had one up last night. What was her name? Louise? No, she had been the one night before last.

The knocking became louder.

"Damn you! I said I was coming!"

Storey found his crutch and hobbled to the table, his right leg swingingly freely. One of the gin bottles had a little left in the bottom. He tilted it high and sucked at the neck. The trickle barely cut through the taste in his mouth. He tossed the bottle toward the overflowing trash container and made his way to the door. It took him a moment to recognize Ortega in the dim hallway.

"You took long time, Roger. The night was bad?"

"Bloody good night until you came around. What time is it anyway?"

"After twelve," the dark little man said. "Will you not invite me in?"

"You wouldn't have a nip of something on you, would you, Luis?"

"I might," Ortega said, smiling.

"Then come in, man, come in."

Storey stood aside and Ortega entered. He was wearing the nondescript overcoat he favored, dark gray-green and made of a heavy wool. The wool cap was almost of the same material but was black. With it pulled well down over his ears, Ortega's shaggy hair looked almost like ravels in the wool where it stuck out from under the cap. To Storey, who had once traveled in better circles, Ortega reminded him of an unkempt rat—black, beady eyes deepset in the dark skin, bushy eyebrows that looked too big for the ferret face, a reedy voice that became a squeal when excited.

"What about that nip?" Storey asked before Ortega could sit down.

Ortega produced a small silver flask from underneath the overcoat. Storey's hand shook a little as he took a long pull directly from the flask. The American bourbon was not to his taste—he almost gagged once—but the effect was what mattered. Ortega smiled, not attempting to recover the flask.

"You have a good party last night?"

Storey took another drink and winked at the little man.

"Good enough, Luis. Good enough."

"You are supporting half the *putas* in Manchester, Roger. Do you wish to fuck yourself to death?"

"And I've heard all my bloody life about what great lovers you Latins are!" Storey laughed, carrying the flask as he hobbled to the window.

"Ah, maybe if I had the time. But all I have is money." Ortega paused. "What about you, Roger? Do you have plenty of money?"

Storey looked out the window. The view wasn't much. The flat was in Salford, off Ordsall Lane. In the gray winter weather, the ship canal and docks looked even more depressing than usual, the smoke from the textile mills, the steam locomotive factories and the armament and machine-tool plants blending with the fog to produce a brownish-gray haze that smothered everything. God, how he longed sometimes for the green meadows and clean air of Lancashire!

"Nobody has enough money," Storey said. "Except maybe the bloody King."

"Then perhaps you would be interested in a proposition."

Storey turned from the window. From across the room, Ortega looked even smaller and more ratlike than usual. He decided that he detested the little man—perhaps even as much as he detested himself.

"Another bloody front job?"

Ortega shook his head. "Not this time."

"What, then?"

"Something easy. Something you will like. All you must do is carry something to America for us."

"What?"

Ortega shook his head. "It is better if you do not know. You will be well paid."

Storey immediately shook his head. "I'm not getting involved in anything that will get me twenty years. You can just find yourself another—"

"This is perfectly safe, Roger. And it is not what you think. Actually, it is a small case for you to put some of your clothes in. You take it aboard ship here and you hand it to a friend inside the American customs. You will not have any trouble. We have taken care of everything."

"How?"

Ortega shrugged. "Some money has been put into the right hands at both ends. But we need a courier, someone who has a reason to go to the United States."

Storey snorted. "I have no reason to go to America."

"Your leg is not mending well," Ortega said. "I notice you still need the crutch."

"So?"

"Would not you like to have it examined by an eminent specialist in America? Would not that be a thing that a personage such as yourself would have done?"

Storey thought a moment. "You said you'd pay well. How well?"

"Five hundred pounds."

Storey managed to maintain his outward composure. "What's in the case?"

Ortega shook his head. "It is better if you do not—"

"Then count me out."

"Do not be foolish, Roger. Where else could you make so much money for just—"

"Either I know what's in the case or you can get the bloody hell out of here right now, Luis."

He screwed the cap back onto the flask and tossed it to Ortega. The gesture had just the proper theatrical flare, Storey thought.

Ortega turned the flask in his hands. "I am not alone in this, Roger. My partners would not like—"

"Bugger your partners, Luis! And get the hell out of here! Find yourself another English gentleman to deliver your goods!"

Ortega smiled ruefully. "You know we cannot do that."

Storey grinned at him. "That's your problem, chum."

Ortega lost his smile. "All right. But you must never tell anyone what you know." He paused, then lowered his voice. "The case contains gems hidden under a false bottom. They are the profits from two years of ... business transactions on these islands."

Storey whistled softly. "Must be a bloody fortune."

"Their worth is not your concern, Roger. You will be put on the ship here and met at the ship in America. I would not advise any attempts to keep the diamonds for yourself. Remember, you still have family here."

Storey smiled. Family? His mother and two brothers, the youngest of which was in Lancashire and the oldest, the one who had inherited the title, somewhere in Italy with Montgomery. Roger was the black sheep, the drunkard, the womanizer. He had always been, and his family no more cared for his welfare than he cared for theirs. One hundred years ago—hell, even fifty years ago—he would have been sent to India or America as a remittance man, one paid to travel abroad, to remove his embarrassing presence from home and hearth. Now, well, the best the family could do was send him a piddling amount each month to stay out of Lancashire. Storey's smile grew.

"Five thousand pounds. And you pay all my expenses."

"Five—I cannot agree to pay that! The others would know that I had told you—"

"Five thousand," Storey repeated.

"One thousand," Ortega said. "And the expenses."

They compromised on two thousand and expenses. Ortega immediately began listing things that Storey must do within the next few days—renew his passport, write a letter to his family telling them that he would be away for three months, notify his landlord and pay him in advance to hold the flat.

Ortega pulled out a roll of bills and counted out one hundred pounds. "This will get you started."

Storey put the money in his robe and asked for the flask again. Ortega gave it to him. Storey took another long drink, almost emptying the container. The situation had possibilities. A fortune in gems, belonging to whomever could manage to keep them. He would give the matter some thought. In fact, he would give it a lot of thought.

4 WREN CORPORAL JENNIFER UNDERWOOD knocked on the door of Major H. Geoffrey Clough's office on the fifth floor of the War Office in Whitehall and waited to be invited before entering. The major was at his desk, reading through a stack of reports from agents working with the French Underground. He lifted his head, and Jenny thought that he looked even more tired than usual. The bags under his eyes were heavier, and the full mustache, liberally sprinkled with gray, seemed to droop more at the tips.

"What is it, Jenny?"

She approached the desk and held out a single sheet of paper.

"It's an intercept, sir. Communications picked it up yesterday. They think it originated in Wohldorf for someone in the United States."

"Then send a copy over to American Intelligence."

"I thought perhaps you'd want to handle that personally, Major. It has ... It mentions Prometheus."

Clough looked up, then took the paper from her outstretched hand. He read through it quickly.

CAPRICORN. PROMETHEUS INITIATED. NOVALIS EN ROUTE. EXPECT WITHIN MONTH. ARES.

Clough read through the message a second time and tapped the paper thoughtfully with one finger. Jenny Underwood gave him a moment, then broke the silence.

"Will you need me further, Major?"

Clough looked up. "No. No, I think . . ." He didn't finish.

She turned to leave.

"Just a moment, Jenny."

"Yes, sir."

"Please close the door and take a chair."

She obeyed, suddenly uneasy. His usually absentminded but good-natured manner was gone. He seemed to focus his entire attention on her, and the effect was a little frightening. She composed herself as best she could and sat very straight in the chair.

"What do you know about the Prometheus Operation, Jenny?"

That was the question which had almost kept her from delivering the intercept to him. She had hoped that he would simply let the matter go, be too interested in the message to question her. She felt herself becoming very nervous, almost trembling, and she could not seem to regain control of her emotions.

"I . . . I was in the outer office when you met with the American Counter Intelligence Officer last week, sir. I came up to bring you those reports on Operation Firefly that you wanted. The door was ajar. I . . . I couldn't help overhearing the American ask you to watch for anything mentioning the Prometheus Operation and send the information directly along to his office."

Clough studied her closely. His expression seemed skeptical. She pressed her hands together to keep them from shaking.

"Why didn't you tell me you'd overheard us?"

"I . . . I didn't hear much, sir. As soon as I realized that I shouldn't be privy to the conversation, I left. I went back to my desk. I . . . I just never could find the right time to mention it."

The major leaned back in his chair. She had a sudden premonition that she had made a terrible mistake. She had admitted to knowing something that no one was supposed to know. Perhaps they would put her in jail, an isolation cell, for the rest of the war. She began to tremble all over, unable to control her muscles.

"I . . . I didn't mean to do anything wrong, sir. I was just afraid that the message might be . . . important and that it might get lost in all the paper that goes through here. I . . . I promise never to mention . . ." She stopped, feeling the tears running down both cheeks.

Clough's expression changed from skepticism to surprise. He found his handkerchief quickly and brought it around the desk to her.

"Easy there, Jenny girl. I didn't mean to—"

"I only wanted to help, si—sir," she managed, crying openly now. "I swear I won't tell anyone ever. I'll transfer out—out of your section or anything else you wish." She could not seem to stop either the crying or the talking.

"Jenny, please get control of yourself. I don't—"

"I mean that, sir. I'll never men—mention the Prometheus Operation to . . . to anyone, anywhere. I . . . I promise on my mother's—"

"Corporal!"

Clough's tone cut through the babble of words. Jenny jerked upright, the words ceasing. Clough pried her clenched hands apart, then held them in his own, feeling the tremors pass through her.

"Jenny, look at me."

"I—I'll be all right in . . . in a minute, sir."

"Look at me, Jenny."

She raised her eyes, suddenly thinking that her face must be a total wreck. His eyes were kind, concerned.

"How long have you been working today? Eighteen, twenty hours?"

"Two . . . Two of the girls are out with the flu, sir. I—"

"And you've been working double shifts or more for the last month, right?"

"I'm all right now, sir. Please let me go back to—"

"You're not going anywhere but home, Jenny. And don't come in tomorrow. That's an order."

"But, sir, the section—"

"I said that's an order, Corporal. I'll arrange for someone to take your place. Just go home, have a good cry if you wish, then a good sleep. The war will still be here when you come back."

"Then you—you don't want me out of the section?"

His eyes widened in surprise. "Good Lord no! Why would I transfer you?"

"Because I know about . . ." She could not make herself say the code name again.

He smiled. "It's not a big secret, Jenny. Or at least it's not one of ours. All I know about it is what you heard. The Americans think it may be an Abwehr espionage operation planned for the United States."

"Then I haven't compromised . . ."

He chuckled. "You haven't done anything wrong. In fact, I'm damned glad you overheard us. We had a long conversation that day and I was tired. I didn't remember this Prometheus business at all until you reminded me." He shook his head slowly. "God knows how many such things we miss. It's not an easy job, is it?"

"No, sir."

He helped her to her feet. Most of the trembling had subsided.

"Now you follow my orders, Jenny. I don't want to see you back here until the day after tomorrow at the earliest. And if you feel the need of it, take another day. As I said, there will be plenty of war left when you return."

She dried her eyes and offered him his handkerchief.

"Thank you, sir."

"Keep the handkerchief. And you'd better fix your face before you leave. I shouldn't want the others thinking you and I were having a lover's spat or something."

She managed a smile. "No, sir."

5 THE TREASURE ISLAND nightclub in Washington, D.C., was packed with people, drinking too much, talking too loudly, dancing almost frantically to the two orchestras as Gregory Allison followed Sheila Warren through the crowded tables. They had just finished a fast rhumba, and her performance in the green silk gown had attracted a substantial number of male eyes. Outwardly, she ignored the looks, but he noticed a more provocative swing to her hips on the trip back to the table.

Five years ago he would have enjoyed the looks, enjoyed the envy of the other men, but now something had gone out of the game. He kept remembering Cynthia, comparing Sheila with her and thinking that this affair was a mistake. Cynthia had no legitimate reason to object—she had been the one who walked out on the marriage—but he still found himself uneasy about the prospect that she might find out, might decide to ask for the divorce that neither had yet dared to mention.

He discovered that he was growing angry again, as he always did when he thought about Cynthia's unreasonableness. But damit, there was a war on! Americans were dying daily in the skies over Germany, along the Gustav line in Italy and on a score of odd-named islands in the

South Pacific. Why couldn't she understand that in such times his work had to take precedence over any personal desires?

They reached the table, and Allison held Sheila's chair for her before taking his own. She took a lace handkerchief from her bag and blotted up the perspiration in the deep vee between her breasts.

"Damn, it's hot in here."

"Have some more champagne," he suggested.

She sipped from the waiting glass and grimaced. "Ugh! That's hotter than I am!"

Allison checked his own glass, then emptied both into the ice bucket and refilled them from the half-empty bottle.

"Would you like a cigarette?"

She nodded, her auburn hair moving against the bare, white shoulders. Allison gave her one of his Camels and held his lighter for her. She inhaled deeply, then added another stream of smoke to the thick blue air. He lit a cigarette for himself and looked up to discover her watching him, her expression serious.

"Something wrong?"

"Just thinking."

"That's the one activity not permitted in this town—or haven't you heard?"

"You're very handsome, you know."

"Why, thank you—"

"And you're tall, are a good dancer. You're even amusing—most of the time—and you're great in bed. But you know all that, don't you?"

"My God, don't stop now," Allison said, smiling. "I think I'm falling in love."

"You're also a bastard," Sheila said abruptly. "One of the kind my mother kept warning me about."

Allison's smile widened. "I liked the tall and handsome part better, but I'll take all compliments wherever—"

"I'm serious, Greg. You *are* a bastard. You lied to me."

He managed to keep the smile in place. "Of course. The male handbook absolutely requires that we lie to all beautiful women at least half the—"

"I said I was serious, damnit!"

Allison inhaled deeply on his cigarette, using the movement to create a short interval for him to think. By the time he had exhaled, he was ready to bluff it through.

"I haven't lied to you, Sheila. But if you wish, I'll show you my driver's license and my law degree. Hell, I'll even have my mother send you an affidavit that I'm her darling boy."

"That's not what I meant. I don't care about—"

"Then what did you mean? Don't you believe I work in the Pentagon? I can show you my civilian employee's ID card. Or you can call Procurement there. They'll tell you that I'm an official procurer for the War Department."

"That's not funny, Greg. And you know what I'm talking about."

Allison dropped the lighthearted façade. "I'm afraid I don't know, Sheila. You'll have to tell me."

"I'm talking about you being married."

He sipped the fresh champagne to cover his relief. She had not broken his cover after all.

"Is that all?"

Sheila flushed, her neck reddening down into the space between her breasts.

"It may not mean anything to you, but it does to me. I'm not a very good Catholic, but I am a Catholic."

"I assumed you were. Most Boston Irish are."

"I think you'd better take me home," Sheila said, reaching for her handbag.

"Easy," Allison said, putting his hand on her arm. "That wasn't a crack."

Sheila pulled her arm free. "Either you take me home or I'll catch a cab. I don't go out with married men." She began to rise.

"My wife and I are separated," Allison said.

She hesitated. "When?"

"Three, almost four months ago. Before I met you."

"Is that true?"

"Your informant must be out of date. You can ask around if you don't believe me."

The anger began to fade. She sank back into the chair.

"But you are still married—technically."

"Yes, I suppose so. Technically."

She was silent a moment, then suddenly became concerned.

"Why did she leave? Were you running around on her? I can't afford to become involved in any divorce suit, Greg. My family would have a fit!"

He took a last drag on the cigarette and snubbed it out. They had been dating for a month and had been intimate for the last week. Sheila was one of those odd combinations of society women, privately liberated from the puritanical sex codes of the nineteenth century but still afraid of public and parental censure.

"You don't have to worry," Allison reassured her. "That wasn't the reason. And she doesn't have any private detectives following me around now, trying to gather divorce evidence."

"How can you be sure? She might."

He suppressed a smile at the thought of a detective trying to trail him.

"She isn't like that."

"All women are like that," Sheila said. "And you still haven't told me why she left."

Allison shrugged. "She didn't like Washington."

"Why? Washington's the place to be now. People are even moving here from New York just to get into the swim."

"Cynthia doesn't want to be 'in the swim.' At least not the kind going on here."

"What is she? Some kind of prude?"

"Let's drop it," Allison said.

Sheila studied him, some of her suspicion returning.

"Are you sure you're telling me the whole truth, Greg?"

"I've told you as much about my wife as I intend to, Sheila."

"And if I ask you to take me home?"

"That's up to you."

She lapsed into silence, wondering whether he meant the statement. He leaned back in his chair, sipping the champagne, waiting for her to decide if she would test his implied threat. The decision was delayed by a waiter bearing a folded note on a small tray. Allison took the note and unfolded it. Inside was one word scrawled in recognizable handwriting: restroom. He tipped the waiter and the man left. Allison put the note in his pocket.

"Fan mail?" Sheila asked.

"Are you jealous?"

"Of course not. Just point her out and I'll claw her eyes out."

Allison laughed. "You are Irish, aren't you?"

"Did you ever doubt it?"

"No. Excuse me a moment. I have to make a telephone call."

"To the woman who wrote the note?"

"It was a man and it's business." Allison rose. "I'll be back in five minutes."

"If you aren't, then don't come back," Sheila said, her tone not as light as she intended.

Allison entered the restroom and looked around. There were several men in the white-tiled room. To his left, one of the black attendants was helping a man get a food stain out of a white dinner jacket. Several of the stall doors were closed, and men were scattered along the rows of urinals and sinks. Allison quickly recognized Neil Davis at the sink on the far end. He was the only man not in dinner clothes. His brown suit was one of the newer single-breasted models with narrow lapels, no pocket flaps and no cuffs. The stylists had been ordered to save as much material as they could for the war effort.

Allison moved down the row of sinks and bent to wash his hands next to Davis. Davis continued combing his hair.

"You're a hard man to find," Davis said quietly. "You know how many clubs I've been to tonight?"

"What's the problem?"

"Chief Kibler wants you in Baltimore the first thing tomorrow morning."

"Why?"

"I don't know. Maybe he found out about you dating Congressman Morrissey's niece."

"I told you, Neil, this is strictly social," Allison said, irritated by the comment.

"Don't tell me. Tell Colonel Kibler. And make it good, because I don't think he'll approve of your dating the niece while you're investigating the uncle."

"I'm not using Sheila to—"

"I know that, but the Chief may not. And if the Congressman finds out—"

"I don't give a damn if Morrissey does find out," Allison said. "I'm not doing anything illegal."

Davis smiled sardonically. "You lawyers. Nothing is right or wrong any more. It's only legal or illegal."

Allison straightened and shook the excess water from his hands.

"You've delivered your message, Neil. Now why don't you just run along and let me handle my own affairs?"

Davis shrugged. "Yes, sir. You're the old pro Counter Intelligence Corps agent, Captain Allison, sir. I respectfully withdraw my unwanted advice."

Allison drew in a deep breath, then began to chuckle, his irritation evaporating.

"All right, Neil, You've made your point. Now I'd better get back to the lady in question before she gets mad and tells her uncle how this civilian named Allison left her stranded in the Treasure Island Club."

6 J. RODNEY POTTS made his way slowly but purposefully through the main lounge on the promenade deck of the Royal Mail Ship *Queen Mary,* his eyes scanning the meager crowd. Two women were playing gin at a table near the locked outer doors, a group of wounded American soldiers were swapping lies at tables near the blacked-out and heavily draped windows, and a dozen or so other mixed civilian and military passengers were scattered around the room.

Potts smoothed his bushy gray mustache with the back of his hand and continued back along the port side to the Midships Bar. The *Queen* looked good. Even with all the troop-ferrying and cargo-hauling she had done since the outbreak of the war, the crew had kept her from deteriorating too badly. True, there were occasional cigarette burns on the carpeting, and the service had fallen off a bit—the result of the younger stewards being pressed into regular Navy service—but her brass still shone, the fifty-six varieties of rare woods used throughout the ship gleamed richly, and her china and silver reflected the subdued lighting in the restaurant.

Potts stopped at the entrance to the bar and surveyed the tables near him, the row of backless stools along the shallow arc of the bar and the small clutch of tables at the far end. There were even fewer people here. Two of the nearby tables were taken by servicemen. Three civilians were engaged in a dispirited conversation on bar stools. A fourth man sat alone at a table on the far end, under the large landscape on the bulkhead. It was probably the weather. The wind was blowing a good twenty knots on the starboard quarter, and the seas were very heavy, imparting a noticeable roll to the great ship.

The *Queen Mary* rose with another swell and plunged down the back side. Even through the thick carpeting Potts could feel the life in her, the subtle sounds and vibrations from her four steam turbines, her double-helical gearboxes with their thirteen-foot-diameter driven gears, her four thirty-two-ton propellers. The bow rose again, and the vibrations changed slightly as she applied a good part of her 160,000 horsepower to the task of pushing her 80,000 tons up the next swell. He estimated that the Gray Ghost—so nicknamed because of her camouflage paint— was making better than fifteen knots, a good speed for these seas.

Potts crossed to the bar and ordered a pint. The three men at the bar glanced at him—noted his thinning gray hair, ruddy features, watery blue eyes, ample girth under the heavy tweed suit—and turned back to their discussion. Potts took a large swallow of the dark beer and brushed the foam out of his mustache.

The man sitting alone at the table under the landscape glanced around, then looked back at his drink. Potts picked up his beer and made his way across to the table, careful to match his gait to the roll of the ship.

"I say there."

The man looked up again. The eyes were a clear, deep blue and the face was slim, aristocratic. The thick brown mustache almost appeared out of place. Potts smiled in his most jovial manner.

"What say I join you, old chap? Been wanting to talk to you since we sailed. Name's Potts. Colonel J. Rodney Potts. Retired, of course."

The man took the proffered hand without rising.

"Roger Storey. I'm afraid I won't be much company, Colonel. I was just having a nightcap before turning in."

Potts pulled out the opposite chair and sat down. "Dashed sorry to hear that, Lieutenant. I was hoping we might have a good chat."

Storey's eyes changed slightly. "I'm afraid you'll have to forgive me, Colonel, but I don't recall meeting you."

Potts smiled. "We haven't met, young man, but there's no mystery about my knowing you were a lieutenant. I asked the Purser about any other British military personnel traveling in First, and he pointed you out. Can't stand much truck with civilians, so I always try to find a fellow soldier when I travel. I have met your father, Sir Henry, though."

"Oh?"

"Oh yes, quite. Met him twice. The last time in Thirty-six at a shoot in Cumberland. He was an MP at the time, as I recall."

Storey smiled. "It must have been Thirty-five, Colonel. Father resigned from Parliament in late Thirty-five and died in early Thirty-six."

"Hmmm. Sure you're right, Lieutenant, but I could have sworn it was Thirty-six. Oh well. How's the leg?"

Storey raised one eyebrow. "The Purser tell you about that too? He seems awfully well informed."

Potts sipped his beer. "Noticed it myself. It explains why you're not still in uniform. What branch?"

"Army. An armored brigade."

"Good show!" Potts said, smiling again. "Knew you'd be the lad to brighten up this voyage. Did you make the doings in North Africa?"

Storey nodded, working on his own drink. He didn't seem particularly anxious to rake it all up.

"I was there too. On Monty's staff until they insisted I retire. Got in on some of the good times, though. Both battles at El Alamein and Rommel's retreat. We sure put it to the old Desert Fox, didn't we?"

"Yes, sir."

"Is that where you got the leg? At El Alamein?"

"No. I had an automobile accident."

"In North Africa?"

"In Kensington."

"Huh! Rotten luck that! Knocked you out permanently?"

"Yes." Storey finished his drink and started to rise. "I'm sorry, Colonel, but I really must turn in. Perhaps we can—"

"Don't be dashing off, Lieutenant. Have another drink with me."

He raised a hand toward the steward. The man started over.

"Really, Colonel, I should be—"

"Stuff and nonsense, Lieutenant! Let me pull rank on you this one time. What are you drinking? Gin and tonic?" He looked at the steward. "Another gin and tonic water for the Lieutenant and another pint for me."

Storey reluctantly sat down again.

"Good lad. Now then, where were we? Oh yes. Talking about El Alamein. That was a good one, especially the second battle. Operation Supercharger. Lasted eleven days I think it was. Rommel finally threw the Sixteenth and Twenty-first Panzer Divisions against us in a pincer movement. They broke through the mine fields on the south end of the line, made a sweep around our flank, then turned north toward the sea to cut us off. But they ran into the First Armored, and those boys fought them to a standstill. The Panzers finally retreated after taking terrible losses, and we broke out shortly afterward. That the way you remember it, Lieutenant?"

"Something like that," Storey said.

"Exactly like that."

Storey shrugged. "I didn't see the entire picture the way you did, Colonel. I was just a—"

"You have permission to disagree if you wish, Lieutenant," Potts said, frowning. "I never browbeat junior officers. I encourage them to speak up."

"I really do have to go, Colonel. If you'll excuse me now, I'll—"

"Let's get this settled first, Lieutenant. I wouldn't want you to think that the old man was unfair. Just tell me what parts you disagree with, and I'll tell you where you're mistaken."

Storey leaned back, eyeing the old man. Finally, he took a sip of the fresh drink and set the glass back on the table.

"You insist, Colonel?"

"I insist, Lieutenant."

"All right. First, the two Panzer divisions were the Fifteenth and Twenty-first, not the Sixteenth and Twenty-first. Second, they turned northward early because of minefield delays and heavy air strikes. Third, they hit the positions southwest of the Alam-al-Halfa ridge which were held mainly by the Twenty-second Armored Brigade, not the First Armored."

Potts shook his head vigorously. "No, you're wrong on at least two counts there, Lieutenant. I remember very distinctly that Monty ordered—"

"Fourth," Storey continued, ignoring Potts' attempt to argue. "The operation was named Supercharge, not Supercharger, and, fifth, you weren't there."

"Weren't ..." Potts stopped, sputtering. "Now listen, Lieutenant—"

"No, you listen, Colonel. General Auchinleck commanded the Eighth Army at the first battle of El Alamein. Field Marshal Montgomery didn't take command until August. So you couldn't have been on Montgomery's staff and present at both battles."

Potts opened his mouth, then closed it under the level gaze of the blue eyes. He looked at the table a moment before speaking.

"Guess I look like a bloody fool, Storey."

"Guess you do, Colonel."

Potts looked up. "I meant no harm. I guess I just like to talk too much."

Storey sipped the drink and nodded. "You should study a little better if you plan to do this again. And don't trust the newspapers too much. They muck the details all up, then don't bother to correct them."

"Oh?"

"Yes, but I'd just forget the whole thing if I were you, Colonel. You've got a bigger problem."

"What's that?"

"Your language. You don't use the current terminology. You don't sound like a soldier, not even a staff officer."

"I don't?"

"No. You sound like the first war, like the Home Guard. Is that what you were?"

Potts nodded, looking down into his beer. "They let me go. Said they didn't need me any more after the old ticker began acting up. I . . . I don't . . ."

"Don't give it a thought, Colonel. Your secret is safe with me." Storey rose. "Now I really must be off to bed. The leg, you know."

Potts rose with him. "Thank you, Lieutenant. You're a gentleman."

Storey left, leaning heavily on his cane. Potts stared after him for a time, then slowly followed. After Storey had taken an elevator down to the main deck, Potts turned into a companionway, unlocked a hatch with a key from a large ring and relocked it behind him. At the top of the companionway he made his way forward to the captain's cabin.

His knock brought an invitation to enter. Commodore Sir James G. P. Bisset was at his desk, making an entry into the ship's log. He asked Potts to take a seat.

"Well, Colonel, how are you this evening?"

"Fine, sir, fine. Not much to do, though. Most of the passengers are under the weather."

Bisset smiled. "You know, Potts, I've come to like heavy seas. They keep the U-boats off us and the passengers quiet. I guess there truly is some good in all things."

"Quite right, sir, quite right. I noticed that you had stopped zigzagging."

"No need when the Wolfpack isn't out, and I don't want to make the passengers any more uncomfortable. She rolls much worse with the sea on her aft quarter." He paused. "Can I offer you a drink, Colonel?"

Potts shook his head. "No, thank you, sir. Just had one with Storey."

"Oh? What did you find out?"

Potts frowned at his hands. "He seems straight enough, sir. Has all the right answers and such. But something about him still bothers me. Just haven't figured out what it is yet."

"And?"

"I was thinking I might get off a query to Whitehall when we get far enough out to break radio silence."

Bisset looked skeptical. "You think that one of Sir Henry's sons, an Army veteran, might try to sabotage a British ship? I'd think that very unlikely."

Potts smoothed his mustache with the back of his hand. "Can't say I think that. Just curious, I guess."

"More likely you're bored, Colonel. How long have you been riding back and forth now? Two years?"

"A little over."

Bisset chuckled. "You just need shore leave, Potts. Like the rest of the crew."

Potts smiled. "Don't doubt you're right, sir. Don't doubt it at all. Still, I think I'll send that query."

Bisset shrugged. "Whatever you decide. You're the MI-five man."

7 LIGHT RAIN was falling from low gray clouds as the taxicab dropped off Gregory Allison at 2327 North Charles Street in Baltimore. He paid the driver, then buttoned his overcoat before hurrying up the walk. Outwardly, the landscaped grounds, the old brick structure still looked like a private residence, although the building had originally been a girls' dormitory at Goucher College. However, since January 1943 the building had been the headquarters of the U.S. Army Counter Intelligence Corps.

Allison showed his credentials to the guard at the desk just inside the front door, then made his way up the stairs to the Office of the Chief. In the anteroom, a pretty brown-haired girl in a plaid skirt and pullover sweater, smiled at him.

"Good morning, Captain. It's nice to see you again."

"Mister, Sandy, Mister," Allison said, his own smile taking the sting out of the reprimand. "Everyone in the CIC is called Mister."

"I'm sorry," the girl said. "They really ground the military system into us during WAAC training, and it's hard to break the habit."

"Just pretend you're a civilian again," Allison suggested. "That shouldn't be too hard."

She laughed. "I'm beginning to feel like one here. No one ever wears a uniform. Everything's so informal. If it wasn't for the secret messages and the classified files, I might as well be working for the lumber company again."

"If you want to learn the difference, just try quitting." Allison gestured toward the closed door to the inner office. "Is the chief in?"

"Yes, but he's on the telephone. Can I get you a cup of coffee while you wait?"

"Fine."

Allison took a seat on the leather sofa. Sandy brought the coffee over, then went back to sorting the morning mail. Allison tasted the coffee. It was strong and black. With rationing, he had learned to drink coffee without sugar, but he still preferred it sweetened.

In an odd way, the minor discomforts and inconveniences of the war bothered him more than the major disruptions in his life. That was because, unlike most other men, he had welcomed those disruptions, had been happy for the excuse to break the pattern of the dutiful son, the respectful junior law partner, the socially acceptable husband. He had been right—despite his family's and Cynthia's objections—to join the service early, to volunteer for the CIC. He had thoroughly enjoyed these last three years.

He was in the first class of the newly created Corps of Intelligence Police Investigators Training School held at the Army War College in Washington, D.C. The instructors, from the Army's Military Intelligence Division, patterned the coursework after the basic FBI courses but had no texts. Instead, they mimeographed their lectures and handed them out so that the students could compile their own training manual as they went through the sixty-one separate courses and practical problems.

They learned methods of working with the detective squads of the metropolitan police forces and agents of the U.S. Secret Service, Alcohol Tax Unit, Customs Agency Service, Narcotics Bureau, and Intelligence Unit of the Treasury Department. In addition, they studied investigative procedures, surveillance, interrogation, undercover

work, "bombs and infernal machines," sabotage and sabo-
teurs, espionage and counterespionage, systems of personnel identification, the laws of arrest, search and seizure, the
history of Nazism and Fascism and other subjects that
their instructors thought they might need. One of those
"other subjects," *Ju Jitsu,* almost convinced Greg that he
had made a mistake when the instructor discovered his
tennis reflexes and thereafter used him as the guinea pig
for all class demonstrations.

Allison had graduated at the top of his class, which re-
sulted in his assignment to the New York office. He spent a
year in New York, doing background investigations for
personnel security clearances, investigating information
leaks and keeping tabs on the activities of German sympa-
thizers. He enjoyed the duty. Cynthia hated it. He was always gone, he never talked about his work, and she had
little to occupy her time.

When the opportunity arose, Allison requested a transfer to the CIC office in Washington, hoping the change
would help. But it hadn't. The workload in Washington
was as bad as New York. She began to mention having
children. He wanted to wait until after the war, when their
lives returned to normalcy. The disagreement became an
argument, each using the child issue to vent other, deeper
grievances. He was the stronger—or at least the louder.
Her family had never indulged in emotional displays,
which put her at a disadvantage. She could not bring herself to fight openly, to release the tensions and frustrations
locked inside her. Perhaps if she had—

"You can go in now, *Mister* Allison."

Allison rose from the couch, smiling. "Let me know if
you break off with that sergeant, Sandy. We'll forget the
fraternization rule and I'll show you Washington."

She smiled, knowing that he was kidding but wishing
that he wasn't.

Colonel H. R. Kibler, Chief of the U.S. Army Counter
Intelligence Corps since May, looked up from a memorandum he was drafting as Allison entered the room.

"Sit down, Greg. I'll be with you in a minute."

Allison took the chair opposite the desk, trying to read

Kibler's expression as he continued writing. Kibler was an odd blend of West Point formality and Yankee practicality, a combination that made him an excellent commander for the CIC. Allison found himself regretting his statements to Neil Davis in the Treasure Island Club last night. He did care what this man thought of him. In fact, he had worried all the way from Washington that Kibler had discovered his indiscretion. Dating Sheila was stupid. He had done it only because—why not be honest?—it had seemed a way to punish Cynthia. Or had he been punishing himself? He was no longer sure.

Kibler finished the memorandum, buzzed Sandy and gave it to her to type.

"You made good time from Washington, Greg. Did you drive?"

"I caught the early train, sir," Allison said.

Kibler nodded. "No matter. You can pick up your car when you go back after your clothes. I'm pulling you off the Morrissey investigation, Greg. As of now, you're working out of this office."

Allison tried not to show the sudden tightening of his stomach muscles.

"May I ask why, sir?"

In answer, Kibler took a slim folder from his center drawer and handed it across the desk. Allison hesitated slightly before opening the folder, then almost sighed in relief. Inside were three standard CIC report forms, each only one page long. Allison read through them quickly. The first, from an agent in the American Embassy in Moscow, said the Russians had intercepted a radio message from "Capricorn" mentioning something called the "Prometheus Operation" and suggesting that Russian Embassy personnel might be monitoring American radio traffic. The second was a relay of a British MI-Five intercept, probably from Wohldorf, telling Capricorn that Prometheus had been initiated and "Novalis" was on the way. The third report was a recent East Coast intercept from Capricorn to Ares stating that everything was ready for Novalis' arrival.

Allison looked up at Kibler. "Is this all we have, sir?"

"That's it. We already knew about the Russians monitoring our traffic, but they picked up the wrong signal this time. Prometheus isn't one of our operations. Instead, it seems to be a planned espionage operation within the States. 'Ares' is an old code name for Abwehr headquarters."

Allison looked over the messages again. "What about Prometheus?"

Kibler smiled. "Analysis couldn't come up with anything plausible. Can you?"

"Not offhand," Allison admitted.

"If it did indicate a particular target, then you could bet that it would be a decoy. The Abwehr aren't fools."

"What about Novalis?"

"Novalis was the pen name of Friedrich Leopold, Freiherr von Hardenberg. He was a German romantic poet who died in 1801."

"What did he write?"

"Poems and treatises on philosophy, faith, nature."

"That's not much help, is it?" Allison said. "Are you sure this whole thing isn't one of those fake paper operations, something to keep us chasing our tails?"

"No," Kibler admitted. "But we can't afford to treat it as anything other than a genuine threat. That's why I want you to give it your full attention."

"Yes, sir," Allison said, his tone betraying his lack of enthusiasm.

Kibler ignored the tone. "I have an office for you downstairs, Greg. Keep me posted on your progress."

"Yes, sir."

Allison rose and started for the door.

"Greg."

Allison looked back.

"Don't take it so hard. It beats Alaskan duty."

"I don't think I understand, sir. Why would—"

"Alaska is where I would be sending you now if the Congressman had discovered that you were dating his niece."

"You know—"

"For more than two weeks now."

It took Allison a moment to respond to Kibler's smile.

"Thank you, sir."

8 STEFAN ROEBLING paid the cab driver and stood a moment on the sidewalk, looking across the street at the bare trees and brown grass of Central Park. He had forgotten how different New York, or at least the island of Manhattan, was from the great cities of Europe and Asia. The buildings were unbelievably tall, crowded together, giving the impression of a dense, brick-and-concrete forest. The park was the one feature of the city that reminded him of Europe, yet it served more to emphasize the differences than to mitigate them.

Watching from the *Queen Mary* as she docked, he had wondered again how the subsoil could support such a great concentration of weight. Almost directly in front of him was the thirteen-building cluster of Rockefeller Center, dominated by the seventy-story RCA Building, which had still been under construction during his earlier visit. Farther south was the metal-sheathed tip of the seventy-seven-story Chrysler Building and, of course, the queen of them all, the Empire State Building. Other buildings filled the areas between the tallest ones, appearing less than they were because of the giants.

The buildings in most European and Asian cities seldom reached beyond five or six stories, the result of having been built long before elevators. Also, most of the important ones were made of stone. These brick and concrete giants, guarding abnormally wide streets filled with automobiles and trucks, gave New York a newer, more modern look than cities on the Continent.

But the structures also seemed less permanent, less timeless, than their European predecessors. In less than 100 years, many of the buildings had deteriorated to the point where they looked unsafe. And even the newer buildings, the skyscrapers, seemed less solid than 500-year-old structures in Germany. Roebling could imagine what saturation bombings, such as London and Berlin had sustained, would do to this city. The buildings would quickly collapse upon one another, leaving massive piles of rubble and millions of people dead.

However, the city's major impact did not come from the buildings, the streets or even the imagined bombings. During the ride from the Hudson River dock to Central Park South, Roebling had been most impressed by the thousands of well-clothed, well-fed people jamming the streets, talking, laughing, Christmas shopping in the gaily decorated stores. He had seen Greeks, Spaniards, Italians, Chinese, a polyglot of Europeans, Asians, Americans, all coexisting peacefully while their fathers, brothers, cousins were fighting and dying daily. It took him some time to realize that he was no longer in the war. He had left the war in Europe and come to a different land, a place where the war was far away.

True, there were signs of the war all around. Billboards carried a variety of pleas to buy war bonds; sidewalk signs depicted a serious Uncle Sam pointing a finger and stating that "I want you!"; and a simple hand-lettered poster in a market window proclaimed that this was a meatless Thursday. Newspaper headlines all bannered war news, and radio broadcasts solemnly pronounced the latest results of the fighting in Italy, the decimation of the Wolfpack in the Atlantic, the rumors and speculations about the coming invasion of France by troops under General Eisenhower, the Supreme Allied Commander in Europe.

But none of these signs and broadcasts carried the urgency of air-raid sirens, antiaircraft guns, exploding bombs that the war had come to mean in Germany. And none of the New Yorkers carried the worried, exhausted look of Berliners trying to eke out a meager existence in the cracks and around the edges of the war. The simple fact was that New Yorkers were not in the war. They were spectators, receiving second- and third-hand accounts of the fighting from correspondents far away. Roebling entered the building and took the elevator to the twentieth floor.

Dr. Ernest North completed the entry in Mrs. Bramsberger's file and closed the folder, stretching to ease the tension in his back muscles. It had been a long day. He had spent the morning in surgery and had seen a steady stream of patients from two to six o'clock. Now all he wanted was a hot bath, a dry martini and a good meal before he collapsed into bed. He rubbed his eyes wearily, hoping that Carol hadn't invited the Ellisons over tonight.

There was a knock on his door, and he looked up to see Mrs. Koscino enter. She was holding a new folder and looking apologetic.

"There's one more patient in the waiting room, Doctor. I told him that you weren't taking any new patients at this time, but he insisted on filling out a form and waiting. The information is in the folder here."

North rubbed his eyes again. "I'm beat, Anna. Can't you get rid of him?"

The plump little nurse held her ground. "He's come a long way. He said you had been recommended to him by a Dr. George Lewis in Manchester."

"Manchester? I don't think I know any Dr. Lewis. Which Manchester? Connecticut, New Hampshire or Vermont?"

"The one in England, Doctor. He's British."

North felt his stomach sink. "Well then, Anna. If he's come all the way from England, I can hardly refuse to see him, now can I?"

Mrs. Koscino smiled. Her thirty years as a hospital-ward supervisor, operating-room nurse and now office manager and major-domo for one of Manhattan's more successful orthopedists had prepared her for every whim of doctor and patient.

"I'll put him in treatment room two."

"Fine. I'll be there in a moment."

North spent the next few minutes rapidly smoking a cigarette, a practice he disapproved of as a doctor but indulged in when under stress. Finally, he snubbed the cigarette out and walked down the hall to the treatment room.

The man was sitting on the edge of the examining table, his overcoat and hat neatly hung on the wall hooks. A large suitcase sat on the floor near the table. He hadn't removed any of his other clothing. North ran over his lean frame with a physician's eye, noting the slight pallor of the skin, the careful way he had propped his left foot on the table step. He opened the folder and glanced at the name on the medical history.

"Mr. Storey, I'm Dr. North. What can I do for you?"

"Dr. Lewis suggested I contact you," Roebling said. "My leg was injured in an accident. He thought you might help me. I brought some X rays of it."

Roebling took a large envelope from inside his jacket and handed it to North. North opened the envelope and held the plates up to the light.

"I'll be back in a moment, Mr. Storey."

He went down the hall to his office quickly, opened the small corner safe and took out a second envelope. Even by the dying light from the window, he could tell that the two plates were identical. He put his plate back in the safe and returned to the treatment room.

"Well, Mr. Storey. You seem to have the right leg, which is of course a bad pun since the left leg is the damaged one. Tell me, have you ever read the early romantic poets?"

"Only one, Doctor. Friedrich Leopold, Freiherr von Hardenburg."

North nodded. "You're three days late. I wasn't sure you were coming."

"The sailing schedule was changed."

"Oh? I wasn't notified. Let's go into my office."

Roebling slid off the table. North noted that he did not use the cane. Mrs. Koscino looked up from the front desk as North stepped into the hall.

"Have Sylvia and Betty left yet, Anna?"

"Yes, Doctor. Do you need something?"

"No. We'll be in my office for a while. I'm recommending another specialist for Mr. Storey. Why don't you leave too? Just lock the outer door."

"Yes, Doctor."

At his office, North let Roebling enter, then waited to make sure Mrs. Koscino was preparing to leave before closing the door. Roebling had used his cane in the hallway, under the eyes of Mrs. Koscino, but he laid it on the sofa with his overcoat now. He took a leather armchair while North extracted another envelope from the bottom of his safe. He handed it to Roebling.

"Do you always keep such information in that safe?"

"Yes. Why?"

"It's the first place the FBI would look. And the information could be taken by any burglar looking for money or drugs. What would happen to you then, Capricorn?"

North flushed with resentment at the reproving tone.

"Where else could I keep it?"

"Don't you remember any of your training?" Roebling asked.

North's flush deepened. Roebling opened the envelope and scanned the information quickly.

"Is this all you have?"

"Yes."

"You know that this is essentially worthless. You haven't even located the target yet."

"It's not that easy," North protested. "I've tried. Believe me, I have. But none of my regular sources know anything about—"

"Then why didn't you develop some new sources?"

"New sources?" North hesitated. "I have to be careful. I just can't—"

"You could get out of this office once in a while, Doctor. Projects require manpower, materiel. Both have to be moved, concentrated in one or more areas. What unusual

movements have there been lately? What new camps have
been developed in the area?"

"I—I don't know," North admitted.

Roebling began to understand why the Abwehr had
needed a special agent for this operation.

"The Abwehr sent you to this country more than six
years ago, Doctor, and it has paid you handsomely for
doing very little. Now you're going to start earning that
money—whether you like it or not."

North flinched visibly. He had almost forgotten the
scorn, the ridicule, that Roebling's tone carried. No one in
New York had ever spoken to him in that manner. He was
a respected—some even said leading—member of his community. He was married to the former Carol Simpson,
whose family owned a chain of drugstores in the city. His
past, his service for the Abwehr, had been reduced to
something more akin to belonging to a secret society rather
than espionage in an enemy country.

But Roebling had brought it all back—the discipline,
the training, the harsh language of the Quenz Lake instructors, their cold-eyed evaluation of his every move,
every word. North felt like a recruit again, standing before
an instructor after having failed to master a simple passing
of notes without being detected.

"I—I'm sorry. I'll get right on it. Maybe Martha has
something more that she—"

"Martha? Who's Martha?"

North hesitated, unsure of whether he had made a mistake.

"I asked who Martha was."

"She—she's the agent who first discovered the existence of the project."

"How do I contact her?"

"You're not supposed to do that. The instructions were
that all contact with other agents was to be through—"

"And my instructions were that you would have everything ready for me when I arrived," Roebling said evenly.
"Now you've mucked this operation up enough. If Martha
might be able to help me get it back on track, then I intend
to contact her—directly."

"But—"

"All I want from you is her name, address and recognition code."

North searched for a way out of his dilemma. "Maybe I could contact Wohldorf. If they okay it, then—"

"Are you questioning my authority as the agent in charge of this operation, Doctor?" Roebling asked.

North flinched again. "No. No, sir. Of course not. I just didn't understand that—"

"Then give me the information I requested."

North hesitated.

"Now, Doctor."

North gave him the information. Roebling made him repeat the address a second time, memorizing it.

"I can contact her for you," North offered. "You can wait in a safe house I have until—"

"I don't need it, Doctor. I intend to leave for Washington immediately."

"But—"

"And I don't want her contacted—understand?"

"Yes, sir. Can I radio Wohldorf? I was supposed to tell them when you arrived."

Roebling considered the request. "All right. But don't say anything except that I've arrived safely."

"Yes, sir."

Roebling rose and began gathering up his things. North watched, afraid to say anything that might earn him another of those scornful stares.

"Do you know how long you might be? I could—"

"I'll contact you when I need you," Roebling said.

"Yes, sir."

9 COLONEL J. RODNEY POTTS leaned against the bow rail of the *Queen Mary,* staring absently at the New York skyline, his mood matching the weather—cold and overcast. The cable from Whitehall had confirmed his suspicions but had not arrived in time for him to do anything about them. If the London people had been just a little quicker, he could have wrapped the whole thing up before the ship docked and presented the colonials with a gift-wrapped package, courtesy of His Majesty. But now—

"Mr. Potts?"

Potts turned to find a young man standing behind him, his overcoat collar turned up and his hat brim pulled down against the wind. The man was clean-shaven, his cheeks rosy from the cold. He could have easily been just another civilian except for two things—the close-cropped hair and the erect way he stood.

"I'm Potts."

The man reached into an inside pocket and brought out his credentials.

"Agent Bill Danvers, CIC. We received a telephone message to contact you."

"I know," Potts said. "I made the call."

The blunt answer put Danvers off a moment. A blast of icy wind came down the Hudson, and Danvers pulled his overcoat collar higher.

"Say, could we get out of this wind? I'm about to freeze!"

Potts started to make a comment about the American's concerns with creature comforts, then thought better of it. That was one of the problems of getting along in years. One kept growing more civil, less inclined to expend the energy to instruct the young when they needed it. Finally, Potts led the way to the drawing room on the starboard side of the promenade deck. He took a comfortable chair near a polished ebony smoking table while Danvers took off his overcoat and tried to rub some life back onto his hands. Potts waited impatiently for him to finish and sit down.

"Shall we get on with it, Mr. Danvers?"

"What? Oh. Yes." Danvers sat down. "Now what is this information you have for us?"

"Perhaps you'd better get out your notebook first. You just might want to jot something down."

Danvers looked embarrassed, then complied.

"Good," Potts said. "Now then. There was a passenger on the voyage over that I thought didn't appear quite right, so I—"

"In what way?"

"What?"

"How did he not seem right?"

Potts fished his pipe out of a pocket and began packing it with tobacco from a leather pouch.

"Perhaps that was a poor choice of words, Mr. Danvers. Perhaps I should have said that he appeared too right, too much the black-sheep Englishman he was pretending to be."

"I'm afraid I don't understand."

"And you probably never will if you keep interrupting me!" Potts said testily. "At the rate we're going, you'll have to make the voyage back with us just to get it all down."

"I'm sorry," Danvers said. "But could we start with a few facts, such as the man's name and description? We have a form for all these reports, you know, and it's much easier if I can just ask—"

"Mr. Danvers," Potts interrupted, "I've been with MI-five since you were in diapers. I don't care to be lectured on proper reporting procedures by a man thirty years my junior."

Danvers paused, his fountain pen hovering over the paper.

"You're with MI-five? Why didn't you tell the secretary that when you called?"

Potts smiled ruefully. "You Americans feel so secure. I didn't even like giving you my name over the telephone, but I had little choice. We're sailing tonight, and I didn't have time for a *tête-à-tête* in the park. My orders are to simply get the information to you and let you 'carry the ball' on this matter. I believe that is the correct expression, isn't it?"

"Uh. Yes, sir."

"Good." Potts lit the pipe, drawing hard until he had it going well. "Now then, let's get this over with. The man is using the name Roger Storey. I have a rather good description of him, along with a radiogram from Whitehall giving particulars about the actual Roger Storey, in this envelope."

Potts produced the envelope from inside his coat and handed it over. Two American officers, advance personnel for the units who would be boarding later, looked in at them, then continued on back to the main lounge. Potts frowned. If he ended up losing his cover because this young American didn't like to stand out in the cold, so help him, he would personally write a letter to Mr. Roosevelt.

"Mr. Danvers."

"Huh?"

Danvers had the envelope open and seemed fully intent on going through the entire contents, piece by piece.

"I would appreciate it if you would hear me out. You can read those items later."

"Oh. Yes, sir."

Danvers put the papers back in the envelope.

"Thank you. I'll be as brief as possible. As I said, your man is using the name of an actual Englishman, Roger Storey. He has Storey's passport and all the proper credentials, including a good knowledge of Storey's background. He even limps—Storey's right leg was damaged in an automobile accident—but he limps on the wrong leg. Do you understand my meaning?"

Danvers nodded. "Someone, probably an enemy agent, has entered the country using Storey's passport and identification."

Potts puffed on the pipe to hide his disgust. "That's rather obvious, isn't it? I was referring to the limp."

"You mean it's fake?"

Potts looked at the ceiling and silently asked the gods what England had done to deserve such allies.

"No, young man. I think the limp is real. You don't think an agent would be dumb enough to limp on the wrong leg if he had a choice, do you?"

"Oh."

Danvers looked down at his notebook, his cheeks suddenly a bit redder than they had been.

"And another thing," Potts continued. "The man had a very believable accent. So good, in fact, that he may have been reared in England."

"I see," Danvers said, making notes swiftly.

"I don't think you do," Potts said. "My point is that you should concentrate on the limp and the accent as much as on the name and description. He can change his name and physical appearance rather easily, but he probably can't change his speech or walk."

"Hey, that's right! Thank you, Mr. Potts. You've been a great help. I'm sure it won't take us long to run down this fellow."

Potts shook his head, puffing on the pipe. "Optimism is the curse of youth."

"What's that, sir?"

"Nothing, Mr. Danvers. Absolutely nothing. I do have one favor to ask, though."

"Of course. What is it?"

"Don't use my name in your report. Just credit it to an MI-five source."

"Well, I don't know. The policy is to—"

"Quite frankly, Mr. Danvers, I would have just mailed the materials to your office anonymously had I not received orders to contact you people personally. I don't have much of a role left in this war, or in this world to be truthful, but I relish what I have. And if you have any leaks in your office—"

"We don't—"

"If you have any leaks," Potts continued, "then my identity could become known and I'd be finished. Now you may see me as a doddering old fool who should have been furloughed long ago, but I don't see myself that way. Do you understand what I'm saying?"

Danvers nodded, his expression serious. "Yes, sir."

"Then you'll respect my wishes."

Danvers hesitated only a moment. "Yes, sir."

"Good. Now run along. I have things to do."

Danvers offered his hand. "Thank you, sir."

Potts shook the hand and Danvers left.

10 ERIKA HUNTINGTON excused herself from the group surrounding Secretary of the Interior Harold Ickes and worked her way through the crowd, looking for Gerald Cavanaugh. She was disgusted. The party was a total waste of time. Ickes was the only Cabinet member there, and the conversations involving him had seldom gotten beyond soil erosion and land reclamation problems.

Erika had spoken to him twice, attempting to shift the conversation to something more productive, such as the fire danger posed by Army installations placed in national forests, but had been interrupted by simpering females, anxious to show off their latest evening gowns from Garfinckel's. She had finally left him to the gaggle of overweight, overdressed Washington socialites, admiring his politician's ability to keep smiling at the meaningless chatter.

She accepted another glass of champagne from one of the roving waiters and began a slow circle of the ballroom. The men's eyes followed her as she passed, the white satin gown rustling. It was a light satin. It clung to her shapely legs, her slim hips, her long waist and full breasts, sliding, tightening, sliding as she walked. She had worn the gown deliberately for its effect on men. The deep vee in the front showed clear, creamy skin from her neck to her breasts. Added to the honey-blond hair, which brushed her shoulders lightly as she moved, and the clear blue eyes, which could promise a man more than she was willing to deliver, the effect was devastating.

However, she could find no one at this party worth the trouble. So the blue eyes ignored the ones staring at her, and the red lips remained composed, not frowning but not smiling. The message was clearly "look but don't speak," and the men let her pass. The women stared after her, trying to think of a casual way to mention that she was married to a naval officer who was now commanding a submarine in the Pacific.

As she passed another cluster of people, a dark-skinned man caught her eye. He was talking to another member of the South American diplomatic corps, but she saw the flash of recognition in his eyes, the almost imperceptible nod of the head. She raised her glass and sipped the champagne in answer. He looked back at the man to whom he was talking. Good. Very good. Everything was set.

In a far corner of the room she found her quarry, Major Gerald Cavanaugh, talking quietly with a brown-haired girl he had trapped between two chairs. Erika recognized the girl as the personal secretary to Mrs. Gracemont, their hostess. She stopped and waited. Cavanaugh finally noticed her and smiled unashamedly. The girl saw her chance and escaped. Cavanaugh sauntered over to Erika, glass in hand.

"She's a little young for you, isn't she, Gerry?"

Cavanaugh's slightly alcoholic smile widened. "Your continuous refusals have just about unhinged me, Erika. I've been reduced to seeking succor from chambermaids."

Erika wasn't amused. Cavanaugh's boyish charm, his glib chatter had long since ceased to impress her.

"I'd like to go home now, Gerry. I don't feel well."

"Lo, the proverbial headache," Cavanaugh said, saluting her with his glass. "Somehow, I expected you to be more original, Erika."

"I thought I was being original," Erika said sweetly. "I came to this party with a pain in the other end—you."

Cavanaugh held up a hand in mock dismay. "Why, Mrs. Huntington. I do believe Washington society is corrupting you."

"Why should I be different?"

She stopped, not wanting to get into a battle of insults with him. His massive ego absorbed every linguistic barb she could hurl at it. He simply could not believe that any woman—not even the wife of his best friend—could successfully resist the Cavanaugh charm, money and social position. So he continued to pursue her, which effectively made him her serf, her errand boy or escort as the situation demanded.

"Please get my coat, Gerry."

He gazed steadily at her for a long moment. Just as she thought he would refuse, he smiled again and moved off toward the checkroom.

The Washington home of Robert Andrew Huntington III and his beautiful wife was located in the northwest section, on Woodly Road not too far from Rock Creek Park. The neighborhood was expensive and genteel, dominated by the Wardman Park Hotel and stately homes and apartment buildings, although it had suffered somewhat from last year's scandal. The Hopkins Institute, a prestigious "medical center" in one of the larger apartment buildings, had been exposed by the FBI and Washington police as one of the largest houses of prostitution on the East Coast. Erika had spent months laughing secretly at the distress of her stuffy neighbors and at the worried looks on some of the capital's most important government and business leaders before visiting Judge Arthur Lederle of Detroit decreed that the famous "black book" of the Institute's clientele was to be returned, unpublished, to the FBI's files. The collective sigh that followed the judge's ruling was almost audible throughout the town.

Despite the alcohol in his system, Cavanaugh managed to squeeze his Lincoln Continental convertible into a narrow space near Erika's two-story brick colonial, then walked back to the house with her. The gate in the iron fence protested at being moved in the cold, but the sound didn't carry far among the heavy snow-laden shrubbery.

He asked for her key and she shook her head. She had made that mistake once and spent twenty minutes wrestling with him.

She saw the change in his eyes and turned toward the door. He caught her shoulders and spun her around. She tried to push him away, then went rigid as he kissed her. He pressed her to him. She stopped resisting, letting her arms fall to her sides, staring through him, beyond him. He finally pushed her back against the door, raising a gloved hand that curled into a fist. She refocused her eyes but didn't move. The only sound was his heavy breathing. Finally, he lowered the hand.

"You don't love Andy that much, damn you! I know you don't! In fact, I don't think you love him at all!"

"That really has nothing to do with it, Gerry."

"Then what does? What does it take to melt a Danish iceberg like you?"

"Only a man, Gerry. Only a man."

His hand came halfway up again, then slowly dropped back to his side. Abruptly, he turned and walked quickly out the gate, slamming it behind him. He was in the car and spinning the rear tires before she got the door unlocked.

As the door swung inward, a sound, a movement behind her, flashed a warning through her nervous system. She started to turn, to duck, but she was caught in a powerful arm, swept up and into the hallway before she could react. She tried to twist away but the arm had her pinned.

The front door slammed shut. The interior of the house had never seemed so black. She could hear something on the wall, a hand moving across the paper. She took a deep breath, preparing to scream.

The entry light came on, filling her eyes, blinding her, and a gloved hand clamped down roughly over her mouth a fraction of a second before the scream. Her lungs were full, but she suddenly felt as if she were choking. The dark edges of panic began to creep in. Suddenly, she was roughly turned and found herself staring into a pair of clear blue eyes not more than four inches from her face. The gloved hand eased its grip slightly, and she could hear the rush of her breath through the gloved fingers.

"Relax, Martha. I bring you greetings from George."

"Wha—"

The hand was removed from her mouth.

"I'll repeat myself. George sends greetings to Martha."

The fear was quickly draining out of her, being replaced by a rising anger.

"Just who do you think you—"

"I'm waiting for your acknowledgment, Mrs. Huntington."

"You jump me at my door, then calmly ask me for . . . I have a good mind to—"

"Are there any servants in the house?"

His voice was calm, pitched low. She shook her head. She couldn't see much of his face. His hat was pulled low and his overcoat collar was turned up. But even while he was looking around the downstairs area, while her anger was threatening to grow beyond her ability to control it, she still kept seeing those icy blue eyes.

"Damnit! Who are you?"

He turned to look at her, and she immediately regretted her outburst.

"I don't have time for games. Acknowledge my greeting, please."

She swallowed the intended profanity and cleared her throat.

"How is George?"

"Not at all well, I'm afraid. He cut his foot with the ax."

"What?"

She searched her memory quickly. His last statement was not part of any recognition signal that she recalled. She looked at him, puzzled. He held her gaze for a long moment, then the corner of his mouth twitched. Was he . . . He was! He was making fun of her! She wanted to fly at him, hit him, punish him for her humiliation, but her muscles only quivered involuntarily as the tension began to drain out of her.

He smiled openly. "You've been leading too peaceful a life, Erika. All you American agents have."

She nodded, a little shaky. He helped her out of her

coat and walked her to the small French sofa in the sitting room.

"Would you like some brandy?"

"No. Just give me a moment."

He watched her a moment, then left. When he reappeared, he was carrying a large suitcase and a cane. After setting the things down, he threw his overcoat across a chair arm and began to prowl the room, examining but not touching. She watched him, regaining her composure. The English tweed was slightly loose on his frame and did not match the erect way he carried himself. Perhaps she had spent too much time with old men, fat government officials, lately, but she thought she saw more than the civilian clothes allowed. She could easily imagine him in a German uniform, one of the impeccably tailored young Navy officers she remembered from her girlhood in Bremen.

"You are Novalis."

"Yes."

"And you were in the shrubbery when I—when we came home?"

"Yes."

"Then you saw—"

"Yes. Very effective. With some men. However, I'd advise you not to try that with all of them. The ones who don't have the major's breeding just might hit you."

"As you would?"

He stopped pacing and looked directly at her. She was immediately sorry she had made the remark.

"From this point on, Erika, your affairs are also my concern. After I leave, you can go back to playing your little games with the Americans."

She could not think of a suitable answer, one that might not draw his anger, so she said nothing. He stopped abruptly.

"Where's the kitchen?"

"In the back."

He motioned her up. "I haven't had anything since noon. You can fix me some eggs."

He started for the door without looking to see whether she intended to follow. She hesitated a moment, then rose. She had not performed domestic chores since marrying

Andrew Huntington, but there were more important considerations than vanity at the moment.

She managed the meal more easily than she had expected, then sat opposite him in the small breakfast nook, confining herself to coffee. He finished the eggs, asked for a second cup of coffee, then pulled a package of Camels from his shirt pocket and offered her one. She accepted. He took one for himself, lit both and left the package lying on the table. She smiled.

"What do you find amusing?"

"Your carelessness with cigarettes. They're very hard to get now. I even have trouble sometimes. American men have gotten into the habit of leaving the package in their pocket, pulling out only one cigarette at a time, so that they won't have to offer the package around."

"Oh? Thank you. I'll remember."

He leaned back in the chair, rubbing his left leg. She had noticed the slight limp during his tour of the sitting room.

"Do you know why I'm here?"

"No."

"I need information. How good are your contacts within the government?"

"What do you need to know?"

"Haven't you been briefed on Prometheus?"

"Prometheus?"

Roebling shook his head in disbelief. Either she was the wrong agent or Jost was making the operation impossible with his paranoia.

"You submitted a report about six months ago on a secret project that had been initiated somewhere in New York City."

She nodded.

"That's the reason I'm here. My job is to locate that project and find out what it is. Prometheus is the code name for the operation."

"I see."

"This operation has top priority, Erika. Headquarters thinks it may involve development of a new weapon. I need everything you can get on it and I need it quickly."

"A new weapon? I haven't heard anything about it. Who told you that?"

"It was part of my briefing."

And the reason why he had been chosen, Roebling thought bitterly. His university training had included a great deal of science and engineering. Jost had finally found a way to use his education against him.

"How long do you think it will take to get something for me?"

She was silent, thinking. "A week. Maybe longer. My source for that particular piece of information isn't aware that he's told me anything. I'll have to pick a natural setting, approach it obliquely."

He sighed. "Great! Just great! You can't bribe or threaten him?"

"Not unless you want to blow the whole operation right now," Erika said angrily. "The source was Major Gerald Cavanaugh, the 'gentleman' you saw at the front door. Just how would you suggest I go about bribing or threatening him?"

He exhaled a stream of smoke. "All right. Do it your way. How many servants do you have?"

"Servants? There's just one, a Negro woman named Mrs. Jackson. She cooks and cleans. Everyone else has gone to work for the government or in the war plants."

"Call her. Tell her to take the next week off. Two weeks if you think it will be necessary."

"Why?"

"Because I'll be staying here and I don't want her to see me."

"You can't stay here! Someone might—"

"If someone should call, my name is Roger Storey. I'm from Lancashire, and I'm an old friend of your husband's. We met in London before the war."

She was silent a moment. When she spoke, her tone carried resentment.

"You're endangering both of us unnecessarily, you know. I'm not Capricorn. I don't have to be pushed or watched to do my job."

He smiled. "You're perceptive, Erika. Now I'd appreciate your showing me to the guest room. I'm very tired."

She wanted to argue, but his eyes, his set expression told her that it would be futile at the moment. Tomorrow, when he had rested, she would try again. She rose.

"All the bedrooms are upstairs."

"Thank you."

He followed her to a guest room, carrying his things, then bowed slightly to her in the Continental manner as he said good night. In her own bed, she lay awake for some time, planning her arguments against his staying in the house, thinking about ways she could get the information for him. But his presence down the hall, his small bow at the doorway kept intruding on her thoughts, reminding her of her homeland. He was not like the other agents that she knew, yet he obviously wasn't an amateur.

She found herself speculating on what his background might be. He obviously had breeding. His English was flawless. She was sure he had served in the military, perhaps on some general's staff. Could that have been where he received the wound that made him limp? But if so, then why had he been transferred to the Abwehr, assigned to Prometheus?

Erika turned over in her bed. Admit it, she finally told herself. He had piqued her curiosity, created an interest that no man had been able to generate since Andy. It might be better if he did remain in the house, out of sight. Mrs. Jackson would be too grateful for the vacation to ever question her motives.

11 GREG ALLISON leaned back in the seat of the unmarked Chevrolet sedan, idly watching Bill Danvers work his way through the New York traffic. He was tired. They had just finished the third day of checking dock personnel, running down bus and taxi drivers, talking to anyone who might have seen Roger Storey after he had left the *Queen Mary*. But the legwork had finally paid off. They had found a cabbie who thought he had picked Storey up and who thought he had let him out along Central Park South.

The line of traffic stopped for a signal light, and Danvers glanced at Allison.

"You want to try the Central Park area before we check in?"

Allison shook his head. "Not tonight."

"I don't mind," Danvers offered. "My wife never expects me home until she sees me anyway."

"Then maybe you should surprise her for a change."

Danvers looked back at the line of cars. Allison caught the tightness of the shoulders, the sudden concentration on the motionless car ahead of them as Danvers tried to hide his disappointment. He had been a little too eager, too enthusiastic, during the three days they had been working together. Allison suspected that this was his first important investigation. He was caught up in the thought of it and hated to quit, even for the night.

"Look, I'd like to check out the Central Park area as quickly as possible, too," Allison said. "Whoever Storey really is, he has a good lead on us by now. But I think it would be a waste of time to try it tonight."

"Why?"

"What time is it?"

Danvers checked his watch. "It's only about eight."

"Yes, but the daytime doormen, cabbies, all the people we want to talk to are off duty."

"I hadn't thought of that," Danvers admitted.

"We can spend all night trying to run them down one by one at their homes or we can catch most of them on the job in about two hours tomorrow morning. They'll be a lot more cooperative then anyway."

Danvers nodded. "I get the message."

Allison smiled. "Don't worry. We'll run him down."

The traffic began to move, and Danvers turned right at the corner. Twenty minutes later, they were entering the building at 50 Broadway where the New York office of the CIC was located. They checked in with the duty officer, who told Allison that Colonel Kibler wanted him to call Baltimore. Danvers had started to sign out but held up. Allison checked the time, then chose one of the empty offices to place the call. The Baltimore switchboard told him that the chief was still in his office.

"Greg? How's it going?"

"Slowly, sir, but we're making progress."

"Have you determined whether Storey might be Novalis?"

"No, sir. In fact, we still don't know whether he's even an enemy agent. He could be nothing more than a smuggler using Storey's name and passport. According to the MI-five report, Storey was suspected of being involved with smugglers and black marketeers before he disappeared."

"That's why I called," Kibler said. "I think we can rule out that theory. We've received a follow-up report from

MI-five. Storey's primary contact with the black market, a man named Luis Ortega, has also disappeared. And on further investigation, Scotland Yard can't find any evidence that Ortega was actually involved in black marketeering or smuggling, although he allowed a number of people to believe that he was.

"MI-five's conclusion is that Ortega's pretended operations were part of a larger scheme to draw the real Roger Storey in and set him up for someone to take his place. They have a Home Guard report of a small rubber boat landing on the Lancashire coast the night before Storey left Manchester for Southampton to board the *Queen Mary*. Someone came ashore, and something was put into the boat before it rowed out again. MI-five thinks that 'something' may have been the real Roger Storey's body being taken out to a German U-boat for disposal at sea."

"Did the Home Guard report contain a description of the man who came ashore?"

"No. It was too dark for the spotter to see him clearly. But MI-five thinks the assumption is reasonable. The identity switch was set up too elaborately, too well, to be the work of smugglers. It carries all the earmarks of an Abwehr operation."

"Then you think it's Prometheus."

"I don't know what else it could be," Kibbler said.

Allison paused, thinking.

"I don't understand why they would go to all that trouble, sir. Why land in England? Why not just make up fake papers and put the agent ashore here, as they did the Operation Pastorius team?"

"I don't know," Kibler admitted.

"Unless the agent needs a better cover for whatever he plans to do," Allison said, thinking aloud. "Which means that he might expect to have his cover story challenged at some point and needs a real person's history to back him up."

"That's an idea," Kibler said. "I'll get Analysis to working on possible targets using that logic."

"Okay. But there's another explanation too. This man may not be Novalis at all. They may simply be bringing in

another *Reiseagent*—a traveling agent—as a replacement
for some of those they've lost. If he plans to spend much
time here, then he would need the more elaborate credentials, the better cover."

"That's a possibility, but I don't really think so," Kibler
said.

"You think the man is Novalis?"

"Yes."

"Then you also think Prometheus is a real operation
and that it's after something big."

"That's right, Greg. At least I want you to treat it that
way until we find out differently. As of now, you've got the
authority to use any personnel or resources you need. Just
keep me informed."

"Yes, sir."

"Any questions?"

"Have you heard anything more from Moscow?"

There was a short pause on the other end of the line.

"I'm afraid there won't be any help from there,
Greg. The contact was caught going though some files,
and our man has been ordered home—all very quietly, of
course."

"I'm sorry to hear that, sir."

"So was I," Kibler said. "Anything else?"

"No, sir."

"Then good night."

Kibler hung up, and Allison spent a few moments
thinking about the conversation. He still wasn't convinced
that Storey was connected with the Prometheus Operation
or that there even was a Prometheus Operation. He had
come to New York to check out the MI-five report on
Storey simply because he'd had no other leads to follow.
He had doubted then—and he still doubted now—that a
German saboteur would choose to sail into New York harbor on the *Queen Mary* and send his bags through customs. They simply didn't operate that way.

Allison rose and walked back into the reception area.
Danvers was still waiting, his expression curious, hopeful.

"Anything new?"

"Nothing that can't wait until morning," Allison said.

"I'd like to hear about it anyway," Danvers said. "Maybe we could—"

"Bill," Allison interrupted.

"What?"

"Go home."

"But—"

"That's an order."

Danvers hesitated a moment, then rose and retrieved his hat and coat. He said good night to the duty officer, looked at Allison once more and left. The duty officer poured two cups of coffee and brought one over to Allison.

"He's a good agent, Mr. Allison. He's still just a little too eager. He wants to work day and night."

"I wasn't knocking him," Allison said. "I was just doing him a favor."

"Oh?"

Allison sipped the coffee, ignoring the question in the duty officer's tone.

12 STEFAN ROEBLING stopped pacing the oak flooring of the study to warm his hands in front of the small fire. The room was masculine yet warm, with dark oak paneling, bookcases, a matching oak desk, leather chairs and the red brick fireplace. In some ways, it reminded him of his father's study on the estate at Mühlhausen, which his mother had kept exactly the same after his father's death in the first war.

The thought broke a barrier he had carefully yet subconsciously built, and the memories came flooding through. He did not remember his father well. He knew him primarily from faded photographs and his mother's stories of an honorable man, a good soldier, a hero killed at the battle of Verdun. He had believed those stories, transferring out of the Abwehr to his father's old regiment when the war broke out. But unless his mother had lied, this war was not like his father's war. There was no chivalry in the soldiers, no humaneness in the methods used to fight this war. The incident in North Africa had taught him that.

It seemed a long time ago now. How could he have ever been naïve enough to take the British officer's word that he would not try to escape if allowed to remain in the field hospital after treatment of the minor wound? That very night the officer had made an attempt and had killed a doctor in the process. Roebling's unit commander reprimanded him severely for his stupidity, then made him personally responsible for recapturing the prisoner—alive. Roebling had brought the man back the next day, escorting him to the commander's tent as ordered. The commander had the guards force the British officer to his knees, then ordered Roebling to shoot him. Roebling objected. The commander repeated the order. This time Roebling refused, citing the Geneva Conventions on treatment of prisoners of war. The commander struck Roebling across the face with his crop, drew his Luger and shot the man in the back of the head. For a moment Roebling thought he would be next, but the commander—remembering the position held by Roebling's uncle—decided that his punishment would be an immediate transfer to a replacement unit destined for the Russian front.

After North Africa, Roebling no longer fought for honor, for glory. After six months in Russia, he no longer fought for the Third Reich. When he was forced to find a reason, he fought for his family—his sister, Fredericka, her husband, Doktor Joseph Muehler, and for their children, Joseph Jr. and Giselda. He fought for Uncle Max and Aunt Kristina. And he fought for his mother, Marlene, until she died of pneumonia during the winter he was in Russia.

Whether or not all the things she had told him about his father, about the proud Prussian lineage of the Roeblings, were true, he was sure that she loved him. To her, he was the last of a very special line which had been decimated by wars, and she guarded that line by protecting him, even to the point of taking him and Fredericka to England during the riots of 1930. She had suffered the life of an outcast there for two years until the country became stable again under Hitler.

She had never really liked Hitler—he was a commoner and a rabble-rouser—but, like most Germans, she eventually came to admire him for giving the German people back their national pride. That had been her excuse for overlooking his occasional, then frequent excesses.

Although she was gone now, there was still Fredericka

and Joseph and the children. There were even the families who tilled the Roebling lands and shopkeepers who rented store space in Roebling buildings. He fought for them. But he also fought for himself—to stay alive until this madness had spent itself.

The iron gate at the front of the house creaked, and Roebling moved quickly to the door of the study. He switched off the lights and looked down the hallway. After a few moments he heard the sound of a key being inserted into the lock and stepped back into the room, pushing the door almost closed. The front door swung inward, and the voices were clearly audible. Erika said good night to the major. Cavanaugh asked to come in. She refused. There was a moment of silence, then he left and she shut the door. Roebling turned on the study lights.

Erika walked quickly down the hallway, and he stepped aside to let her enter. She threw her mink coat on a chair, then crossed to the liquor cabinet, chose a crystal decanter and poured two fingers of Scotch into a glass. Roebling returned to the fireplace, waiting. She sipped the drink slowly.

"Well?"

"I didn't get anything."

Roebling tried to keep his irritation out of his tone.

"Why not?"

"Because the time wasn't right to ask."

"The time . . ." Damn the woman! "You didn't do it, did you?"

"Take Gerry Cavanaugh to bed? No, I didn't."

"Why didn't you?" Roebling asked angrily. "All you have to do is give the man what he wants, then keep him from sleep until he tells you! I thought the cadre at Quenz Lake would have instructed you in these matters!"

"They tried!" Erika said, equally angrily. "But they know even less about the matter than you do! This isn't nineteen-sixteen! Mata Hari went out with high-button shoes!"

"I still think—"

"I know my business! I'm as good an agent as you are!"

"I didn't say you weren't." Roebling replied. "But I can't stay here forever. I need that information!"

"And you'll get it!"

Erika stopped, breathing rapidly. She sipped the Scotch while she recovered control.

"Listen to me a minute. I know Gerry Cavanaugh very well. He may be a jackass, but he's no fool. I've been fending him off for over a year now. If I suddenly jump into bed with him, then ask him about a secret project, that'll ring every alarm bell he has."

"Perhaps not if you—"

"Believe me, I want to get the information for you as badly as you want me to get it. However, it will take more time."

"How much time?"

"I have another date with him Friday night. The timing should be right then."

"Are you sure?"

"Of course not!"

Erika sipped the drink again.

"Look, Roger, or Novalis, or whatever your name is, I'm going to do this my way. And no matter what you say or think, I'm not a prostitute!"

The statement surprised him, stopped any immediate reply. He realized that he had been thinking of her in just that way, that he thought of all women agents as little more than prostitutes.

"You're right. I apologize, Erika. Do it your way."

Now she was the one who was surprised.

"Do you mean that?"

"Yes."

"Then your apology is accepted."

"Good. Would you like a snack before bed?"

She lifted one eyebrow.

"I'll do the cooking," Roebling offered. "I can scramble eggs fairly well."

She shook her head in disbelief. "This I have to see."

He offered her his arm, and they went out toward the kitchen.

13 IT WAS ALMOST ten o'clock Wednesday morning before Greg Allison and Bill Danvers tracked Dennis Conner to his apartment on Manhattan's West Side, just off 72nd Street. The apartment building, within five blocks of the decidedly more expensive apartments fronting Central Park, had threadbare carpets in the halls and tricycle gouges along the baseboards, on the doors.

Allison knocked on the door of Apartment 432, which was on the back side of the building. Danvers waited beside him, his hands jammed into his overcoat pockets. In the adjoining apartment a small child began to cry. Allison knocked again. The door opened to the length of the night chain and a tired woman's face appeared.

"Mrs. Connor?"

The eyes became wary, frightened at the hats, the overcoats.

"Who are you?"

Allison held his credentials up close to the crack in the door.

"We're with Army Counter Intelligence, Mrs. Connor. Is your husband home? We'd like to talk with him."

"You don't want him for the Army, do you? He's got a bad back. They said he wouldn't have to go."

"We're not here for anything like that," Allison reassured her. "We'd like his help. Is he here?"

Again, the woman looked from Allison to Danvers. "Let me see."

She closed the door. Both men waited, Allison suppressing a smile at the woman's behavior. In a few minutes the door opened again and a sleepy-eyed man peered at them. Both agents introduced themselves again while Dennis Connor, a short man with a heavy belly under his dirty undershirt, peered at their credentials. Finally, Connor took the chain off the door and let them inside. His wife ushered two small children into the kitchen and stood in the door, watching.

"Mr. Connor, we won't take any more of your time than necessary," Allison said. "We're here because we're checking all the cabs who worked the Central Park area last week. We're looking for a particular fare you might have picked up."

Connor scratched his belly, yawning. "How'dya know I worked the park? I'm an independent. I don't have no particular territory."

"We know," Danvers said. "Now about that fare. It was a man who would have had—"

"D'you guys know how many fares I pick up each week?" Connor asked in an irritated tone. "How'dya expect me to—"

"This fare would have been different," Allison said. "The man we're interested in is English, has a bad left leg which forces him to use a cane, was wearing a dark wool overcoat, gray Homburg, Harris tweed suit and dark-brown shoes."

"Look. I been up most of the night and you guys—"

"Are you telling us that you don't want to cooperate?" Allison asked, his tone suddenly very cool, very business-like.

Connor hesitated, looking from one man to the other.

"I don't haveta answer any questions if I don't want. I know my rights."

"Is there some reason why you don't wish to help your country, Mr. Connor?" Allison asked.

"I—"

"We thought you'd want to do the patriotic thing," Danvers said, taking his cue from Allison. "However, if you don't ..." He left the sentence hanging, an unspoken threat.

Connor swallowed. "I didn't exactly say I wouldn't help. I'm as patriotic as—"

"Then what did you say—exactly?" Allison asked. "We wouldn't want to misquote you in our report."

"You gonna make a report on this?"

Connor cleared his throat, sneaking a glance at his wife.

"Well, in that case, I'll tell you what I can. I wanta do everything I can to help the country. I wanted to join the Army, but my back ... Just ask anybody. They'll tell you that Dennis Connor is—"

"Have you seen the man we described?" Allison asked. "He's about six-one or two, brown hair, blue eyes—"

"Yeah. Yeah, I seen him. I picked him up in front of one of those apartment hotels on Fifty-ninth, along the south side of the park."

"Which one?"

"I don't remember for sure. I think it was between Fifth and Seventh."

"How do you know it was the same man?" Danvers said.

"He was wearing the kinda clothes you said. And he had a bad leg. I remember noticing when I took his bag. And he had an English accent."

Allison and Danvers exchanged looks. "Do you remember where you took him?" Danvers asked.

"Yeah. Yeah, I took him to Grand Central. I remember because he was in a hurry and didn't even wait for his change."

"Did he say where he was going, which train he was taking?" Allison asked, watching Danvers make notes on a small pad.

"Yeah. Well, not right out, but he asked which ticket counter to use—you know, so he wouldn't lose any time. I asked which direction he was going, and he said south. There's only one train which leaves Grand Central south at six-oh-five. That's the one to D.C."

"Is there anything else you can remember?" Danvers asked.

"No. Not right offhand. Why are you after this guy?"

"Thank you very much," Allison said. "Mr. Danvers will leave you a card. If you remember anything else, I'm sure you'll call him."

"Yeah. Yeah, I'll do that."

Out in the hallway, Allison could no longer suppress the smile.

"Mr. Connor is a very tough customer, isn't he?"

"He was," Danvers said admiringly. "Until you called his bluff."

Allison started down the stairs. "I didn't do anything but ask a few questions. He did the rest himself."

At Grand Central Terminal they spent over three hours questioning ticket sellers, concessionaires and others who had been on duty that day before they finally found a porter who remembered carrying the bag of a lame Englishman to the Washington train. Danvers questioned the man closely, almost cross-examining him, until Allison finally stepped in and thanked the man for his help. On the way back to the CIC office Danvers was silent, moody.

"What's the matter?" Allison finally asked.

"I still think it may have been a trick. It just doesn't stand to reason that a spy wouldn't cover his tracks better."

"He feels safe," Allison said. "And a good agent knows when to avoid getting too tricky. It's best to act normally whenever possible. Otherwise, you just might call the attention to yourself that you're trying to avoid. We've been lucky, you know. Our chances of tracking him this far were slim, and we still don't know where he went. He may not have stopped in Washington. He may have just switched trains there and continued down the coast."

"But you're sure he did take the Washington train from here."

Allison nodded.

"And you're going after him."

"That's my job."

Danvers shifted his hands on the steering wheel.

"Look, Mr. Allison. Can you get me assigned to you, to this case? I could be a big help, and I don't want to go back to routine security-clearance investigations when a German spy is running loose in Washington or wherever."

Allison thought of the blanket authorization that Kibler had given him to use any and all personnel, but he also remembered that Danvers was married.

"Sorry. But with the field offices being switched over to the Service Area Commands, I don't think the First Area Commander would like me pulling out any of his people."

Danvers looked up at the traffic, the muscles in his jaw working. He started to say something else, then changed his mind and was silent all the way back to the office. The office personnel noticed Danvers' frown but didn't comment. Allison chose an empty office and placed a call to Kibler.

"Glad you called, Greg. I've got something more for you."

"And I've finally got something for you, Chief," Allison said. "We've traced the man to Grand Central. He took the Washington train ten days ago at—"

"He's in Washington?" Kibler interrupted, his tone betraying an uncharacteristic excitement.

"We're not sure of that, but he took the Washington train. A porter remembers putting him on it just before it pulled out. The man then watched the train leave. There was no way he could have gotten off before—"

"I want you on the next plane to Washington, Greg," Kibler said. "We've intercepted and decoded another message from Capricorn to Ares. It stated that Novalis had arrived safely and that he was proceeding with Prometheus as planned."

Allison paused. "Then Storey is Novalis."

"Unless they have two operations on a simultaneous schedule," Kibler said.

"Yes, sir, but he still might not—"

"Hold it, Greg. Let's scramble this call."

"Yes, sir."

Allison pushed the red button on the telephone. From that point on, the words he spoke would be broken down, changed into a series of electronic tones which would sound like nothing more than static to anyone tapped into the line. A similar device in Kibler's set at Baltimore would change the tones back into words. The electronics people were getting very sophisticated these days.

"Can you hear me?"

"Yes, sir."

"Good. I want you on the next plane to Washington. I'll alert our Washington office."

"Why?" Allison asked.

"Because it has just occurred to me that Novalis' mission may be to assassinate the President."

"Assassinate . . . Isn't that highly unlikely, sir?"

"Maybe," Kibler admitted. "But we can't afford to ignore the possibility. Prometheus was a fire god, right?"

"Yes, sir."

"Isn't that somewhat analogous to an assassin—a man who 'fires' at another man? Also, the operation fits the pattern—one man, completely unknown to any Allied intelligence agency, an elaborate cover—isn't that what you want in an assassin?"

"Yes, sir, generally, but—"

"I know it sounds unlikely at first, but who would have expected Hitler to attempt a rescue of Mussolini from that hotel on the Gran Sasso d'Italia? That was supposed to be impossible too. But the German Commandos pulled it off. No, I think we have to assume that this might be an attempt to assassinate the President. Hitler's not only a madman but an increasingly desperate one."

Allison took a deep breath. "I'm still not sure, sir. If the man is an assassin, then why didn't he bring in any weapon?"

"With guns as easy to get as they are here?" Kibler asked.

There was a short silence. Kibler broke it.

"Greg, we can't afford not to act on the possibility. The President is scheduled for a trip to the Maryland retreat this weekend."

Allison whistled softly, finally understanding Kibler's concern. He looked quickly at his watch.

"If I hurry, I can make the five-o'clock plane. I'm leaving now."

"Good. I'll alert our Washington office and the White House Secret Service."

14 ERIKA HUNTINGTON smiled to herself as she watched Major Gerald Cavanaugh drive away. It had been surprisingly easy to get the information from him, especially since they had never talked about his work for General Groves. Cavanaugh was not one of her primary sources of information, and she had not tried to turn him into one. He was more valuable as an escort, a source of invitations to the right parties, a highly placed officer who could testify to her lack of interest in military secrets if anyone ever became suspicious of her.

As she locked her front door, Erika allowed herself a quiet chuckle, remembering. He had been holding forth again on her frigidity, claiming that it was destroying his manhood. She had suggested that, if there weren't enough other women in Washington, he might try his New York girlfriend again. He denied having a girlfriend in New York, and she reminded him that he had regularly taken trips to the city until a few months ago. Then he had laughed and told her that that particular girlfriend had moved. In fact, he had jilted her and she—poor thing—had fled to the top of a mountain in New Mexico to become a female hermit. He had thought the whole conversation very amusing, and she had played along, pretending not to understand the joke.

Erika started down the hall to the study. She had expected to feel only relief at having something to give Novalis, something that would get him out of her house and her life, but that relief was tempered by other, unanalyzed feelings. They had come to know each other somewhat during the week he had been her unwanted guest. For the past few nights they had sat in front of the fire and talked about the war, about Germany.

She had been home only once—to visit her parents in Bremen—since marrying Andy Huntington. That had been in the fall of 1939, and she had been there less than a week when she received a call from a Dr. Frolich. He had recruited her as an agent for the Abwehr, skillfully playing on her natural sympathies for her homeland while also darkly hinting that her parents might have to bear the brunt of any refusal. She stayed in Germany a month longer than she intended, most of the time being spent at Quenz Lake.

The instructors there expertly overcame the last of her reluctance to work against her husband's country. As she mastered the necessary skills, her enthusiasm for the game grew until they no longer bothered to remind her periodically that despite being married to a German national, her father, Erik Thorvaldsen, was still a Danish citizen and subject to deportation.

She returned to the United States in November 1939 with the code name Martha—a whimsy of Dr. Frolich's that designated her station—Washington. In Berlin, she was known as A.2495. The "A" prefix indicated that she was a regular, a professional. The "2" indicated that she worked for the Bremen subbranch, and the "495" was her number in the Abwehr registry.

By the time America finally entered the war against Germany, Erika was a fixture in Washington society, protected by the Huntington name and the carefully cultivated impression that she was Danish, not German. That deception—and thus her value to the Abwehr—was enhanced by the Huntington family's disapproving silence about their alien daughter-in-law. After Andy's transfer to submarine duty in the Pacific, Erika continued to make the social rounds, providing a sympathetic ear for the harried Congressional staffer, the impressed Naval intelligence officer, the other war widows whose husbands were being shifted from one combat theater to another. As a result, she almost always had something of value for Rudolph to put into the Argentine Embassy diplomatic pouch. She would pass along this latest tidbit too, after she had had "Michael" check it out.

The conversation had finally turned to Novalis, his private life. He told her very little, only that he wasn't married and had little family left. She kept asking questions, but he would not tell her more, not even his real name. She knew that he was following standard procedure, but she also suspected that he did not completely trust her. The thought bothered her, but she had not let him see. She reached the study door, put on a smile, then went in.

The following night, Saturday night, Erika dropped Roebling off two blocks from Union Station. The lobby was crowded with people, mostly servicemen and young women clerks trying to get away for a day. He stood in line for a ticket to New York, then walked around to kill time until the train was called.

Passing through the crowd, Roebling kept his eyes moving, trying to spot anyone who might be watching him. The people looked tired but happy. The loudspeakers were playing Christmas carols, and a good number of people were carrying brightly wrapped packages. Back home, the radios would also be playing Christmas music—between the propagandized news broadcasts and the Führer's speeches—but it would not have the same happy ring in cold homes with empty pantries. He had almost forgotten what peace was like, how normal life was lived.

Roebling caught himself not putting any real weight on the cane and corrected his walk immediately, rebuking himself. He must not forget again, succumb to the lure of peace and normalcy, however tempting. He shifted his grip on the suitcase, his eyes sweeping the faces around him.

None were watching. He crossed to a bank of chairs and found a seat. By Storey's watch, a Rolex, he had fifteen minutes more to wait before the train to New York would be boarding. He fished one cigarette out of the package in his coat pocket and lit it. A young man in a dark-blue overcoat, a folded newspaper under his arm, strolled by, glanced at Roebling and stopped.

"Pardon me, but I wonder if I could have a light?"

Roebling looked up at the face. The brown eyes were clear, the skin healthy, the hair trimmed short. From the way the man moved, he was in excellent physical condition. Roebling found the matches in his coat pocket and handed the box to the man. He lit a cigarette and puffed on it before handing the box back.

"Thank you very much. Is this seat taken?"

Roebling shook his head. The man sat down.

"What outfit were you with?"

Roebling lifted an eyebrow. The man pointed to the cane.

"I assumed you had been wounded and sent home."

"That's partially right," Roebling said in clipped British tones. "It wasn't your army though, and this isn't my home."

"You're English?"

"Yes."

"Well then, welcome to America. I'm Neil Davis."

He held out his hand, and Roebling shook it perfunctorily.

"Roger Storey."

"Been here long, Mr. Storey?"

Roebling shook his head.

"Well, I hope you like us. I admire your people's courage. You held on through the German blitz when we all thought you had to go under."

"We managed to muddle through," Roebling said. "With very little help from you Yanks, I might add."

The mild rebuke was calculated. If the conversation was truly casual, Roebling wanted to cut it as short as possible. If not . . .

Davis shrugged, shifting the folded paper onto his lap.

"You have a point, Mr. Storey. However, we weren't at war then, if you'll recall. We did send you—"

"You should have been," Roebling said, rising. "You owed us that much, Yank."

Davis rose as Roebling picked up his suitcase, the cane ready in his hand. Davis had all the signs—the youth, trim appearance, even the single-breasted suit favored by men who wore shoulder holsters. But Davis was better than Roebling expected. He did not try to reach into his coat. He simply turned the folded paper over and dropped his right hand into the crease, onto a short-barreled Smith & Wesson .38 revolver.

"Let's do this quietly, Storey, and you won't get hurt. Just walk toward the main entrance in front of me."

"What in the bloody hell is this?" Roebling asked, trying to sound both indignant and innocent.

Davis reversed the paper so that it covered his hand and the gun. The muzzle lifted slightly, from Roebling's stomach to his chest.

"The bluff won't work, Novalis. Move or die. Take your choice."

Roebling stood a moment, then turned and started for the entrance, limping noticeably, using the cane. Davis followed. As they reached a row of telephone booths, Davis ordered him to halt. Roebling stood as Davis opened the door to an empty booth and slid inside.

"Stand right in front of this door and don't move. If you try to run, I'll shoot."

Roebling moved to within six inches of the open door. Davis tried to reach the change in his right pocket with his left hand.

"You wouldn't have a nickel, would you?"

Roebling leaned on the cane, his face a mask.

"It wouldn't have bought you anything anyway," Davis said, reaching under the paper to transfer hands on the gun. The paper started to slide off his arm. He reached for it reflexively, his left hand momentarily pushing the pistol to the side, his eyes darting to follow the falling paper.

Roebling swung the cane up and planted the rubber tip against Davis' chest. Davis forgot the paper and grabbed the pistol with both hands, bringing it back into line. Roebling twisted the handle of the cane sharply.

Inside the ebony wood, a small catch clicked and a heavy spring was released. The spring drove a slim steel spike with a needle point through the rubber tip and into Davis' chest with the force of a bolt from a crossbow.

Davis' mouth dropped open, his eyes widening in shock. For a long second, the eyes stared, unable to comprehend, then the body began to relax. Roebling quickly withdrew the spike and stepped into the booth. He caught Davis by the overcoat lapels and held him on the padded seat, propping him against the wooden back of the booth. Davis' eyes were already glazing. The pistol slipped from his relaxing hand and thumped Roebling painfully on his left arch. He picked it up quickly and looked around.

He was drawing a few glances from passers-by, but only the fleeting curiosity associated with seeing two men in the same telephone booth. His body and the loose overcoat blocked any clear view of Davis from the outside.

Roebling slipped the pistol into an inside pocket and placed two fingers on Davis' neck. He couldn't find a pulse. He reached into Davis' coat and found a wallet and a leather credentials case. Roebling put the wallet into his overcoat pocket and opened the case. Alfred Neil Davis, Special Agent, U.S. Army Counter Intelligence Corps. The picture was a good likeness. Roebling slipped the case into the pocket with the wallet, took the telephone receiver off its cradle and propped it between Davis' ear and the wall. It held his head up, made his posture more natural.

There was surprisingly little blood around the small hole in the white shirt. Corporal Becker had told him that there would not be, if he hit the heart. He moved Davis' tie to one side to cover the spot. As a last touch, Roebling propped Davis' left elbow on the ledge, wedged the fingers of his left hand under the receiver, then recovered his cane from the corner of the booth. He set the point against the floor of the booth and pushed downward. On the second try, the catch clicked and the spike was reset.

Roebling picked up the fallen newspaper and slipped both Davis' wallet and credentials inside, then backed out of the booth, lifted a hand in casual goodbye for the benefit of the curious and pulled the door shut. Through the glass panels, Davis looked almost natural. Roebling picked up his suitcase and walked quickly to the front entrance, remembering to use the cane. As he passed a waste container, he casually dropped the folded newspaper into the wire basket.

15 SMALL ICE CRYSTALS in the air were making yellow rings around each streetlight as Roebling reached the Huntington residence. He had ridden two buses on odd routes, then walked a half mile to reach the house. The cane, wiped clean of fingerprints, was lying at the bottom of a storm drain, and the suitcase, the first item to be jettisoned, was behind some trash cans in an alley only two blocks from the station. It would probably be found rather quickly, but there was nothing left in it to connect it with him.

At Erika's gate, he paused, his left leg aching, his mind still examining each step, each move, for a mistake that might lead the CIC to this house, to him. Several lights were on. Erika should have left for the party by now. Roebling strolled on down the street casually, looking for Major Cavanaugh's Continental. He did not see it or anything that looked like a police car. At the end of the block, he turned back. When he reached the gate, he opened it and went directly up the walk to the door. After ringing the bell, he pulled off his right glove and put his hand in his overcoat pocket, on the .38 revolver he had taken from the CIC agent.

Erika opened the door, her eyes widening in surprise.

Roebling looked past her. The hall was empty. He stepped inside and she closed the door behind him.

"Is anyone else here?"

"No. What's wrong?"

"Why aren't you at the party? Is Cavanaugh late?"

"I decided not to go. I called Gerry and canceled."

He glanced down at her floor-length robe. She involuntarily followed his eyes. Before she could move, he pulled the belt loose and jerked the front of the robe open. She was wearing only a blue nightgown underneath. The material was silk. It clung to her breasts, her thighs.

"What are . . ."

He released the robe and walked past her to the open door of the study. A reading lamp was on beside one of the big chairs facing the fireplace. A book lay open on the table that held the lamp, and a half-filled glass of Scotch sat on a coaster beside the book. The fire had burned about halfway down. He looked back at her. She had retied the belt on the robe and was facing him, her lips set, her face slightly flushed.

"Does everything meet with your approval, or am I to receive five demerits for this inspection?"

He ignored the sarcasm. "Get some clothes on and put some things in a bag. We're leaving."

She folded her arms across her breasts, her expression angry, obstinate.

"What's the matter? Couldn't you get a seat on the train?"

"Don't argue," he said quietly. "I don't know how much time we have. I'll need some of your husband's things. I have to get out of these English clothes."

The angry expression changed to concern. "Something did happen. What?"

"I was spotted in the station," Roebling said. "A CIC agent. He must have recognized me from a description, but I think he also knew Roger Storey's name."

"But how? Who could . . ." She stopped.

He admired her quickness.

"I can think of only two possibilities."

"Capricorn and me."

"That's right."

He turned and started up the stairs. She hesitated a moment, then hurried after him. He reached the top and walked quickly down the hallway to the master bedroom. She changed while he shaved off the thick mustache. He was quicker than she anticipated and came out of the bathroom while she was clad only in a brassiere and panties, about to step into a pair of gray wool slacks. He looked at her a moment, then turned to the large closet holding her husband's clothes. She put on the slacks but deliberately left off her blouse until she had finished redoing her makeup.

He went through the closet carefully, finally picking a dark-blue suit, a white shirt and gray tie. He glanced up to see her watching, then stepped behind the closet door before changing his shirt and pants. Modesty was only part of his reason. Primarily, he didn't want her to see the money belt.

After completing the change, he began to fill a leather suitcase with a second suit, underwear and additional shirts, ties and socks. He looked at the rows of shoes but discarded the thought. The clothes fit fairly well, except that he was several pounds lighter than her husband, but the shoes were obviously too big and he didn't want to add blistered feet to the bad leg.

He was ready before she was and paced up and down the carpet, running over his mental checklist again. But his eyes kept straying to the clear, creamy skin of her back and the highlights in the blond hair. From this angle, she reminded him of Gretchen, but her waist was slimmer, her hips flatter. She checked her face one last time in the mirror, then slipped into a long-sleeved blouse with lightly padded shoulders.

He glanced at his watch as she began filling a suitcase from various drawers of the French bureau. He stopped pacing and picked up the discarded English clothes.

"I'm going downstairs and get rid of these. Hurry up."

He made a quick turn of the house, checking both front and back, then went down into the basement. The coal furnace still had a good bed of coals. He added a fresh shovelful from the bin, got a fire burning, then added all his Roger Storey credentials. When they had burned, he threw in the tweed suit, made sure it was burning well and closed the door.

When he reached the bedroom again, Erika was putting bottles into a large cosmetics case. She looked different, and he suddenly realized that she was wearing glasses and a dark auburn wig that completely hid the blond hair.

"That's too much. You're only going as far as New York."

"I'll still need everything here."

He hesitated. "All right, but you'll have to carry that case."

He picked up both suitcases and started out. She hurriedly dumped several other items into the cosmetics case and shut the lid. On the first floor he turned back toward the kitchen. She caught up with him there.

"Ready?"

"Just a minute. I have to write a note."

"To whom?" he asked in a tone that caused her to look up.

"My houekeeper, Mrs. Jackson. She comes back Monday, and she has a key. If I'm not here, she may get worried and—"

"All right. But don't tell her anything except that you're going shopping and will be back in a few days. Will that cause her to be suspicious?"

"No. I often go to New York to shop."

"Just the same, make it convincing. And ask her to clean the place thoroughly, wash the woodwork and windows and things. That should get rid of any fingerprints."

"If she does it," Erika said, writing hastily on a notepad.

Roebling watched, reading over her shoulder. When she had finished, he nodded approval.

"Leave her some money for her trouble. What do you pay her?"

"Ten dollars per week. It costs a lot to get help now."

"Then leave her two weeks' pay. That should keep her

happy. It might even keep her from talking too much about your being gone."

Erika rummaged through her purse. "I don't think I have that much. I didn't cash a check this week and—"

"Here." Roebling pulled out a money clip and peeled off a twenty dollar bill.

Erika took the bill and put both the note and the money on the dinette table.

"She'll love that. It's new."

"Let's go."

They made their way through the snow to the double-car garage. She unlocked one of the doors and then the trunk of a big Buick, a touring car with a covered spare tire mounted in each front fender well. Beside it sat a lower, slimmer shape under a tarpaulin. The outline seemed familiar. After putting the suitcases in the trunk, he took a moment to lift the front end of the tarp.

Underneath was the familiar latticework grille and three-pointed star on the radiator cap. A Mercedes-Benz 500K roadster. The silver exhaust tubes coming out of the side of the hood and disappearing through the fender gleamed dully in the dim light. He had raced one a little once, a long time ago.

"I haven't driven it much since America entered the war," Erika said from behind him. "Andy's family disapproved even of my keeping it. And the last time I parked it on the street, someone slashed all the tires."

He dropped the edge of the tarpaulin and turned back to the Buick.

"You drive. I'll lie in the back and pretend to be asleep if you're stopped."

"What name should I give for you?"

"Stevens. Paul Stevens. I'm a friend of your husband from Virginia but now live in New York. I've been down visiting old friends, and you're driving me back so that you can go shopping."

"You have papers to go with that story?"

"A Navy discharge and a New York driver's license."

"What about your English accent?"

He smiled. "Well now, ma'am. Y'all don't have to worry 'bout that."

She laughed, surprised. "You do that very well. How did you learn?"

"It wasn't hard. The American Southern dialect is rooted in Victorian English. And I've been in the country before."

"Oh? When?"

He took her arm. "We're wasting time."

He helped her into the driver's seat, waited for her to back the car out of the garage, then locked the door and climbed into the back. When they were in the street and moving, she glanced over her shoulder.

"One more question, Roger—uh, Paul."

"Yes?"

"What do you want me to do if a policeman stops us and doesn't believe our story?"

"Nothing. Except stay out of my line of fire."

16 SERGEANT WAYNE HIGGINS of the Washington police was a stocky man with slightly bowed legs and a pugnacious expression that couldn't quite conceal the intelligence in his eyes. He seemed quite young for a homicide detective—especially a sergeant—but he could have been promoted after the men ahead of him had been drafted into the service. However, after spending less than an hour with him, Greg Allison was sure that Higgins' rank was earned, not achieved by default.

They had just come from the city morgue, where Allison had identified the body of Neil Davis, then spent a few moments fighting back his nausea. The deputy coroner had waited boredly for Allison to get his color back, then recited a good part of his preliminary report for them. The examinations made thus far revealed that Davis had been killed with a sharp instrument that pierced his heart and barely exited the skin on his back. Death was almost instantaneous. The instrument might have been a switchblade, but it would have had to be an unusually long one. The wound suggested an *epée*—a fencing sword—or some similar blade, as did the straight-on angle of entry.

In the car riding back to central police headquarters, Allison parried Higgins' questions about Davis. He needed time to think, to get over the shock of Davis' death and get his mind functioning again. However, Higgins recognized the symptoms and pressed his opportunity.

"How did you hear about the killing?"

"On the radio—a news flash. Have you reported it to Baltimore yet?"

"'No. We didn't know he was an agent until you called. He didn't have any credentials on him. In fact, he didn't even have a wallet."

"He should have had his credentials," Allison said. "The killer must have taken them."

"I see," Higgins said, thinking. "Something bothers me here. You heard about a killing at Union Station on the radio, so you immediately called us. That sounds like you stationed Davis at the station to watch for some-one—someone who probably killed him."

Allison looked up. "That's good reasoning, Sergeant."

"Then you know who killed him."

"I think I do."

"Who?"

"Let's take a look at those things you have at the labo-ratory first," Allison said. "If they confirm my suspicions, then I'll cooperate to the extent that I can."

"We're wasting time," Higgins said. "If you tell me what you know right now, we'll have a much better chance of picking the killer up before he gets out of the city."

Allison shook his head. "It's already been almost three hours since Neil was killed. He's long gone by now."

"You could be wrong there," Higgins said. "You may just be giving the killer the extra time he needs to get clear."

"Even if he's still here, Sergeant, I doubt very much that you'll catch him in any dragnet."

"Oh? Why not?"

"I'll tell you after we see the clothes."

They rode the rest of the way in silence, Allison berat-ing himself for leaving Davis alone, ordering the other men to converge on that shooting near the bus station. But who would ever have thought that Neil would turn cowboy, try to bring in Novalis alone instead of calling the contact in and waiting for the others? Allison shook his head slowly, wondering how things could have gone so wrong.

At police headquarters, Higgins led the way to the elevator, then down a hall to a door with "Crime Laboratory—Authorized Personnel Only" painted on the opaque glass. They went inside and made their way past small cubicles where examining tables were piled high with tagged items—everything from weapons and stolen merchandise to one bent headlight rim. In the third cubicle from the end, Higgins introduced Allison to Sergeant Patrick Fisher, a gaunt man with thick-lensed glasses and the look of a tubercular. Fisher shook hands with a surprisingly strong grip.

"How're you doing on those things?" Higgins asked, indicating the suitcase and pile of clothing on Fisher's work table.

"I'm about finished," Fisher said. "I've been over everything three times, but there's very little to add to what I've already told you."

"Where did you get them?" Allison asked.

"A patrol car picked up a bum who was trying to sell the suitcase and clothes to people on the street," Higgins said. "He told the officers that he'd found the suitcase in an alley only two blocks from Union Station. The officers brought the things to us, thinking there might be some connection with the killing."

Allison looked at Fisher. "What did you find?"

"Not much. The case is leather, expensive. The clothes are fairly expensive too, and they're all English-made. The labels are from London shops, and they fit the style and the stitching."

"Can I look through them?" Allison asked.

"Be my guest," Fisher said. "We've already lifted all the prints off the case." He looked at Higgins. "All of them belonged to your drunk upstairs, except for two made by one of the patrolmen. I'd say the case was wiped clean before it was dumped."

Allison went through the clothes carefully. He didn't recognize any of the pieces individually, but they did fit the impression given by the description of Roger Storey. None of the pants or jackets contained anything, but one jacket had a small cut in the lining near the inside pocket. Allison turned the lining inside out and held it up to the light. The material showed slight traces of a green smudge.

"I noticed that too," Fisher said. "I'd say whoever owned that coat had some money sewn into the lining there. Probably new bills. Getaway funds?"

"Could be," Allison said.

"Well, what about it?" Higgins asked. "You ready to talk to me now?"

Allison looked around. "I'll tell you what I can, Sergeant. But I want something in return."

"What?"

"This jacket—and a pair of those pants."

"Why?"

"I'd like to have some people go over them, make some measurements and come up with a better description of the size and weight of the man who wore these."

Higgins thought about the request a moment.

"You'll pass the information back to us?"

Allison nodded.

"How about you, Pat? You ready to turn loose of those things?"

"I might as well. Unless you want me to check them chemically for bloodstains. I didn't see anything under the magnifying glass, though."

"I don't think the man stopped to change clothes in that alley," Higgins said. "In fact, I don't think the man got any of the victim's blood on him at all. All right, Mr. Allison. You answer my questions to my satisfaction, and I'll have Pat sign out those two pieces to you."

"Fine. Shall we go down to your office, Sergeant?"

17 ERIKA HUNTINGTON watched as Stefan Roebling took the pen from the clerk and wrote "Mr. & Mrs. P. Stevens, Richmond, Va." in the hotel register. The clerk, a white-haired little man who had never quite made the step to one of the first-class hotels, made change for the twenty and waggled the room key toward a black bellhop in a faded red jacket. The bellhop took the key, put the bags on a small cart and led them to the elevator. Roebling took Erika's arm and followed.

They didn't speak in the elevator or the narrow corridor that followed. In the room, she made a slow circle, inspecting the double bed, the old four-drawer bureau, the single armchair and the adjoining bath while the bellhop placed the bags on two stands and opened the valve on the steam radiator. It hissed loudly, knocked twice, then settled down into a relative silence, emitting only a watery gurgle from time to time.

Roebling tipped the man a quarter, then followed him to the door and checked the lock. Erika sat down on the edge of the bed. The springs squeaked faintly.

"This isn't exactly what I had in mind after driving all night."

Roebling crossed to the window and looked out. The view wasn't much, mostly the dirty brick of the adjacent building and a rusting fire escape. He closed the drapes and the room darkened substantially.

"If you're as tired as you claim, the room shouldn't matter," Roebling said, taking off his overcoat.

"It doesn't—for now," Erika replied. "But I'd hate to spend a week here."

"You won't. We'll be here only a day—two at the most."

"And then?"

He looked up from the suitcase he was rummaging through. "Then you can move into one of the big hotels, do some shopping, drive back to Washington."

"Just like that?"

"Yes."

"And what if the CIC tracks you back to my house?"

He straightened, pajamas and toilet kit in hand.

"They won't. I covered my escape from the train station very well. Now if you don't mind, I'll take the bathroom first."

"Be my guest."

She smoked two cigarettes while he bathed and changed into the pajamas. Her eyes were getting heavy before he came out, carrying the suit pants. She watched him fold the creases neatly before draping the pants over the back of a chair. He went around to the other side of the bed and began to pull the coverlet back. She rose.

"Are you taking the bed?"

He smiled. "Are you always this cross after being out all night?"

"Where do I sleep?"

"Wherever you wish," he said, getting into the bed.

She watched him settle under the blankets, then found a nightgown, picked up her cosmetics case and carried both into the bathroom. By the time she had completed her bath and donned the nightgown, she had made up her mind. If Novalis, currently alias Mr. Paul Stevens, thought she intended to spend the next eight hours in that sagging chair, he was wrong. And he was also wrong if he thought she was available for his pleasure, at his pleasure. They would see who ended up with the bed.

While brushing her hair, she noticed that her anticipation of the contest, perhaps even the struggle, had hardened her breasts, pointed the nipples under the thin fabric. She turned off the bathroom light and stepped into the darkened room. He lay with his back toward her on the far side of the bed.

"Paul?"

He didn't answer. She listened a moment. His breathing was even and deep. He was asleep.

When Roebling awoke, Erika was snuggled against his back in the bed. He lay quietly a few minutes, enjoying her touch, her warmth, then slid out of bed. She stirred but didn't waken. The room was dim. He checked his watch, saw that it was almost five o'clock and began to dress.

On the street, among the remnants of late shoppers heading home through the gathering darkness, Roebling looked both directions, then walked eastward. He had picked a hotel on West 47th Street, close enough to be within walking distance of Central Park. The neighborhood was a variety of small stores and restaurants, shopkeepers and transients.

He ignored most of the faces but found himself covertly inspecting two Jews in traditional Hasidic dress, with their black hats, long coats and uncut ringlets hanging on either side of their faces. It was strange to see such people walking openly down the street, talking, mingling with the crowd, unafraid. Traditional Jews had been gone from the streets of Berlin so long that he had almost forgotten what they looked like. It was a surprise to rediscover that they weren't really different from all the others.

He was waiting in the lobby as North exited the elevator shortly after six-thirty. Roebling followed him across the lobby, letting him get outside before coming up alongside.

"Just keep walking, Doctor."

"What? Oh. Nov—Mr. Storey. I didn't expect—"

"Where's your car?"

"It's in a garage near the apartment. Why?"

"Can we walk it from here?"

"Yes. It's not far. What do you want with my car?"

"We're going to your radio station. I've got a message to send."

"Now?"

"Yes."

"But I can't drive out there now. I have to be home by seven. We have guests coming over for—"

"Tell them an emergency arose and you didn't have a chance to call."

"But—"

"Just keep walking, Doctor."

The traffic was relatively light and the streets clear, but it still took more than an hour for them to clear the city. North drove in silence, concentrating on the road, the other traffic. Roebling found himself wishing that the man would hurry, then being grateful for his caution.

"Just where is your station?"

"In a house on the north side of the island. It's not too far out."

"Do you rent the house?"

"No. I bought it. I didn't want any landlord snooping around."

"In your own name?"

North glanced at him. "Of course not. I used the name of a dead man—one of my former patients. And I was very careful, working through two attorneys. One of them is dead now, too. I keep a post-office box in the dead man's name and pay the taxes by mail. Even if someone should accidentally find the radio, there's no way it could ever be traced to me."

Or you to it, Roebling thought.

The road to the house had not been cleared, but the snow wasn't deep enough to require putting on the tire chains. The heavy Cadillac wallowed somewhat as North negotiated two small bends but did not slide off the narrow track. They stopped in front of a weathered old house with shiplap siding and a rock chimney. A grove of trees surrounded the house, shielding it from the distant neighbors.

North unlocked the door, flipped a light switch and led Roebling inside. The house was fully furnished but dusty, cold, unheated. North made his way to the kitchen with Roebling following. This room was also furnished, even including a set of heavy glass canisters on the sink counter. North noticed his interest.

"An old man owned the place. When he died, there were no heirs, so all the things came with the place."

"What's your schedule with Wohldorf?" Roebling asked.

"I normally check in only on Sunday afternoons unless a different time is arranged beforehand. Of course, I can send a message at any time by using one of the constantly monitored frequencies."

North opened the door to a large pantry and pulled the chain for the overhead light. He moved several cans off a shelf about three feet above the floor, then grasped the shelf firmly and pulled. The section of the wall to which the shelf was attached came free and North set it aside. Behind it was a large recess which contained a powerful radio. North smiled up at Roebling proudly.

"How do you like that? I built it myself. See those spring-loaded catches on the wall section? The antenna goes up the chimney."

"Very good," Roebling said. "Have you a pad and pencil?"

North reached in beside the set and lifted out a pad, pencils and his code book. Roebling wrote his message quickly and handed it to North.

ARES. HAVE BEEN DISCOVERED. AM CANCELING PROMETHEUS.
HAVE U-387 PICK ME UP AT RENDEZVOUS POINT C, 0100 HRS, 12-26. NOVALIS.

North's expression of surprise was very well done, Roebling thought.

"My God! What happened?"

"I'll tell you later. Get that off."

North turned on the set to let it warm up while he translated the message into code. When he was ready, he asked for one of the kitchen chairs and sat down to tap out the message. Roebling watched, making sure the radio was tuned to one of the Abwehr's frequencies.

North finished the message, received an acknowledgment and turned off the radio. While he ws replacing the wall section and putting the cans back on the shelf, Roebling took off his gloves and slipped his hands into his overcoat pockets. North came out of the pantry, wiping the dust off his hands with his handkerchief.

"Are you ready to go? I need to get back."

"In a minute," Roebling said. "How long has your nurse been with you?"

"Mrs. Koscino? Four—almost five years. Why do you ask?"

"Could she suspect that you might be an agent?"

"What! No. No, I would have noticed. She's not a deceptive woman. Despite all her years as a nurse, she still can't hide her feelings. Do you think she had something to do with—"

"No. I was just making sure."

"Then who . . ." North stopped, beginning to comprehend. "You don't think that I . . . But I couldn't inform on you without informing on myself!"

"You could be working both sides of the street."

"No! I swear!"

"Or you could have simply made an anonymous telephone call. You have a very good life here, don't you, Doctor? The Allies are winning the war. If the coming invasion of France is successful and Germany is eventually overrun, you know the Abwehr will destroy all its files. Right now, your only problem is me, my mission. I might force you to do something that would ultimately expose you, destroy that fine life, all your plans for the future with your rich wife and lucrative practice. That would be worth one telephone call, now wouldn't it?"

"No! I swear I didn't! I'm loyal to the Fatherland, just as you . . ."

Roebling lifted the .38 out of his pocket. North's eyes widened. He backed a step, shaking his head. The sink counter stopped him.

"Please. Oh, please!"

"How much does the CIC know about me? What did you give them besides my cover name and description?"

"Nothing! I gave them nothing! I swear on my oath as a doctor! I didn't tell anyone—"

"What about your oath as a member of the Abwehr?"

"That too! I'll swear on my father's life! You have the wrong man! I'm innocent!"

Roebling watched the eyes, the facial movements. North continued to beg for another few moments, then fell silent, staring at the muzzle of the pistol. Roebling held it motionless. The silence grew. North began to tremble. A light appeared in the kitchen window, a car passing on the main road. Roebling's eyes flicked in that direction involuntarily. North grabbed for the big flour canister. Roebling shot him twice before he could throw it.

North stumbled back against the counter, then staggered forward, his hands clawing at the air, his face distorted. The canister hit the floor and rolled away, not breaking. On his third step, North's muscles collapsed and he fell heavily. Roebling shook his head, watching the small, involuntary spasms die away.

"You were a fool to the end, Capricorn. For a few moments there you had me convinced."

His own body suddenly jerked, and he barely made it to the sink before he vomited. The spasms racked his stomach, and he kept vomiting until there was nothing but a trickle of stomach acid and a burning in his throat. He had never executed a man before. He had killed many—most at long range—but he had never executed an unarmed man. As the spasms subsided, Roebling found himself wondering whether there was now any difference between himself and his commander in North Africa.

It took a good deal of self-control for him to go through North's pockets, to carry the body out to the car and place it in the trunk. He found a medical bag in the trunk and rifled it, taking a small bottle of morphine and several bottles of pills, which he threw as far into the night as he could. The more he could make it look like a robbery, the more time he would have.

He left the car in a Brooklyn alley and rode the subway

back to Manhattan. By the time he arrived back at the hotel, it was almost midnight. Erika was still up. She raised one eyebrow questioningly.

"I wasn't sure you were coming back. I almost left."

"Why didn't you?"

"Did you want me to?"

"No."

She watched him a moment. He seemed restless, edgy.

"Staying in this flea trap isn't a good idea, you know. Capricorn's safe house would be much better."

He ignored the suggestion. "I need some additional identification papers. Where can I get them?"

"How good do they have to be?"

"The best."

"Then they'll have to come from Cleveland. There's a printer out there who makes the best forgeries I've ever seen. Capricorn can get whatever you need from him."

He nodded absently, thinking. She decided that this was as good a time as any.

"I think we should split up, Paul."

His eyes shifted back to her. She met his gaze levelly.

"After Gerry Cavanaugh told me about New Mexico, I sent a message to our Los Angeles agent, Michael, instructing him to get more information about the project location for you. He's very good at that sort of thing. I think you should move into Capricorn's safe house until you hear from him. It shouldn't take too long."

Roebling nodded. "Do you know how to contact the man in Cleveland?"

"The forger? Yes, but—"

"Good. We'll catch tomorrow morning's plane."

"We? Now wait a minute—"

"I need your help," Roebling said.

"I can't go to Cleveland with you!" Erika said, then quickly lowered her tone. "Now look. I got the information you wanted and I got you out of Washington. From now on, Capricorn and Michael can give you all the help you need. I advise you to stay in the safe house and let Capricorn—"

"Capricorn's dead," Roebling said bluntly.

Her face reflected her shock.

"How?"

"I killed him."

"You what!"

"I killed him," Roebling repeated.

The shock began to be displaced by anger. "In God's name, why—"

"It was him or you. I chose him. Was I wrong?"

She stared at him, thinking that someone had fouled up very badly when they picked this man for Prometheus.

"Well?"

She took a deep breath. "No. No, you weren't wrong."

"Then we'll leave for Cleveland in the morning."

She was quiet for a time, then began to chuckle mirthlessly.

"What's funny?"

"Just what I've always wanted."

"What's that?"

"To spend Christmas in Cleveland."

18 IT WAS WEDNESDAY, December 22, before Greg Allison got the break he had been needing. He had spent a fruitless day and night directing the other agents in the search of Davis' killer, interviewing possible witnesses and coordinating the CIC and police efforts with Sergeant Higgins. Each group had developed additional eyewitness descriptions of the man seen with Davis, and those descriptions—the limp, dark-brown hair and blue eyes—removed any doubt in Allison's mind that Davis had been killed by Novalis.

Higgins had men on all the terminals, freeing the CIC agents for investigative work, but no sightings had been reported. Allison knew there wouldn't be. By now, Novalis was out of the Washington area or hidden so deeply that no ordinary measures would uncover him.

The telephone on Sergeant Higgins' desk rang and the switchboard operator said she had a call for Allison. Higgins told her to put it through, then handed the receiver to Allison.

"This is Allison."

"Greg, this is Marty Goldman. I have the lab results for you on that stain in the jacket."

"Good. What did your people find?"

"Enough to stir up quite a few people here. Can you get over here right away?"

"Can't you just tell me what you have over the phone?"

"I'd rather not. How long will it take you to get here?"

"Twenty minutes. Maybe less."

"Fine. I'll see you then."

Goldman hung up. Allison did likewise and discovered that Higgins had been listening attentively.

"Something I should know about?"

"I don't know, Sergeant. The man wouldn't tell me anything over the phone."

"What man?"

"A friend of mine. I'll get back to you."

"You promised to cooperate, remember."

"I remember," Allison said. "Any way I can."

Allison made the drive from the police station to the Treasury Building—just across from the White House—in fifteen minutes. Inside, he took the elevator to the fifth floor, then walked quickly down the marble corridor toward Martin Julius Goldman's office.

Marty Goldman, a wiry, intense man with light olive skin, a scholarly look and the wry humor that often grows out of generations of persecution, met Allison at the door and ushered him into the well-appointed offices. They had been acquaintances since their college days at the University of Chicago and had met again six months ago. Goldman had joined the Secret Service after college and had been assigned to Washington for almost two years now. Since running into each other again, Allison had been to dinner at Goldman's house once, but they were not really friends. Each recognized that the other moved primarily in circles where he would not be fully accepted.

"Well, I'm here, Marty. Now what's all the secrecy about?"

"It's not secrecy, Greg. I'm just making sure that I get as much information as I give."

"Oh? Then the stain on the jacket was currency ink?"

Goldman nodded.

Allison sighed. "I thought so. The man was carrying some extra money sewn into the lining of his coat."

"And what else?"

Allison looked at the dark eyes, puzzled. "And nothing else. I just wanted your laboratories to confirm that fact. The police lab could have made the analysis just as easily, but they don't have the secret formula for our inks to make the comparisons." He sighed again. "Quite frankly, Marty, I was hoping that it wasn't money."

"Why?"

"Because it doesn't help. Almost anything else—bonds, stocks, anything—might have given me something to trace the man with, but not money."

Goldman was silent a moment, his right forefinger tapping his desk blotter absently.

"What's the problem?" Allison asked. "Did you think someone had duplicated the formula for the ink used on our currency?"

Goldman shook his head.

"Then what?"

"You really don't know, do you?"

Allison frowned. "I'm not in the mood for games, Marty."

"Neither am I, Greg." Goldman paused, then decided to lay it all out. "You were partially right. The stain was ink, and the ink did come off currency. But it wasn't our currency."

"Then whose currency was it?"

"The spectrographic analysis showed that the ink is close to the base formula we use, but it isn't a perfect match. However, it does match some bills that have been showing up in the country recently. And because of that, I have to know exactly where and from whom you got that jacket."

It took a moment for the import of what Goldman had said to register in Allison's brain.

"Are you telling me that the money in the jacket was counterfeit?"

Goldman smiled. "You must be tired, Greg. You're normally quicker."

"Counterfeit." Allison rolled the word on his tongue. "Counterfeit!" He looked quickly at Goldman. "Are you sure?"

Goldman nodded. "The first of it showed up about two

weeks ago. A New York bank official spotted a fifty and sent it to us for confirmation. So far, we've gotten three other bills—two tens and a twenty—all from the New York area. It's good, Greg. It's so damned good that it scares us. The engraving is top-notch and the inks and paper are—"

"It's German," Allison said.

Goldman slapped the desk with his palm. "I was afraid you were going to tell me that. We've been waiting for the Germans to try to flood this country with counterfeit, the way they did in England. They almost ruined the British pound. The government finally had to change the paper, engraving, inks, even the size of the notes. They also passed a bunch of American counterfeit in Mexico in Forty-two, but this is much better. If they flood the country with this stuff, they'll ruin the public's confidence in the dollar. Everyone will be afraid to take a bill in payment for anything because it may be counterfeit. I don't have to tell you what that could do to the war effort."

"I don't think you have a problem," Allison said. "The jacket belonged to a German agent, but so far as we can tell, he's the only one who's come into the country."

"But what if—"

"He's here for an entirely different reason," Allison said.

"How do you know?"

"His method of entry, his movements since that entry. He couldn't have brought a large amount of money in with him."

"He could be here to set up a distribution network," Goldman said.

"That's possible," Allison admitted. "But if so why would he be passing the counterfeit now?"

"As a test run?"

Allison shook his head. "They have to know that it would be spotted eventually, and that would tip your people off before they could get a large amount in circulation. No, I don't think he's here for anything like that."

"Then what?"

Allison paused, thinking. When he spoke again, it was more to himself than to Goldman.

"This doesn't make sense. Why would the Abwehr go to all that trouble, set up such an elaborate cover, then give the man counterfeit money?"

"You've lost me entirely, Greg. What in the hell are you talking about?"

"Sorry," Allison said. He told Goldman quickly about the discovery of the German agent by MI-Five, his attempts to track the man and the killing of Neil Davis. Goldman listened intently, not interrupting.

"So you see how important it is that we run this agent down," Allison finished. "And you've just given us the means to do that. As long as he keeps spending those bills, we can track his movements. Have you gotten the word out about the counterfeit yet?"

"Every bank in the Federal Reserve System has been sent full descriptions and color photographs of the bills we have. We're now in the process of getting the same information to state banks, savings and loan companies and other organizations. Within another week the entire country should be alerted to watch for the bills."

"Good," Allison said. "Then it should be just a matter of time before we know where he's gone."

"I already know," Goldman said. "I received a call from a bank official just before you arrived. Another bill has shown up."

"Where?"

Goldman paused. "I want in on this, Greg."

"No problem. I'll keep you fully informed."

"That's not what I mean," Goldman said. "Have you heard the stories about what the Nazis are doing to Jews in their concentration camps?"

"Yes, but—"

"Those stories are true," Goldman said. "A number of people, my father among them, have personally spoken to refugees from Europe. They confirmed everything you've heard and more. Much more."

"What are you trying to say, Marty?"

"I'm telling you that I have reasons for wanting this Nazi even more than you. And I intend to be one of the people who get him."

Allison hesitated. "This is primarily an Army matter, Marty. I don't know—"

"He's passing counterfeit bills, Greg, so it's my job too." He paused again. "You don't really have a choice, you know. Either we work together or I'll go alone."

"You'd refuse to share your information?"

"Of course not. You can submit a request for what we have through channels. My chief will take it under advisement and let your chief know what he decides."

Allison took a moment to think although he knew Marty was right. He really didn't have a choice. Marty obviously meant what he had said. And that bothered Allison. Marty had never expressed a desire for revenge before. Maybe he didn't know Marty as well as he thought.

"All right. We go together."

"Your word?"

"My word," Allison said. "Now where do we go?"

"New York."

19 STEFAN ROEBLING paid the cab driver and stepped out on the walk in front of the Cleveland Museum of Art. The wind off Lake Erie quickly began to numb the skin on his cheeks, but he took a moment to imprint the scene in his memory—the white stone structure set well back from the street, guarded by its stone wall, wide steps, four Doric columns. The reflected glare from the snow on the building, the wall and the expanse of lawn was broken by patches of dark evergreens planted inside the wall, adjacent to the building. The trees out front, near the empty fountain, were bare, their limbs ice-covered. Roebling thought he would like to come back sometime, see the scene in a green month.

He turned his overcoat collar up and moved quickly up the circular walk to the front steps. Inside the building it was warm, but it still took a few minutes for the numbness to leave his cheeks, his ears. He smiled at the receptionist, a pleasant, gray-haired woman, signed the register as "Robert Adams, N.Y.", then allowed her to sell him a printed guide for five cents. After listening to a short description of the main sections of the museum, Roebling thanked her politely and made his way to a showing of modern paintings in the north wing.

He wandered along casually, noting that the exhibit consisted primarily of works by the precisionist painters—Demuth, Dove, Hartley, O'Keeffe. A small card stated that the exhibit was made possible through the courtesy of Mr. Alfred Stieglitz, his An American Place gallery in New York, the New York Museum of Modern Art and a few other institutions that Roebling did not bother to read. He did not particularly like the abstract paintings, as he had not liked the cubism of Picasso, Braque and their followers.

The museum seemed deserted, at least in this section. Roebling made his way into the next room, which contained a group of lesser known abstractionists. The man was standing in front of a particularly violent painting, mostly slashes of reds and yellows. He tilted his head first one way and then the other, the thick neck not moving very far. Roebling checked the nearby rooms, then approached the man quietly.

"Personally, I prefer the impressionists."

The man's head jerked around. Up close, he was even shorter, heavier, with pale, sallow skin and permanent ink stains on his fingers. The bloated face was dominated by large hyperthyroid eyes that—combined with the small mouth—gave him the look of a giant guppy.

"You scared me. I didn't hear you come in."

"Sorry," Roebling said. "I didn't realize you were so involved with that painting."

"I like the way he uses color."

"I prefer more subtlety. You're Herder?"

The man nodded. "And you?"

"I'm a fan of Monet," Roebling said. "Can we get down to business? I'd like to keep this as short as possible."

"Fine with me," Herder said. "Whadda you want?"

"Two complete sets of identification papers—driver's licenses, Social Security cards, the works."

"For who?"

Roebling took a slip of paper from his overcoat pocket and handed it to the man.

"It's all here, including the descriptions and other information you'll need."

"You want birth certificates too?"

"No. Just the things written there."

Herder studied the list.

"These real names?"

"No."

"Then they ain't gonna stand up to much of a check. I can give you real people's names—along with genuine birth certificates. Course, it'll cost more."

"I don't need the birth certificates."

Herder looked at him. "Not lamming outta the country, eh?"

Roebling stared at him coldly.

"Sorry. I was just thinking out loud."

"How much for everything there—not including the birth certificates?"

"Real people's names and a little information on their backgrounds?"

Roebling nodded. "All right?"

"Two thousand for the lot."

Roebling shook his head. "That's too much."

"Hey, you wanna buy junk, you go to somebody else. With me you get artistry. Maybe not the same as these people hanging here, but artistry just the same. I can make you an FBI identification card that will have the Feds sending you a check each month."

Roebling smiled. "All right, two thousand. But I'm buying your best work—right down the line."

"For two G's, you got it."

"When can I have the things?"

"Ten days. Maybe a week if—"

"Two days," Roebling said.

Herder chuckled softly. "No way. I can't put everything aside to—"

"How much more?"

"For what?"

"For delivery in two days."

Herder chuckled again. "Boy, you're really hot, ain't you?"

"How much?"

"Hey, I'd like to accommodate you, friend. But it ain't

possible. I'm outta the right kinda paper for the Social Security cards, and I got other problems too. A week is tops."

"Make it three days, and you've got another thousand."

Herder stopped smiling. The little mouth puckered as he sucked on his lips, thinking.

"Four days. But it'll cost you fifteen hunnerd more."

"Three."

Herder shook his head. "Hey, I got my pride. You want these done right or you want me to use a cookie cutter?"

Roebling nodded. "All right, four days."

"Half now."

Roebling took a roll of bills out of his pocket and counted out five hundred, then put the roll away.

"Hey, that's only—"

"That's all you get until you deliver."

Herder started to argue. Roebling silenced him with another cold stare.

"Another thing. No foreign names and no Smiths or Joneses."

"You want a lot for your money," Herder complained, putting the five hundred in his pocket. "How do I contact you when they're ready?"

"You don't. I'll contact you in four days."

Herder shrugged. "And I thought I was a cautious man."

Erika was not in the hotel room when he returned. He checked her things quickly, found everything except her purse, then stopped, listening. A key was being inserted in the lock. He drew the pistol from the overcoat pocket and moved quickly, silently to the wall behind the door. The door opened and Erika came into the room. Through the space between the door and jamb, he could see only empty hallway. As she turned to shut the door, she saw him and stopped.

"Close the door."

She obeyed. He put the pistol back into the overcoat pocket.

"Where have you been?"

"Just downstairs to get something to eat. I didn't know when you'd be back. Is something wrong?"

He didn't answer. Instead, he listened at the door for a moment.

"Something is wrong. What is it?"

"You tell me."

"Tell you what?"

Again he didn't answer but turned to hang the overcoat and hat on the door hooks. When he turned back, her face was set, angry.

"You still aren't sure, are you? Where did you think I was? Out informing the CIC? Leading them back here?"

"The thought occurred to me that North may have been more desperate than guilty," Roebling said.

Erika took a deep breath, then let it out slowly. He thought she was going to say something further, but she suddenly picked up her purse and began pawing through it for her cigarettes.

"All right, I was wrong," Roebling said. "But when I found you gone—"

"You can't really trust anyone, can you?"

"I'm trying to apologize."

She stopped rummaging through the purse and looked at him.

"That's fine for now. But what happens the next time I do something you can suspect? Do you give me the benefit of the doubt or do I get the same treatment as Capricorn?"

"It's not the same thing," Roebling said, his own anger rising.

"Isn't it?"

"No."

She glared at him a moment, then suddenly lifted a small, nickel-plated automatic out of the purse. The muzzle reached only an inch beyond the end of her forefinger, which was curled firmly around the trigger. He froze in position.

"Step away from that overcoat."

Her tone was quiet, deadly. He took two careful steps and she stopped him—too far away ever to reach the .38

and just beyond the range where he might have a chance if he lunged at her. He cursed himself for being a total fool.

"In case you haven't noticed, this is a thirty-two-caliber on a twenty-five frame. Andy had it made especially for me before he shipped out. At this range, it's very deadly."

Roebling forced himself to relax, to think.

"What now?"

"Now you get it through your head that if I was a double agent you would never have gotten as far as New York."

"Maybe."

"Give me a good reason why not."

"You could have been ordered to stay with me, to learn more about my mission."

It was a stupid thing to say while looking at the steady muzzle of the automatic, but he was mad—at her, at himself.

She couldn't suppress the smile. "You forget that I already know as much about the operation as you do."

She was right. He had no answer, no further reason. She shook her head slowly.

"For an intelligent man, Paul, you can be awfully dumb."

She suddenly dropped the automatic back into the purse and tossed it on the bed. He didn't move. She came to him, pulled his head down and kissed him deeply, fully. It took him a moment to react, then he was holding her, kissing her in return. All the anger, the tension of the past few days focused suddenly in a need for her, a hunger that would not be denied. He forgot logic. He forgot caution. All he knew was that she was alive under his hands, against his body.

She broke the embrace and began unbuttoning her blouse, breathing rapidly. He slipped out of the jacket and began taking off his shirt, unable to take his eyes off her. Each article that she discarded heightened his desire. Her breasts were full but firm, with dark, pointed nipples. Her waist was smaller than it looked in the woolen skirts. Her legs were long and tapering, smoothly muscled.

She pulled back the coverlet on the bed and slipped between the sheets.

He slid in beside her. Immediately, she was in his arms, kissing him, stroking him, responding to his touch. Her skin was unbelievably smooth and soft over the delicate ribs, the muscles of her back, her buttocks. He could not touch her enough, hold her sufficiently close to fulfill his need. With surprising strength, she suddenly rolled him over on his back and climbed atop him. He tried to roll back, but she held him, reaching down to guide him inside her.

She began a rocking, elliptical motion, and he thought for a moment that he would not be able to contain himself. As he began to match her rhythms, she leaned forward and kissed him deeply without interrupting her movements. He was drowning in her. Her movements increased, her motion becoming more violent. His hands found her breasts, and he stroked the hard nipples. She added a slightly different stroke and he felt himself losing control.

He called her name softly, through clenched teeth. Her breathing was deep, strong, in time with her movements. He gripped her breasts, exploding into her. She made three more rapid strokes and went rigid also, digging her nails into his arms, emitting one long, low sound that was more than a moan.

He sank back into the bed slowly. She stayed rigid for another moment, then slowly settled onto his chest. Her breasts were no longer hard. He put his arms around her and she tucked her head up under his chin, her breath sending small waves of warm air across his chest. She shuddered once, squeezed him tightly, then was still. He felt totally drained of all tensions, all doubts, everything except a deep, deep warmth for her.

Neither spoke for a long time. Finally, she snuggled deeper against him.

"Darling?"

"What?"

"It will be better next time. Neither of us will be so hungry then. We'll have time to explore, to learn more about each other."

He kissed the top of her head, burying his face in the mass of golden hair.

"Will there be a next time?"

She raised her head to look at him.

"Why not?"

He smiled. "Aren't you in a hurry to get back to Washington?"

"Are you telling me I can go?"

"Yes."

She studied his face. "What convinced you? The gun?"

"No. I made the decision before I ever got back to the hotel." He laughed softly. "That act with the pistol was totally unnecessary. In fact, it almost convinced me that I had made a mistake. For a moment there, I thought you intended to shoot me."

"I should have," Erika said, laughing with him.

Roebling brushed some loose strands of hair away from her face and touched her cheek softly.

"Can you wait until tomorrow to catch a plane or do you need to leave tonight?"

She kissed him lightly.

"There's nothing I'm doing that can't be put off a few days," she said, telling herself that she wasn't lying. "I can stay at least until you get the new papers. You'll need the extra cover until then."

"Are you sure? It'll be four days."

"Four days!" She raised up on one elbow. "Why so long?"

He smiled sheepishly. "Probably because I did something foolish. I ordered you a Christmas present."

"A Christmas present! What?"

"A new identity—just in case I've made any mistakes and you have to get out quickly. I was going to send the papers to you with a note of apology."

She began to laugh again. He could not keep from laughing with her. When their laughter had subsided, he shook his head ruefully.

"It's not much of a Christmas present, is it?"

"But it's perfect," she said. "What better present could one agent give another?"

"It was just a whim," Roebling said.

She snuggled against him again. "You know something, darling?"

"What?"

"I never thought I'd see the day, but I think I'm going to love Christmas in Cleveland."

20 THE DESK CLERK'S name was Peter Bouska, and he was nervous. Greg Allison watched that nervousness grow from a minor apprehension to a trembling of the hands under Marty Goldman's questions. Harry Franklin, the hotel manager, also seemed nervous, although he hid the symptoms better than the white-haired little clerk. Allison watched both, letting Goldman carry the brunt of the interrogation.

"And you say the man had shaved off his mustache when they left?"

"I think so," Bouska said. "I—I can't remember for sure."

Goldman looked at Franklin. "You made your bank deposit just before closing time on Tuesday. When was the last deposit before that?"

"Monday morning, just before noon," Franklin replied, toying with the pen set on his desk. "I make daily deposits. I don't like to keep much money here."

"Then you didn't ask him to pay for the room in advance, Mr. Bouska? I thought you said that was hotel policy."

"Yes, I did get ..." The clerk stopped, looking at Franklin.

Goldman also looked at Franklin.

"If they paid in advance on Monday morning, then why didn't the bill show up in your Monday deposit?"

Franklin cleared his throat and managed to cough twice. It gave him time to think.

"We keep some money out to make change. I guess the bill was left in a drawer until the Tuesday deposit."

Allison lit a cigarette. The man was quicker than he seemed. His reasoning was plausible, noncontradictory with his earlier statements.

"I see," Goldman said. "I don't think I have any more questions. What about you, Greg?"

"I'd like to ask Mr. Bouska whether he thought the woman's hair was real."

"What?" Bouska fidgeted in the chair. "What do you mean?"

"You must have seen a lot of people in your years behind a hotel desk, Mr. Bouska, developed some ability to spot phony mustaches, wigs, things like that. Would you say the hair was real?"

Bouska licked his lips. By Allison's count, that was the fourth time the man had needed to wet the dry skin.

"Well, sir, it's hard to say. The hair looked real. If it was a wig, then it was an expensive one."

"How about a henna rinse?"

"No, sir. The color was too dark, sort of auburn. It didn't look orange like the rinses used by . . ." He stopped.

"Could you tell me about the woman's skin again? You said her eyebrows were dark."

"Yes, sir. They were very thin and arched, like one of those movie actresses. I think she had put something on them to make them dark."

"Probably. But her skin was fair?"

"Very fair, sir. I remember thinking that it was—"

"Was what?"

"Well, it was . . . It seemed too fair for a redhead."

"I don't follow you," Allison said. "Most redheads are very fair."

"Yes, sir," Bouska said, nodding quickly. "But what I mean is that her skin was very clear. She didn't have any freckles."

"None?"

"No, sir."

"How much makeup was she wearing?" Allison asked.

"It's kinda hard to say," Bouska said, licking his lips again. "She had on powder and some rouge, but I don't think it was enough to cover freckles, if she had any."

Allison nodded. "That's all I have, Marty."

Bouska relaxed, obviously relieved.

Goldman rose. "We won't take any more of your time, gentlemen. Thank you for your cooperation."

The men shook hands with Bouska and Franklin, then left. In the unmarked sedan, driving back downtown, Allison mulled over the interview.

"What do you think, Marty? Why were they so nervous?"

"I'd say the two of them have a sideline, one they don't want the police or the hotel owners to know about, and they were afraid we'd pick up on it."

"What's your guess? Prostitutes? Numbers?"

"Could be both. It could also be a dozen other things. I hear the dope racket is beginning to boom now. The war's producing a lot of addicts. Did you see the newspaper story on that doctor who was killed for a bottle of morphine?" He shook his head in disbelief. "Of course, it could be something as simple as a rake-off. Half the time when I flash my Secret Service credentials, people think I'm from Internal Revenue. It scares the hell out of them. Everyone still remembers that the IRS put Al Capone in prison when the FBI couldn't. If those two did hold anything out of the till last weekend, they'll be afraid to spend it now, afraid that one of their bills is also counterfeit."

Allison chuckled. "Serve them right."

Goldman laughed with him. "What now?"

"Now I suggest we both get out supplements to our notices, adding the woman and changing the man's description. I'll send a teletype to the Washington police, giving them her description. They might have something on her in their files, although I doubt it."

"You think he picked her up in Washington?"

"Yes. My office there can't find anyone who saw them get on a bus or plane. I think she drove him up."

"The bellhop didn't see any car."

"They probably left it in a garage or dumped it. We need to have the Washington police send us the stolen-car reports for Sunday night, then start checking abandoned vehicles and garages in the area. If we're lucky, we might come up with the car and some identifiable prints."

"That's a good idea."

Allison dropped Goldman in front of the Federal Building, then drove on over to the CIC office. A message was waiting. Chief Kibler wanted him to call Baltimore. He found a telephone and placed the call.

"Greg? What have you found?"

"They checked out of the hotel yesterday morning, sir. We don't have a lead on where they went yet."

"Do you think they're still in New York?"

"I don't know. I doubt it."

"We've intercepted another message from Capricorn. It says that Novalis is scrubbing the mission and wants to be picked up by a U-boat on Thursday night."

Allison was silent a moment, thinking. "Do you believe it?"

"I don't know," Kibler said. "The other Capricorn messages were accurate."

"Yes, but Novalis knows we're onto him now." Allison paused, unconsciously shaking his head. "I don't think he'd quit that easily, sir. He got away clean after killing Davis."

"He could be beginning to panic," Kibler suggested. "In a way, that makes sense."

"How?"

"If he really was sent in to kill the President, after the killing he'd know that we would blanket the entire Washington area. He wouldn't get another chance. So he could have just decided to forget the whole thing."

"If so, then why would he come back to New York?" Allison asked. "Any rendezvous would have to be along the southern coast. This area's too heavily populated."

"Maybe he had to make personal contact with Capricorn for some reason."

"Maybe. But I don't think he's quitting," Allison said.

"So unless you order me to do otherwise, I plan to stay here and follow up on what we've got."

"It's your choice," Kibler said. "I'll alert the Coast Guard."

"Thank you, sir."

21 MAJOR HEINRICH JOST hurried along the corridor, then turned into the stairwell, ignoring the elevator. By the time he had climbed the two flights of stairs to the top floor, he was panting a little but warmer than he had been all morning. The basement furnace had been cut back again—to conserve fuel for the war effort—and he could put his hand on his radiator without burning it. He was certain that the temperature in his office was no more than fifty degrees.

The director's suite of offices on the top floor seemed warmer, but he could not be sure whether that was because of his exertions. The mannish-looking secretary informed the admiral of his arrival. He tried to read the expression on her face, but she had been with the admiral too long. In a moment the intercom buzzed, and she told him to enter.

Jost had been in the admiral's office before and loved the dark paneling, the thick rugs, the polished desk and matching conference table. In fact, he had occasionally daydreamed about the changes he would make when he became director of the Abwehr. Of course, the brassbound ship's clock would have to go. He would also remove the pictures of the *Bismarck*—now sunk—and the other ships, replacing them with paintings. Perhaps he would add a metal sculpture of the German eagle on the wall behind the desk and a large flag on the wall behind the conference table. All in all, he would make substantial changes.

Jost crossed smartly to the desk and came to attention, clicking his heels.

"Major Jost reporting as ordered, Herr Admiral."

Admiral Wilhelm Franz Canaris—a tall, hawk-faced man with a lean frame and tired blue eyes—ignored the salute. He had taken over as head of the Abwehr in 1935 after serving in the Imperial Navy in World War I. Jost had heard of criticism by members of the Foreign Ministry and the Sicherheitsdienst—Herr Himmler's internal security police—against Canaris' conservatism, his traditional military background, his heavy agent losses in England and the United States, but the Führer still backed him. Of course if the criticism continued to grow . . .

Canaris picked up a message from his desk and handed it to Jost.

"Can you explain this, Major?"

Jost recognized it immediately, inwardly sighing in relief.

"*Ja,* Herr Admiral. It means nothing."

"Nothing? This states that Novalis is canceling Prometheus!"

"*Ja,* but the message is false, Herr Admiral. It does not contain the proper code word to make it so."

Canaris leaned back in the leather chair, studying Jost.

"And just why is Novalis sending false messages?"

Jost hesitated. "I do not know, Herr Admiral. Perhaps he is testing Capricorn's radio security."

"Are there any serious problems with Prometheus?"

"*Nein,* Herr Admiral."

Canaris extracted another message from the papers on his desk and handed it to Jost.

"Then how do you explain this?"

Jost took the message form and read it quickly. He had not seen this one. It was marked for Canaris' eyes only. Jost began to sweat a little under his jacket. He hadn't known that Canaris was monitoring radio traffic on the Prometheus Operation. In fact, he hadn't known that a message could be sent or received on Prometheus without passing through his hands.

He read the message quickly. It was from Martha, transmitted through Rudolph, her contact in the Argentine Embassy in Washington.

ZEUS. NOVALIS KILLED CAPRICORN. NOW ON WAY TO
CHICAGO. WILL SEND DETAILS LATER. MARTHA.

Jost read the message a second time, trying to think of an acceptable explanation. Canaris waited impatiently.

"I was not informed of this, Herr Admiral. I did not know—"

"Why did you not know, Major? You are in charge of the American Desk, are you not?"

"*Ja,* Herr—"

"Did you not select Hauptmann Roebling personally for this mission?"

"*Ja.*"

"Then are you not personally responsible for his killing Capricorn?"

Jost hesitated.

"Are you or are you not?"

"*Ja,* Herr Admiral."

"Then I suggest you find out what has happened immediately and make a full report to me, Major. You know the importance of this operation. If Roebling has caused it to fail, I will hold you personally responsible. Now leave me!"

"*Jawohl,* Herr Admiral!"

On the way back to his office, Jost walked slowly, reading and rereading the two messages. Damn Roebling! Why hadn't he followed orders? Why had he killed Capricorn? Why was he headed for Chicago? Jost felt his hatred of the man rise in his throat like stomach acid.

He had hated Roebling since their first day at Quenz Lake, the rural training facility known as "The Farm." Roebling was one of the aristocrats whom Jost's family had been born to serve. Only the Führer's rise to power, his Youth Corps program had kept Jost from spending his life working the land, grubbing in the dirt and doffing his hat as the owner of the farm rode past in his Mercedes-Benz.

When the Party had rewarded his work, his loyalty by se-
lecting him to attend secondary school, he thought he had
finally escaped. He worked hard, very hard, using his native shrewdness to make up for his lack of background, following his superiors' orders to the letter, finally graduating
with honors and winning a place in an Abwehr training
class.

But there he had met Roebling and his friends, recent
graduates of the University of Göttingen. They had joined
the Abwehr for a lark. He had come in deadly earnestness,
determined to aid the Führer—his idol—in whatever way
possible. The contest had quickly narrowed to Roebling
and him. The others—aristocrat and peasant—were con-
tent to let the two settle the differences of class.

But Roebling had defeated him at every turn—in the
coursework, the exercises, even the physical training. He
set a new camp record for push-ups. Roebling broke it. He
devised a new method of sabotaging an industrial plant.
Roebling devised a better one. He stumbled over foreign-
language syntaxes; Roebling corrected him in front of the
entire class. He came to hate Roebling as he had never
hated another human being—not even the landlord in the
Mercedes. All his frustrations, his former hatreds coa-
lesced on one man. He would have challenged him, killed
him, except that the cadre strictly forbade any such personal competitions.

Mercifully, graduation had separated them, sending
Roebling overseas and keeping him within the country because of his language problems. A year later he had heard
of Roebling's transfer to the Panzers and had gotten very
drunk toasting Roebling's stupidity, his certain death. He
had almost forgotten Roebling until Gretchen Jahnke had
suddenly began dating him. Then it had all returned—all
the small defeats, the humiliations. He swore that he
would never lose anything to Roebling again, not even
something as unimportant as Gretchen.

He had been working on a plan to remove Roebling
quietly yet permanently from his world when he had been
handed the Prometheus Operation. It was so perfectly
suited to his needs that he had known the gods were finally

smiling on him. But Roebling had now crossed him again. He had done something totally unexpected—disobeyed an order—and in doing so had jeopardized the entire operation—and perhaps Jost's career. Now there could be no more restraints. He could not let Roebling survive this time.

Jost stopped suddenly, smiling to himself. The Americans had been stupid so far—more stupid than he had expected. All he needed to do was help them a little more, and they would take care of Roebling for him. But it would have to be done subtly. He could not endanger the operation in a way that would get back to the admiral.

He took a deep breath and marched on down the stairs. He would think of something that was just right. His only regret was that Roebling would never know whose hand had placed the rope around his neck.

22 NOTHING, GREG ALLISON thought, staring at the pile of reports on his borrowed desk at the New York CIC headquarters. Three days' worth of dawn-to-midnight work, checking hotels, talking to cab drivers, poring over each abandoned car report. The New York police had been enlisted in the search and were also checking all area parking for cars with Washington, Virginia and Maryland plates, but none of them had matched any of the stolen-vehicle reports thus far.

As the reports came in, he sent the tag numbers to the district and state motor vehicle offices for information on the owners, but checking all of them out would be slow work. Still, it had to be done. At the moment, they had nothing else going for them.

Yesterday he thought they had something. The First National had found another counterfeit fifty in a United Airlines deposit. But the trail had ended there. There was simply no way to trace it back to any particular flight, and the clerks were too busy this time of year to notice any particular passenger. So he was left with the same feeling that he had lived with for two days. Novalis was gone, either down south to meet a German submarine or to some other area to continue his mission. The woman and the car were probably gone too, back to where they had come from, untraceable.

Allison leaned back, rubbing his eyes. When he looked up, Bill Danvers was standing beside his desk, holding another stack of reports. He also looked tired, and his cheeks were showing dark stubble. Allison's own face felt like sandpaper.

"Here's a fresh batch that just came in. Want me to help you go through them?"

Allison looked at his watch. It took a moment to focus on the hands. It was almost midnight.

"Thanks, but let's catch them in the morning. Just stack them in the basket there."

Danvers piled the stack neatly and placed a paperweight on it.

"Say, Mr. Allison, would you mind if I came in a little late tomorrow? I'd like to wait until my son opens his presents."

"Presents? Is tomorrow Christmas?"

"Sure. Didn't you know?"

Allison glanced quickly at the desk calendar.

"I thought this was the twenty-third."

Danvers smiled. "You forgot to turn the calendar."

"Damn," Allison said absently. "No. Take all the time you need. In fact, why don't you take the day off? We're not doing any good here."

Danvers hesitated. "Are you sure? I'd like to spend the day with my family, but if you need me—"

"I may not even be here myself," Allison said. "The duty officer can do what I'm doing."

"Thanks," Danvers said. "And Merry Christmas."

"Merry Christmas to you. And to your family."

"I'll tell them."

Danvers left. Allison rubbed his eyes again, wondering if it was too late to call Cynthia. He had intended to take the time to buy presents for her, for his parents, but he had forgotten. He smiled ruefully. Cynthia would love hearing that story again. Cynthia. The only Christmas present she really wanted was for him to transfer out of the CIC.

Maybe he should call her. It had been almost six

months since he had come home to the Washington apartment to find her gone, the note on the mantel. Maybe she
was ready to listen now, really listen to his explanation of
the way he felt, why he had volunteered for the CIC and
why he could not transfer back to the Judge Advocate
General's Corps.

When America had entered the war, he was within two
months of being thirty years of age—probably half his
life—and he had never really *done* anything. His entire life
had been a series of proper schools, proper grades, proper
sports, proper dating, a proper wife and a proper career in a
proper legal firm. Everyone had nothing but praise for the
proper Gregory Edward Allison, a rapidly solidifying pillar
of the community. Everyone except Greg Allison. As the
milestone year bore down on him, he began to analyze his
life, to see the pattern clearly, to feel the years passing with
a sameness that frightened him. But he had not known
how to change it.

Were it not for the horror of it, he could have cheered
when the Japanese bombed Pearl Harbor. He wanted to
volunteer for the Army the next day, but his father—the
proper Edward Allison—persuaded him to wait until he
could arrange a commission. However, when the commission came through, Greg found himself assigned to the
Judge Advocate General's Corps at Sixth Area Headquarters—in Chicago. He went to work each day and returned
home each night to Cynthia, the only noticeable difference
being that he now wore a uniform with gold lieutenant's
bars. The nation, the world were at war and he was still
doing routine legal contract work.

Within two months he could no longer stand the routine and quietly volunteered for the newly formed Corps of
Intelligence Police. He waited until the day before he left
for the first class of the new training school before telling
anyone. His father had railed at him. His mother had almost fainted. Cynthia had cried. And he had never been
happier. Even now they did not understand, and he still
could not explain it adequately. He only knew that CIC
work made him feel useful, important, alive.

But that feeling was becoming increasingly expensive

to maintain. He had already lost the close contact he had always had with his family, especially his father. And now it was threatening his marriage to Cynthia. He loved Cynthia. He didn't want to lose her. But he could not transfer back to the Judge Advocate General's Corps, go back to what he had been. He simply was no longer that person. There must be some middle ground. If he could only find it.

Allison sighed heavily and turned off the desk lamp. He was too tired to worry about it tonight. He would call Cynthia tomorrow and apologize for not sending her a present in time for Christmas.

He never made the call. There was a good lead on his desk when he arrived at the office the next morning, and he spent the entire day tracking down an auburn-haired Washington resident who was in town visiting her parents for Christmas. Sunday morning he thought about calling again, but he knew she would be attending church services with her family. Sunday afternoon—well, it was too late to call by then. Monday morning there was a message from Goldman on his desk. He dialed the number, and Goldman answered immediately.

"Where've you been, Greg? I called more than thirty minutes ago."

"Trying to pry my eyes open," Allison said shortly. "What's up?"

"We've got another bill at the Federal Reserve in Cleveland. I've booked us on the first flight out of La Guardia. Can you make it?"

"How soon?"

"Forty-five minutes."

The duty officer entered and motioned to him. The chief was on line three. Allison nodded.

"Let me call you back, Marty."

Goldman hesitated. "All right. I'll give you five minutes, but then I'm gone."

"Thanks."

Allison punched the button for line three.

"Yes, sir."

"We've intercepted another message to Capricorn, Greg. It orders him to tell 'Sampson' to expect Novalis' arrival in Chicago within the next few days."

"Chicago? It actually names Chicago?"

"Yes."

"Another decoy?"

"That's very possible, Greg. It was sent twice last night at different times without any acknowledgment from Capricorn."

"Sure sounds fishy," Allison said. "But another counterfeit bill has just surfaced in Cleveland."

"That's strange. If the message is a decoy, why would they send us in the same direction? They have to know we would alert everyone along the line."

"That was my thought too, sir. It just might be genuine. I'll fly out."

"To where?"

"I think I'll try the long shot," Allison said. "We just might get in front of him for a change."

"Chicago?"

"Yes, sir."

"Good luck. I've already alerted both detachments."

"Thank you, sir. I'll report in as soon as I have anything."

He hung up and called Goldman back. Goldman was skeptical.

"You aren't trying to run something on me, are you?"

"All I'm doing is keeping you informed as we agreed, Marty. I'm not asking you to go to Chicago with me."

"There's something you're not telling me, Greg."

"That's all I know, Marty. I told you it's a long shot. I wouldn't try to decoy you."

"Like hell you wouldn't."

Allison hesitated, surprised at the new tone, the intensity, in Goldman's voice.

"What's the matter with you this morning, Marty? You sound mad about something."

"I am," Goldman said.

"What?"

"It's a family matter," Goldman said curtly. "Are you sure this isn't a dodge to keep me away from Cleveland?"

"I give you my word," Allison said.

"I meant what I said about wanting a crack at that Nazi, Greg."

"I know you did, Marty. And, frankly, that worries me a little."

"It should. Are you still going to Chicago?"

"Yes. But go to Cleveland if you like. Don't let me stop you."

There was a pause on the other end of the line. Finally Goldman spoke.

"I'll change my reservation."

23 THE TWENTIETH CENTURY LIMITED arrived at Chicago's La Salle Street Station at two-thirty Monday afternoon after the run from Cleveland. Its route had taken it along the shore of Lake Erie to Toledo, then across the northern part of Ohio and Indiana to the shore of Lake Michigan. Once around the tip of that lake, it had proceeded past Gary, Indiana, up the shoreline through miles of factories—iron and steel works belching heavy black smoke—across the Illinois state line and finally into the heart of the city.

Stefan Roebling had never been this far west in America before, but he could see the growth, the development spurred by the war. The suburbs were new, clean, in contrast to the inner city, the factories, the old buildings and streets. The distances between Gary, then Hammond, then Chicago were short. People were crowding into the cities. If the boom lasted another three years, the cities might grow together, combine into one large metropolis.

Roebling handed Erika down to the station platform and looked around. The station was too crowded to pick out any particular person who might be watching. She took his arm, lovely in a beige traveling suit, the dark auburn wig reaching below her shoulders in front and back, peeking out from under a pillbox hat in front. She shouldn't be here. They had both agreed that it was dangerous for her to stay with him, that she should go back to Washington. Then she had thought that he might have trouble locating Sampson, that Sampson might not accept his authority without her to introduce him, so she had offered to accompany him to Chicago. He didn't think it was a good idea, but he had allowed himself to be convinced. In truth, both wanted, needed all the time, the memories that they could steal from the war.

They went through the gate and crossed the main concourse of the station, a black porter following with their bags on a small hand truck. Roebling walked quickly, picking his way through the crowd, keeping his eyes moving. Perhaps it was only the delay in Cleveland, but he was uneasy, edgy. He shouldn't be. They had not had any trouble in New York or Cleveland, but he kept feeling a presence somewhere behind him, moving, closing the distance.

They came out the front of the station and the porter waved up one of the waiting cabs. He helped the cabbie put the bags in the trunk, then came back to Roebling, flashing a white smile. Roebling handed him a fifty-cent piece and got a salute in return.

"Thank you, suh."

As Roebling was helping Erika into the cab, a man in a dark overcoat came out of a door farther down and trotted to a black Ford Sedan. Roebling could see no markings on the car, but it was parked in a no-parking zone, its motor idling, another man behind the wheel. Roebling slid into the cab and shut the door.

"Where to?" the cabbie asked, looking over his shoulder.

"A good hotel. Do you have a Sheraton here?"

"Yes, sir."

"Then take us there."

The cab moved off. Roebling turned and saw the Ford move out, keeping pace with them. Erika pressed his arm and smiled.

"So you finally decided to take my advice."

"About what?"

"About hotels, darling. It only costs a few thousand dollars more to go first class."

Roebling smiled. "You're very free with our employer's money."

"I'm sure he can afford it."

The cabbie made good time through the afternoon traffic, not taking any side trips that Roebling could tell. Still, the meter read almost $1.25 before the cab stopped in front of the hotel. Roebling helped Erika out and watched the street as the cabbie unloaded the bags on another cart brought out by a bellhop summoned by the doorman. The black Ford was double-parked halfway up the block. The passenger got out and strolled up the sidewalk, taking his time.

Roebling paid the cabbie with two one-dollar bills, waving away the man's thanks for the large tip. The bellhop followed them inside and turned toward the desk. Roebling caught his arm.

"Where's the back entrance?"

"Pardon me?"

"The back entrance. Where is it?"

"There's a delivery entrance, sir, but that's for employees only. You must mean the side entrance. That's down through—"

Roebling showed the man the corner of a ten-dollar bill he had pulled from his pocket.

"Look. I think I saw my friend's husband following us. This ten is yours if you point out the door to the delivery entrance, then check those bags into your cloakroom."

The bellhop nodded. "I understand, sir. Of course, there'll be a storage charge."

Roebling found another ten and added it to the one in his hand.

"What shall I do with the claim check?"

"Mail it to John Smith, care of General Delivery at the Main Post Office."

"Yes, sir. The back entrance is through there. Turn left before you get to the coffeeshop, then left again. It's marked 'employees only.' "

Roebling handed the man the two bills.

"Thank you, sir. Come again."

Roebling walked quickly through the lobby, Erika matching his stride. They found the door, went through a storage room, into an area littered with cartons, then came out on a dock where several kitchen busboys were carrying in crates of vegetables that had just been unloaded from a truck backed up to the dock. The men, mostly Negroes, turned to stare as Roebling jumped down from the dock, then helped Erika down. They walked quickly around to the front of the truck and looked up and down the alley. Roebling started down the alley. Erika stopped him. The truck driver was sitting in his cab, a clipboard braced on the steering wheel, watching both of them.

Erika smiled. "We've got a problem."

"I can see that, Lady, but don't look at me."

Erika's voice took on a helpless tone. "Would you be a gentleman and give us a lift? We only want to ride a few blocks."

The man shook his head, pointing to the sticker on his windshield.

"Company don't allow no riders."

"You don't look like a man who's afraid of breaking a rule now and then," Erika said, still smiling. "We'd pay you."

The man glanced at Roebling, his eyes skeptical. "I ain't no taxi." He put the clipboard aside and started the engine, racing it unnecessarily.

"How about fifty?" Roebling asked.

"Dollars?"

The engine settled into an idle.

Roebling took out his money clip and held up a bill. The truck driver looked both ways in the alley.

"You runnin' from the cops?"

"Hardly," Erika said, losing her smile. "If you're afraid—"

"Hand it here," the man said. Roebling gave Erika the bill. She handed it to the driver. He looked at both sides.

"I'm only goin' a few blocks before my next stop. I can't take you no farther than that."

"That's fine," Erika said.

"Then get in."

They went around the front of the truck and Roebling helped Erika up on the high running board. Both slid down in the seat as the man negotiated the narrow alley and turned into traffic. After two blocks, he told them they could sit up. At the edge of another alley, five blocks away, they thanked him and got out.

It took Allison and Goldman almost thirty minutes to get to the hotel from Midway airfield. All the way in, Allison had been cursing himself for not foreseeing that the man would switch to the train. But this might work out better after all. All the hotel entrances were completely covered. The back-up units had arrived within minutes after the train-station team had radioed the location. An arrest in a hotel room should be much easier than in a crowded airfield terminal. He settled back in the seat, smiling.

"You look like the proverbial cat," Goldman said.

"Not yet. But give me another ten minutes," Allison replied. "Then you'll really see feathers on my chin."

"Aren't you counting your chickens a little early?"

"Aren't you mixing metaphors or proverbs or something?"

"Okay. So you guessed right about Chicago. But we haven't got them yet."

"We will," Allison said, still smiling. "You always were a pessimist."

"Of course," Goldman said, checking his pistol. "I'm a Jew."

Allison lost his smile. "You're beginning to act like a Comanche. I told you I wanted the man alive."

"I remember. But you forgot to tell the Nazi. He may have a different idea."

"And if he does, you intend to oblige him. Is that it?"

"An agent has a duty to protect himself and his partner. That's in the manual."

"It's in ours, too," Allison said. "But I still want him alive, Marty."

Goldman put the gun away. "Greg, do you know that there are people who claim the American Indian is part of the lost tribe of Israel?"

"No. But right now i could believe it."

24 STEFAN ROEBLING paced the living room in the small frame house, pausing occasionally to look through the crack between the edge of the shade and the window. The area looked the same each time—weathered, ugly houses, small yards, a narrow asphalt street with dirty snow along the gutters. Occasionally, a car passed, its occupants usually housewives with heavily bundled children on the way to or from the market, the laundry, wherever housewives went in this cold, windy city.

The house was on the Near Northwest Side—not far from the North Branch of the Chicago River—in an area of older workers' homes, remnants of another era now being crowded out by industrial expansion. He could hear an almost constant rumble, interspersed with the puffing of steam engines, the banging of cars in the nearby railroad switching yard. Truly, as Kipling had written of Chicago: "Having seen it, I urgently desire never to see it again."

But Kipling had not had his problems, Roebling thought. That gentleman could simply catch the next train out. They were trapped. He looked across the room at Erika. She sat in a well-worn armchair near the open heater, filing a broken place on one nail and listening to a small radio. Her clothes were showing two days of constant wear. The skirt was badly wrinkled and the blouse was limp, but she still managed, without her cosmetics case, to appear fresh and lovely.

However, she was the only thing in the room that looked fresh. The wallpaper, once a bright, flowered pattern, had succumbed to age, the vibrations of the trains and the coal smoke that covered the area. The linoleum on the floor was cracked and worn down to its dark base in heavy traffic areas. The furniture was tired and sagging, with dirty cotton padding sticking out of the occasional rip or tear. The other three rooms were more or less the same. The house, the area depressed him, but not as much as his thoughts, his knowledge of what lay outside this temporary haven. Erika noticed him watching her.

"When will Sampson be back?"

"Soon."

Harold Owen, code name Sampson, was their temporary host. He had responded to Erika's call from the drugstore, after their second bus ride, and brought them here. Now, he was out picking up additional food and trying to learn what he could about their pursuers. Erika tapped the nail file on the wooden chair arm absently.

"What are you thinking?"

The tapping stopped. "That they'll be able to trace my clothes. Almost everything has a label—Garfinckel's in Washington or Saks in New York."

"I know," Roebling said. "I shouldn't have let you come."

"It was my choice," she said. "It's just that . . ." She didn't finish.

"Just what?"

"Nothing. What do we do now?"

"I haven't decided yet."

"We can't stay here long. We need to keep moving, make our way to Mexico."

"Mexico? You think I should abort the operation?"

She met his eyes. "Yes."

He smiled ruefully. "Suddenly it's not a game any more, is it?"

She frowned. "All right, then, what do we do?"

"We concentrate on immediate problems."

"Such as?"

"Such as figuring out who is helping them. I've been going over every step I've made since leaving Washington, and I keep coming back to the same conclusion. Someone is giving them information. Otherwise, there's no way they could have traced us, known where to wait for us."

"Could Herder have sold information about us to the police?"

"It's possible, but he didn't know where we were going."

"He could have guessed. Or they could have just covered all the stations where we might show up."

He shook his head. "There wasn't anyone at the Toledo or South Bend stations. No, they knew our destination."

"Then what about our host?"

"Sampson didn't know we were coming, remember?"

"And North's dead," she said. "So that just leaves me."

He denied the statement almost immediately, but she caught his slight hesitation.

"Don't lie to me, Stefan. If we're back to that, I want to know."

He didn't respond. Her eyes changed, became wary.

"I still don't have a plausible reason. That's what's stopping you, isn't it?"

"No. I trust you."

She didn't believe him. They stared at each other. The silence grew slowly, then was suddenly broken by a car turning into the graveled driveway beside the house. He checked the window quickly.

"It's Sampson."

As he looked back, she had her purse open, her hand inside. She withdrew the hand slowly, lifting a package of Camels out of the purse.

Owen cursed aloud as he fumbled with the two bags of groceries at the door. Roebling let him unlock the door himself—in case anyone should be watching—then closed it behind him. Owen was under six feet but thickly built, with a loud voice, close-cropped hair and a naturally belligerent manner. He was German, born in Düsseldorf but brought to America by his family at age ten.

He had retained his loyalty to his native land, however,

and had become a member of the German-American Bund, rising to drillmaster at Camp Nordland in Andover, New Jersey, before the Bund had been broken up. Without help, he had successfully changed his name from the original Herman Otto, eluded the surveillance of the FBI and volunteered his services for sabotage work. The Abwehr had accepted him reluctantly, after several of their trained agents had been caught, but had used him only for minor operations. His most valuable assets were his contacts with the American underworld.

Owen carried the bags into the kitchen and came back with an orange, which he promptly bit the end off and began to suck out the juice. Erika didn't try to hide her disgust.

"What did you find out?" Roebling asked.

"The downtown terminals are heavily covered, and your descriptions have been circulated to all police patrol units."

"We could have guessed that," Erika said. "How did they track us?"

"I don't know," Herder said. "Most of my sources have gone underground and the rest ain't talking. They think it's another crime clean-up campaign."

"You're a lot of help," Erika said.

He gave her a look of contempt and sucked on the orange.

"I got the stuff you wanted. How long're you gonna be here?"

"I don't know," Roebling said.

"You're really hot," Herder said. "I think you oughta get outta town right away."

"My sentiments exactly," Erika said.

Roebling ignored her. "We need some things first. Some different clothes, some hair dye, some—"

"Hey, whoa," Owen said. "I don't mind getting the stuff for you, but I got to have some cash. I ain't exactly rich, you know."

"That's no problem," Roebling said, pulling out his money clip. He counted out two hundred and handed it to Owen. Owen looked at the bills.

"What'd you do, rob a bank?"

He rubbed one of the new bills, then looked at his thumb.

"Ain't you got something a little more used? I'm gonna attract enough attention buying women's clothes in some dress shop without paying for 'em with brand-new money."

"I asked for used currency, but the unit didn't have enough," Roebling said. "They had to mix in a lot of new. They were supposed to rub them down, make them looked used, but they didn't do a very good job."

"That's your problem," Owen said. "How many used bills can you gimme?"

Roebling checked the bills remaining in his money clip. He had only sixty dollars in used bills.

"I'll have to check to see if I have any more."

He flashed a look at Erika. She rose and came over to distract Owen while he went into the bedroom to take off the money belt. It took him a few minutes to find enough used bills. When he came out of the bedroom, Erika was examining one of the new bills, comparing it with one of the used ones.

"Stefan, take a look at this."

"What's wrong?"

"These new bills don't feel right. They don't really look right either."

Roebling took the two bills from her and made his own comparison.

"I don't see any difference."

"Don't look at the numbers or backgrounds. Look at the portraits. Hold one just above the other."

He changed the position of the bills.

"Now examine Franklin's mouth and eyes. See the difference?"

"Damn!" Roebling said, then uttered a better curse in German.

"Counterfeit!"

She nodded. Owen was examining two of the other bills, holding them up to the light.

"These are queer too," Owen said. "Why would they give you this stuff? Did somebody foul up?"

Erika looked at Roebling. He already had the answer to that question.

"No."

"They wanted you to be caught?" Erika asked.

"Yes," Roebling said.

Owen suddenly looked uneasy. Roebling smiled.

"It's not what you're thinking. This isn't the work of the section but one man. It's personal."

"You sure?"

"Yes. I didn't think he'd go this far, jeopardize an entire operation just to get me, but he obviously has."

"You ain't spent any of that here, have you? I mean, they can't ... No, I paid for the groceries myself." Owen grinned in relief. "and I almost hit you up for some dough before I left. Good thing I didn't, huh?"

Roebling ignored the man, unbuttoning his shirt. Owen's eyes widened at the sight of the thick money belt. Roebling carried it into the small kitchen with Owen and Erika following. As Roebling began emptying the pockets on the table, Owen whistled softly.

"How much you got there?"

"I started with fifteen thousand," Roebling said. "And now I know why my friend was so generous."

"What're you planning to do?" Owen asked.

"Separate the good from the bad. Sit down and help me."

With three of them working, it took less time than Roebling expected. Once they learned to recognize the bills, the work went rather quickly. He doubled-checked the others' work, then counted the pile of good bills. It was depressingly small.

"How much?" Erika asked.

"Four hundred and change."

Erika sighed. "Well, I guess I'll have to get accustomed to going second class."

"It's not enough, even for second class," Roebling said.

She looked at him. "You're not thinking of trying to continue Prometheus? Surely now, you—"

"Hey," Owen interrupted. "I don't think I wanna hear this. I ain't getting involved in no fouled-up operation that might—"

"Sit down," Roebling said. "All I want you to do is get rid of this counterfeit for me."

"That's easy," Owen said quickly. "there's an incinerator out back."

"No good," Roebling said. "We need this money. I want you to exchange—"

"I ain't about to walk into no bank with that stuff!" Owen said adamantly. "And I damned sure ain't gonna sell it to the mob!"

"That wasn't what I had in mind," Roebling said. "I don't want either these bills or the new ones to be traceable to any of us." He looked at Erika. "Any ideas?"

She smiled. "Since I became a member of the Huntington family. I've spent money just about every way that money can be spent. Let me think about it for a while."

He squeezed her hand. "I owe you an apology for what I was thinking earlier—and for not leaving you in New York."

She squeezed his hand in return. "Your first apology is accepted. The second one is unnecessary. As it turned out, you did me a favor by bringing me with you."

"A favor? How?"

"I just remembered that twenty-dollar bill we left for my housekeeper."

25 THE CIC TRAINING SCHOOL had changed drastically since Greg Allison and his classmates had put together their own training manuals from mimeographed instructors' notes at the Army War College. In November 1941, after holding classes in various Washington locations and at the Arlington Cantonment, the school had been moved to the Tower Town Club hotel at 820 North Michigan Avenue in Chicago. With these facilities—and cooperating agreements with the Chicago police laboratory, the criminal laboratory of Northwestern University and the Underwriters Laboratory facilities—the school had grown rapidly in stature and professionalism.

Instead of the crowded billet at the Arlington Cantonment, the students had enjoyed comfortable two-man rooms within the hotel. The food, prepared in the hotel kitchens, was as good as the fare at any of the hotels in the area. The recreation facilities included a swimming pool, exercise room and various reading and study rooms. The Chicago students, on hearing descriptions of the first school, reacted like Thunderbolt and Mustang pilots listening to World War I aviators talk about Spads and Sopwith Camels. They simply could not empathize with the earlier group because their experiences were so different.

Now there was a third group of trainees who could not empathize with the second group. By late 1942, almost a year after Pearl Harbor, the number of agents being processed by the school had tripled. The two-man rooms had four or more men in them, classroom space had been stretched to the limit and the ratio of instructors to students had declined sharply. In addition, the Navy had been assigned space in the Tower Town Club, and the hotel bulged with non-CIC personnel. In the Navy way, everything had promptly been renamed, and the Army personnel got off the elevators at "decks" instead of floors.

So in November 1942 the CIC school was moved to 66 East 11th Street on Chicago's South Side, and the curriculum was revised again. The Chicago school was now an advanced training facility. The initial instruction of agents was delegated to preliminary CIC schools within all Departments and Service Commands, then those students selected for advanced training were sent to Chicago for specialized training.

Greg Allison had been aware of these changes, but he had not really been prepared for the change of attitude that had taken place along with the change of quarters. He had driven down to the school after a concentrated five-day search had failed to turn up Novalis or the woman with him at any of the hotels in the downtown area. He planned to enlist the aid of the school commandant, Lieutenant Colonel William B. Parsons, but had not been able to talk with him. Instead, he was shown into the office of the executive officer of the school, Major Theodore J. Walker. Allison did not know the man, and Walker didn't know him. As a result, Walker's first reaction to his request was completely negative.

"I don't see how we could do that, Mr. Allison. You should know that our training schedule here is very tightly drawn so that we can get the maximum training into the minimum time."

"Yes, sir, but—"

"We also have very few people here now that are scheduled for Zone of the Interior work. In accordance with the recent decisions of the General Staff, we're training most of the people for overseas duty. In fact, the men here will soon start wearing uniforms just like other Army personnel. And once they get overseas, they'll be wearing bright red armbands with 'CIC' emblazoned on them. They simply aren't being trained to do the type of thing you want them for."

"I'm sure they could handle it," Allison said. "I have four men from the Sixth Service Command detachment who could direct them. We just want them to help us check on the tourist courts outside the downtown area. If I can get enough men, it shouldn't take too long. Probably only a few days."

"Have you tried the Chicago police? We've found them very helpful."

"I contacted Captain Petrain shortly after we lost the agents at the hotel," Allison said. "He's put men at all the transportation terminals, which released our men for the investigative work, but that's about all he can do—other than passing out our descriptions and artist's sketches of the two agents to his patrolmen. We also have four Secret Service agents from the Chicago office working with us, but they can't spare any more."

"Won't that be sufficient?"

"It should be," Allison said. "But this agent is very good. We've run him to ground for the first time, and I don't want to lose him."

"I understand. And I sympathize. But I'm afraid we can't let you have any of our trainees."

Allison sighed. "I was hoping it wouldn't come to this, but I have verbal authority from the chief to use any CIC personnel I need to run this agent down. So I'm afraid I'll have to insist."

Walker regarded him skeptically. "You realize that Colonel Parsons will want to confirm that statement with the chief before giving you the men."

"Of course," Allison said, rising. "Just have the men report to the detachment office. Mr. Hooper will brief them and assign them to areas. Good afternoon, sir."

Allison left the school and drove back to the Federal Building complex on Adams Street. He parked the car in an official slot next to the Treasury Building and took the elevator to the third floor, where Marty Goldman had managed to get a temporary office as a command post. He was tired. Right now, he would like to forget Novalis, the woman, the whole affair. The familiar sights and sounds of Chicago had been intruding on his concentration these past two days. The streets, the stores, even the snow and cold winds kept reminding him that he was home, that just five blocks over was his father's law offices, that on the near North Shore was his family home, that in twenty minutes he could be pulling into the driveway of his own house.

But he had not allowed himself to dwell on those thoughts. He had not even taken the time to call his parents. They would not understand why he didn't have time to drop by, to have dinner with them. Cynthia would not understand either. Cynthia. She had been the hardest to keep out of his thoughts. He wanted to see her, to talk with her. Was she planning to file for divorce? Had she been seeing someone else? Would she even talk to him?

Goldman was reading the third page of a teletypewriter message when Allison entered his office. He glanced up.

"Any luck?"

"Yes, but they want to contact Chief Kibler first."

"Good." He paused. "My headquarters has identified the woman."

Allison brightened. "Who is she?"

"Mrs. Andrew Huntington the third."

"What!"

"Do you know her?" Goldman asked, watching him.

"I know who she is," Allison said. "Are your people sure they have the right identification?"

"She left one of those counterfeit twenties as a tip for her maid just before they left Washington. The maid saved it to make a payment on her refrigerator. Otherwise, we'd have known two weeks ago."

Allison shook his head. "Erika Huntington. That's hard to believe. It must be a mistake. She must have gotten the bill in change from a store or something."

Goldman handed the TWX to him. "Your people also

traced the clothes to her. This just came over from your Sixth Area office."

Allison took the TWX, noting the CIC restriction against unauthorized readership. Goldman's expression was defiant. He had no intention of apologizing for reading the message.

Allison read the three pages quickly. Baltimore had moved very quickly after identifying Erika Huntington. The three pages contained a good, concise history of her background.

She had been born in Bremen, Germany, in 1919. Her father was Erik Thorvaldsen and her mother was Karen Wendt Thorvaldsen, a German national. Thorvaldsen was a native of Esbjerg, Denmark, but he had been educated as a naval architect in Germany and worked in a Bremen shipyard. She had met Andrew Huntington in 1936, while he was an aide to Admiral Leahy. Leahy and a party of other high-ranking officers and civilians had been touring European shipyards, ostensibly to exchange information on the latest maritime designs but in reality to assess the various countries' shipbuilding capacities should the possibility of a second world war grow more probable. Within a month of their meeting, Huntington had her agreement to marry him. His family objected strongly, especially after discovering that her father had once been a suspected Communist, but Andy Huntington had been adamant.

Baltimore doubted that Erika had been an Abwehr agent at the time of her marriage. More likely she was recruited during an extended visit she made to her parents in 1940. However, that did not matter. She was an agent. Allison smiled, imagining the embarrassment of one Major Gerald Cavanaugh, who was probably on his way to Alaska by now.

"What's so funny?" Goldman asked.

"Nothing. Did the office send over the photograph mentioned here?"

"It's downstairs. I'm having twenty-five pocket-sized copies made."

"Better up that to two hundred. Let's get a copy in every police patrol car as soon as possible."

"All right. Then what?"

"Then we continue our search pattern of the hotels and tourist courts."

"Do you really think they've holed up in a public house?"

"No," Allison admitted. "But unless you have a better suggestion, I'm going with standard procedures."

26 IT WAS ALMOST nine-thirty when Greg Allison reached the quiet neighborhood on the North Side and turned down the winding, snow-packed street. Only an occasional evergreen broke up the stark, wintry look of the bare-limbed trees under the yellow streetlights. He drove slowly, looking at the houses, the snow-covered yards, the lighted windows. Through the partially open vent window the air carried an occasional whiff of wood smoke, feeding his memories of warm fires in the cozy den of the house just down the block.

He rounded another slight curve and there it was, sitting well back on the lot, the front lawn and hedge covered with undisturbed snow. He pushed in the clutch and the sedan idled to a stop. There was a light on in the entry and a thin plume of smoke rising out of the brick chimney. He sat for a moment, debating with himself, then eased the clutch out and guided the car into the driveway.

Just before he was ready to ring the doorbell a second time, the porch light came on and the door opened to the limit of the night chain. Allison took off his hat so that she could see him clearly.

"Greg?"

"Hello, Cyn."

She hesitated a moment, then closed the door and slipped the chain out of the groove. He wiped the snow off his shoes and came inside, closing the door behind him. For a moment they stood silently, awkwardly. She was prettier, more petite than his memory of her. Her robe was new, made of a blue silk that brushed the floor as she moved. She blushed faintly under his examination, running a hand quickly over her hair, smoothing back the loose strands.

"I wish you'd have let me know you were coming. I could have been more presentable."

"You look fine," Allison said. He remembered the gift and took it out of his overcoat pocket.

"I'm sorry about Christmas. I didn't have a chance to mail this in time."

She hesitated, then took the package from him. "I have yours in the bedroom. I sent it to the apartment in Washington, but it came back. You should have let me know that you'd moved."

"I'm sorry."

There was another short, awkward silence.

"I hope you don't mind my coming by this way."

"No. Of course not. Take off your coat and come into the den."

He hung his things in the entry closet and followed her into the room. Everything was as he remembered, the wood paneling, oriental rug, leather sofa, his big chair and ottoman drawn up near the hearth. The fire was small and only one lamp was lit. From the open book on the table, she must have been curled up on the end of the sofa, reading. The picture came easily to mind. He had seen her like that many times. But now the picture carried a tinge of loneliness.

She put another small log on the fire while he took a place on the couch, deliberately avoiding the big chair. Her movements were tense, nervous.

"You must be cold, Greg. Would you like a drink?"

"No, thank you."

They were being too polite, too formal. He wanted to ask her how she had been, how she now felt about him, but he could not think of the right way to get into the subject.

Perhaps this visit was the mistake that he had been telling himself it would be. She came back to the couch and sat down.

"Well now, what are you doing in Chicago?"

He hesitated and she recognized her mistake.

"I'm sorry. I shouldn't have asked."

"I'd love to tell you, Cyn, but I can't."

"Well, at least that tells me that you're still in the CIC. How long will you be in town?"

"I don't know."

"Have you seen your parents yet?"

"No."

There was another silence. She smoothed a wrinkle in the robe. He tried to think of something to say. Finally, she looked up.

"Why did you come by, Greg?"

"I just wanted to see you, to make sure you're all right."

"I see."

"Do you need anything? I could see that you get it before I leave."

"I'm fine. My parents check on me regularly. Your parents do too."

Allison smiled. "You sound as if you wish they wouldn't."

"Sometimes I do wish that," Cynthia said. "I'm a big girl now, Greg. I can take care of myself."

"I'm sure they don't mean anything by it. They just want to make sure you're all right." He chuckled softly. "To be truthful, I think my parents like you better than they do me."

She didn't answer. He tried to find another topic of conversation.

"Aren't you going to open your gift?"

She looked around, discovered that she had put in on the lamp table and touched it briefly.

"I'll get yours out of the bedroom first."

She rose and walked quickly out of the room. He lit a cigarette and stared at the fire. Why wasn't there a way he could say what was on his mind? Maybe he should leave as soon as they had exchanged the gifts. He could write her a letter. Or maybe he should just forget this idea of patching up everything. She didn't seem very receptive. All he seemed to be doing was embarrassing them both.

She took more time than he expected. When she returned, she had brushed the loose strands of hair back into place and put on lipstick. She was the same and yet she was different, like a person he had known very well but long ago.

Her package for him was not very large. It still had its Christmas wrapping, but the bow and corners showed the effects of shipment across the country and back. He hefted it. It wasn't very heavy and it didn't rattle. He pulled off the ribbon and opened it. Inside was a pair of leather gloves, fur-lined, with stitched ribs along the backs. He tried the right one. It fit perfectly.

"I didn't know what to get," she said apologetically. "I thought about getting you a silk scarf with your initials, then I remembered that you wouldn't be able to wear it if you were using a different name."

He smiled at her. "They're fine, Cyn. Really fine. I needed a pair of good gloves. Thank you."

She nodded and began opening her gift. The store, Marshall Field, had been out of Christmas wrapping, but they had found some green paper and a red bow. She unwrapped the package carefully. Inside was a gold locket in the form of a heart. She held it up by the chain, looking at the delicate carvings on the locket, the matching chain.

"It's beautiful! Thank you, Greg."

"Do you really like it?"

She smiled at him. "Of course I do. Why wouldn't I?"

"I just thought you might not, that it might be the wrong kind of gift under the circumstances."

She slowly lost her smile.

"I'm sorry, Cyn. I didn't mean to spoil it for you."

"That's the reason you came by, isn't it? To talk about us."

"Yes."

She took a deep breath and let it out slowly, putting the locket and chain back in the box.

"I wanted you to come, Greg. I wanted that more than

anything. But I wanted it to happen five months ago, even three months ago. Now—"

"I would have come, Cyn. I wanted to come the minute I discovered that you'd left, but I couldn't. You know I was tied up on that—that problem. And after I was transferred to Baltimore—" He stopped. "I didn't tell you about the transfer, did I?"

"Your parents told me."

"Oh. Well, I was put on another assignment. It's important, Cyn. It's very important to the country that—"

"They're all important, Greg. They're always more important than me or anyone."

"I'm sorry, Cyn, but it's true. There's—"

"Please don't tell me there's a war on, Greg! Just don't say anything about the war!"

"I'm only—"

"I know all about the war. That's all I heard from you for two years! And that's all I hear now from the radio, the neighbors, even our parents. I'm sick to death of the war!"

"That won't make it go away, Cyn."

"And stop calling me Cyn! I hate that nickname. I've always hated that nickname. My name is Cynthia!"

She stopped, breathing rapidly.

"You never told me."

"I told you. You just didn't listen."

He nodded again. "You're right. I apologize. I won't call you that any more."

"Oh hell!"

She covered her face with her hands and he thought she was about to cry. He reached out to put a hand on her shoulder, then drew it back.

"Maybe I'd better leave."

She took her hands down. Her eyes were red but there were no tears.

"Maybe you'd better, Greg. If you stay, I just might say some things you don't want to hear."

He rose, feeling awkward, unsure. "I'm sorry, Cyn—Cynthia. I didn't want this to happen. I thought ... Well, I just wanted to see you."

"You've seen me," Cynthia said. "And I'm all right. I don't need anything, and I don't want anything, and ..."

Her voice caught and she looked away from him quickly.

"Why did you come by anyway? You don't need me. You never needed me. All you need is that damned job, running around, chasing spies, playing Dick Tracy. You don't have any room in your life for anything but that."

"That's not true."

"Isn't it?"

"No. I need you. I love you."

"Then will you transfer back to the Adjutant General's Corps?"

He hesitated. "I can't do anything until this job's finished."

"When will that be?"

"I don't know."

She shook her head. "You won't transfer. You love playing counterspy too much."

"I don't—"

"You want to know something, Greg? I don't hate the CIC any more. I admit I did in the beginning, in New York, but after we moved to Washington I finally learned that the CIC wasn't the problem. The problem was you. You put everything you had into the job. You worked all day and all night and when you came home you brought it all with you. I just wasn't part of your life any more."

"You know why I couldn't tell you about—"

"That's not what I'm talking about," Cynthia said. "I never expected you to tell me any government secrets. But I did expect you to think about something else, about me, occasionally."

"I did think about—"

"Can you really tell me that one—just one—of those mysterious jobs you did in New York and Washington wouldn't have gotten done just as well, just as quickly, if you had taken a Sunday off occasionally, had spent just a little time with me when you weren't thinking about the job?"

"It wasn't that way, Cyn. I—"

"It was that way, Greg! And it'll be that way again if I come back to you. I don't want that. I don't want any man ever again making love to me while he thinks about something else."

Allison stared down at her, his face hot from a sudden rush of anger. Her words surprised him, hurt him, because they carried a grain of truth that he could not deny. He had spent two years feeling that she was unreasonable in not accepting the necessity of his work coming first. Now she was telling him that he was the unreasonable one. He had put the job first, second and last, leaving nothing for her. He wanted to refute the statement, but he couldn't. There had not been a single job that did not leave him some time for her—if he had taken it. He took a deep breath, looking at the pattern on the rug.

"I'm sorry you feel that way, Cynthia. I guess I'd better go."

He turned and walked quickly into the entryway. She followed more slowly. He had his overcoat and hat on by the time she got to the door. She held onto the knob for a moment.

"Greg, I'm sorry. I shouldn't have said those things to you—"

"Don't apologize. If you'd said them a year ago, maybe we wouldn't be here now."

"And now?"

"Give me some time. I've got to think about it."

"Okay."

She opened the door. He started out. She caught his arm.

"Thank you for the locket. It's lovely."

"You're welcome."

Tears welled up in her eyes, and she reached up quickly to kiss him on the cheek. He had a sudden urge to gather her in his arms, slam the door and tell the world to go to hell. Instead, he told her goodbye and went out. He was in the car before he remembered the gloves. He started to get out, then changed his mind, reaching for the ignition key.

27 THE APPEARANCE of the new counterfeit bills took Greg Allison completely by surprise. The information came in over the teletypewriter into the communications center of the Treasury Building in Chicago, marked for Martin Goldman's attention, and the report was brought directly to him. He read it first, then passed it to Allison. Allison shook his head.

"I don't believe it! They couldn't have gotten out of the city. We've got it bottled up tight!"

"They could have driven out," Goldman said. "The police can't cover every road going out of this city."

"But they don't have a car, Marty! And they haven't bought one or we'd know. The minute they spend any of that money—"

"They could have borrowed one—or stolen it. If you'll read that again, you'll see that the three bills came from two gas stations and a roadhouse. They have to be driving."

"All right, but if they are, why are they going the wrong way? This says the bills turned up in South Bend, then at Battle Creek and Ann Arbor. Why would they double back? Why would they come all the way to Chicago if their target was in Michigan?"

Goldman shrugged. "You should be able to answer that question better than me. Maybe they were just laying a false trail. But whatever the reason, I think we'd better move. That Ann Arbor station took the third bill last night. If they're heading for Detroit, they're already there."

Allison shook his head. "Something's not right here."

"What? You know how many targets there are in Detroit. All the auto companies are building tanks and aircraft engines and—"

"I still don't think—"

"Look," Goldman said. "Stay if you like. I'm going. I'm having the secretary book me on the first flight to Detroit. If you want to go, meet me at the airfield. If you don't, fine."

Allison nodded. "I'll meet you there as soon as I get my bag packed."

Special Agent Paul Pearson, commander of the local CIC detachment, met them at the door of the plane in Detroit and grabbed Allison's arm, pulling him toward a waiting car.

"Let's go! We've got him spotted in a tourist court on West Grand Boulevard."

Goldman ran after them and was barely in the car before it lurched into motion. Allison took a moment to catch his breath, then turned toward Pearson.

"Are you sure it's Novalis?"

"Positive," Pearson said, grinning. "The car fits the description given by that service-station attendant in Ann Arbor perfectly. He even had the license number right. We got the call over the radio while your plane was landing." Pearson paused, his grin widening. "I almost left you stranded at the terminal when I heard it."

"If you had, I'd have shot you," Allison said.

"Why do you think I waited?"

"Who's watching the suspect's cabin?" Goldman asked.

"A local police unit. They spotted the car. I made them promise not to move in until we get there."

"Good," Goldman said, his tone drawing looks from the other men in the car.

Pearson looked at Allison. Allison belatedly introduced them. The radio in the car came to life, and all the men fell silent. Two cars of CIC agents had reached the tourist court and all was quiet. They confirmed the police identification of the car and the tag number. Allison could feel the increased pounding of his heart.

"Can't you get a little more speed out of this thing?"

"We're almost there, Greg," Pearson said.

The tourist courts were a series of separate cabins—with spaces for cars in between—forming a rectangular horseshoe around a graveled drive. The driver pulled to a stop at the curb behind two other unmarked sedans which were parked several yards short of the entrance, behind the office. Two city patrol cars sat farther down, also out of sight of the cabin. Allison and Goldman were out immediately, walking in long strides to the group of men congregated on the sidewalk. Pearson introduced them quickly.

"Bob, what's the situation?"

One of the agents stepped out of the group.

"He's in the next to last cabin on the far side. The owner says he came in about three hours ago and hasn't been out since. He looked beat, like he had been driving all day and all night. The shades are all drawn, so he's probably asleep."

"Good. Is anyone in the office?"

"Harry and Claude."

"Is there any back entrance to the cabin?"

"No. The owner didn't want any deadbeats sneaking out on him. There isn't even a window in the back."

"I think we should cover it anyway," Allison said. He looked at the uniformed officers. "Would you mind doing that?"

The men looked at each other and shrugged.

"Thank you. We'll give you five minutes to get into position."

"Okay, Paul and I'll go across to the other side and work our way down to the cabin. Two of you follow us at an interval, and two of you take this corner. When we get into position, we'll wave. Then I want three of those cars driven into the entrance crosswise just before we go in. I don't want any chance of this man getting away. Any questions?"

The men looked at each other, then back at Allison.

"If you have to fire, try for the legs," Allison said. "I want this agent alive."

"And watch where you're shooting," Pearson warned. "We're going to have people scattered all over in there."

Marty Goldman had been checking his pistol. He snapped the cylinder back into the frame and put it away.

"Let's do it before he dies of old age."

Allison frowned at Goldman. "We'll handle this, Marty. Our way. You stay here."

Goldman looked at him, then walked away, crossing the drive toward the other side. Allison started to call him back, then went after him, walking quickly but trying to appear casual. Pearson followed. By the time they reached the other side of the drive, Goldman was moving down the front of the row of cabins. Allison began to run and caught him just before he reached the suspect's cabin.

"Damn it, Marty," Allison said, his voice pitched low. "You mess this up, and I'll—"

"Go to hell," Goldman said, also keeping his voice low.

He tried to pull out of Allison's grasp, but Allison dragged him into the space between the cabin and the car. Pearson came up. Allison nodded to Pearson, still holding Goldman. Pearson waved, and the idling cars began to move. Goldman jerked loose and started for the cabin door, drawing his pistol. Allison pushed him aside at the last instant and kicked the door himself, hitting it just beside the knob.

The jamb gave with a crack of broken wood, and Allison was inside, his .38 sweeping the area in front of him. The bed was to the right, against the wall. A figure that Allison saw only dimly in the darkened room sat up in the bed abruptly. Allison swung the gun to cover him.

"CIC! Hold it right there!"

The man moved. As Allison swung the pistol to cover him, he was almost deafened by three rapid shots from his right. He pivoted, managing to knock down Goldman's arm before a fourth shot could be fired, then looked quickly back toward the bed. The man had been knocked back against the wall, his arms out, his eyes staring at the ceiling. Just as Allison got to him, he emitted a long sigh—a sound not unlike a strangled cough—and relaxed, lifeless. Allison whirled on Goldman.

"God damn you, Marty! I ought to strangle you with my bare hands! I told you I wanted him alive! I—"

"He was reaching for a gun," Goldman said evenly.

"I had him covered! He couldn't have—"

"Look at this," Goldman said, pulling the sheet back. The blue steel of the pistol was clearly visible, even in the dimly lit room.

"I'd say he saved your life," Pearson said, looking over Goldman's shoulder.

Allison gritted his teeth, trying to control his anger.

"Let's get some light in here."

The other agents were crowding into the room now. Someone flipped on the bare overhead bulb and another man began raising the shades. Allison bent over the body, studying the face.

"This isn't Novalis!"

"What?"

Goldman elbowed him aside, staring at the man.

"He doesn't fit the description at all."

"It's him," Goldman said.

"Look at him," Allison said. "The hair's wrong, he's too short, he's—"

"It's him," Goldman said adamantly. "The hair could be dyed. The descriptions could be wrong about the height."

"How about the eyes?" Allison said. "Did he change the color of those too?"

Goldman and Pearson bent over the man again.

"Well?"

"If it isn't Novalis, then who is it?" Goldman asked defensively.

"I don't know," Pearson said. "But let's all hope to God that it isn't just some traveling salesman from Chicago."

28 MAJOR HEINRICH JOST was surprised to find Kapitän Karl von Schroeder, the Abwehr deputy director, in Admiral Canaris' office when he entered. Von Schroeder, a heavyset man with the salt-burned skin of the professional seafarer, watched as he closed the door and came to attention in front of Canaris' desk.

"Major Jost reporting as ordered, Herr Admiral."

Again, Canaris ignored the clicked-heel salute.

"What is the current status of the Prometheus Operation, Major?"

The admiral's tone was brusque. Jost cleared his throat.

"I have been unable to contact Novalis, Herr Admiral. I believe—"

"I am not interested in what you 'believe,' " Canaris said sarcastically. "What do you know?"

Jost glanced quickly at von Schroeder. The deputy director's face was a mask, but the blue eyes reminded him of a man watching a hawk circle a chicken. Jost looked back at Canaris.

"Herr Admiral, I *know* that Novalis has bungled the operation very badly, but I have thought of a plan to salvage it. I believe that Martha can—"

"Martha? Tell me, Major, just what can Martha do?"

"Herr Admiral, I have devised a strategy which will allow Martha to remain in Washington yet cover Prometheus—"

"Martha has returned to Washington, then," Canaris said, glancing at von Schroeder.

"*Jawohl,* Herr Admiral. I sent specific order to Rudolph to have her—"

"You *know* that, Major?"

Jost hesitated only momentarily. "I expect confirmation from Rudolph at any time. I—"

"Did you send this message to Capricorn?" Canaris asked suddenly, taking a Wohldorf radio form from his pocket and tossing it on the desk.

Jost picked up the form and scanned it quickly.

"I can explain this, Herr—"

"Can you also explain why Martha was with Novalis when he arrived in Chicago?"

"Martha? But—"

"Silence!"

Jost jerked back to attention, his eyes staring straight ahead.

"Now I will tell you what *I* know, Major. I know that Capricorn was already dead when you sent that message. I know that you wanted the message to be intercepted by the Americans. And I know that you wanted Novalis to be picked up the moment he arrived in Chicago."

"Herr Admiral, I can explain—"

"I ordered you to be silent, Major!" Canaris paused. When he spoke again, his tone was quiet, controlled, even more frightening.

"You are the one who has bungled this operation from the beginning, Major. You have allowed personal animosities to interfere with your judgment and with your duty."

"Herr—"

"Martha has been identified by the Americans, Major. Both she and Novalis were almost captured in Chicago and are now attempting to reach our contacts in Mexico. The entire operation has been destroyed by your petty attempts to revenge yourself against Hauptmann Roebling."

Canaris suddenly looked away, as if he could no longer stand the sight of Jost. Jost's mind raced frantically, but he could not think of anything that the admiral might accept in his defense. Canaris suddenly flipped a switch on his intercom.

"Sergeant Krause! Come in here!"

The door opened almost immediately, and the burly security man entered. Jost could not keep himself from looking around.

"Major Jost is under arrest. Take him to the security cell immediately. He is to communicate with no one without my personal permission."

"*Jawohl,* Herr Admiral."

"No! Wait!" Jost screamed.

Krause moved in. Jost tried to fend him off, screaming at the admiral to let him speak, explain. Krause easily blocked the outstretched arm, twisted it up behind Jost and marched him out of the door on tiptoes, still screaming. The secretary reclosed the door quickly. Canaris slumped down in his chair, sighing. He remained in that position for a few moments, staring at the closed door, then looked up at Von Schroeder.

"Well, Karl?"

"There was nothing else you could do, Herr Admiral."

"I know. Do you think he may have been deliberately collaborating with the Americans? Giving them other information as well?"

"*Nein,* Herr Admiral. My investigation showed no other such contacts. I will have Sergeant Krause question him fully, of course, but I am sure that his actions were solely the result of his personal hatred of Hauptmann Roebling."

Canaris pulled his center desk drawer open and took out the message from Martha, relayed through Rudolph. He reread it for the tenth time.

"This is a tremendous loss, Karl."

"I know, Herr Admiral. Prometheus could have been very valuable in blunting the criticisms of our political enemies."

"I was also thinking of the loss of Martha. She was by

far the most valuable of our remaining agents in America."

"*Ja.* But at least both were well-kept secrets. And if they remain secrets, it would be to our advantage."

Canaris looked up. "Are you making a suggestion, Karl?"

"*Ja,* Herr Admiral. Only three persons know that the Prometheus Operation ever existed—yourself, me and Major Jost. I do not believe that leaves us any choice as to what Major Jost's punishment should be. Since we cannot use the success of Prometheus against our critics, we must ensure that our critics cannot use its failure against us."

Canaris didn't reply immediately. Instead, he looked at the message again, this time not reading it but simply staring at the individual words. Finally, he sighed.

"You are right, Karl. I will leave the details to you."

"I will take care of it, Herr Admiral."

GREG ALLISON slumped wearily in the chair at the Detroit CIC office, waiting for the Baltimore switchboard to connect him with Colonel Kibler. He wasn't anxious to talk to the chief, but he hadn't reported in for three days, and the Chicago office had relayed a message that Kibler was trying to get in touch with him. Kibler came on the line.

"Greg? What are you doing in Detroit?"

"We tracked some counterfeit bills here, sir. We got a description on the man and the car he was driving, and the local police spotted the car at a tourist court."

"That's great! Did you get him?"

"Yes, sir, we have him. Or, rather, we have his body. Marty Goldman killed him."

"Killed him! Why?"

"To save my life, he says."

"You don't sound convinced."

"I'm not, but I can't prove anything. The man did have a gun."

"Well, as long as you have Novalis, I suppose—"

"It's not Novalis, sir."

"It's not? Then who is it?"

"A decoy."

"Do you want to explain that, Greg?"

"Yes, sir." Allison took a deep breath and let it out tiredly. "Novalis knows about the counterfeit, sir. He sent a substitute by car from Chicago to Detroit, dropping just enough fake bills along the way to pull us in, then he pulled a new one."

"What?"

"He walked into a Chicago telegraph office, bold as brass, and wired the counterfeit to the decoy in Detroit. The total was almost ten thousand. We forgot to cover the telegraph offices, Chief. It just never occurred to either of us that—"

"How did the decoy get the telegraph company to pay him ten thousand in cash? Didn't anyone question such a large wire?"

"Yes, sir, but he simply waited in the telegraph office while the manager confirmed the Chicago wire, then had the money brought over from a bank. He spent the time telling the manager about this business deal he could sew up if they got the cash to him before three o'clock. The man was well rehearsed. The manager believed every word of it—and he had the confirmation that the Chicago office had taken in the cash to cover the wire. So he paid the decoy in good bills and sent him on his way."

"Well, at least you recovered the money," Kibler said. "That means Novalis doesn't have the funds to—"

"No, sir."

"No what?"

Allison took another breath. "No, sir, we don't have the money. It wasn't in the room or the car, and we haven't been able to find it anywhere."

"What are you trying to tell me, Greg?"

"That I think Novalis has the money back—only in good bills this time. I'd bet my next month's pay that the decoy went straight from the telegraph office to a post-office substation and mailed the money to him."

"In Chicago?"

"No. To some other place they had agreed on."

Kibler was silent a moment. "Have you tried to confirm that?"

"Yes, sir. We've checked all the substations near the telegraph office that he used, but no one remembers him. Of course, there's no particular reason why the clerks would remember just another customer mailing a package, much less the address to which it was sent. Frankly, sir, I think it's a dead end."

"So what do you plan to do?"

"Fly back to Chicago. See what the detachment there has on the car and the man Goldman killed. Maybe—"

"They haven't identified him yet?"

"No, sir. His identification was phony and the license plate on the car was taken off a wreck in a junkyard. The Illinois motor-vehicle people are checking the serial number on the car's motor against their records in an attempt to identify the car's real owner, but it's a slow process."

"I see," Kibler said. "Well, I wish we could help, but we haven't intercepted anything more from Ares. If we do, I'll let you know."

"Thank you, sir."

After hanging up, Allison stared at the telephone for a time, then reluctantly dialed Marty Goldman. The phone rang several times before the night duty officer answered. Allison identified himself and asked if Goldman had left for the night.

"No, sir. He's left town."

"Left? I thought he was working with the local police, checking—"

"I don't know what he was doing, but he's no longer here."

"Where did he go?"

The man hesitated. "He didn't sign out."

Allison caught the evasion in the tone. "That wasn't what I asked. Do you know where he went?"

Again, there was a slight hesitation before the man answered.

"I don't think he wanted anyone to—"

"You know who I am," Allison said. "If you make me call my chief and have him call your chief, I don't think either of them will like it. Now where did he go?"

Allison could hear the man take a deep breath and let it out.

"Cleveland. I heard him make plane reservations."

"When?"

"About three hours ago. He barely had time to make the last flight."

"Why?" Allison asked.

"I don't know. And that's the truth."

"Okay," Allison said.

"Uh, Captain, if you plan to go after Mr. Goldman, I wish you wouldn't tell him who told you where he went."

"It's like that?"

"Yes, sir."

"Okay. He won't hear it from me."

"Thank you, sir."

Even catching the early plane, it was still after eleven the following day before Allison arrived at Cleveland police headquarters. Lieutenant Horace Gambrell, a sandy-haired veteran with a worried look, met him at the desk. Allison showed him his credentials.

"How's the CIC involved in this, Captain?" Gambrell asked.

"We're after the same German agent that Marty Goldman is," Allison said. "Is he still here?"

"Yes, sir. But this Herder we picked up isn't any German agent. He's just a local hood. He has a small printing shop, but he's a known forger. We've been after him for years, but until this we could never prove anything."

"Then why did Marty come here?"

"I don't know," Gambrell said. "We got word from the First National that Herder had just deposited some of that queer we've got all the flyers on, so we had a squad car—"

"He passed some of the counterfeit?"

"That's why we picked him up," Gambrell said. "We notified the Secret Service. A few hours later this Goldman shows up and starts acting like the guy had just murdered President Roosevelt. He demanded to be allowed to question him alone. What the hell? It's a Federal matter, so we complied. He was at him half the night and back at six this morning, but I don't think Herder is telling him anything." Gambrell paused. "Do you know what this Herder did— besides pass the queer, I mean?"

"He probably made some forged identification papers for a German agent," Allison said. "The agent is the one who passed him the counterfeit."

"And that's all?"

"As far as I know. Will you show me where the interrogation room is?"

"Sure," Gambrell said. "Follow me."

Two detectives—big men in loose-fitting suits—were lounging in the hall outside the interrogation room as they approached. Gambrell nodded toward the closed door.

"He still at it?"

One of the men shrugged. "It's been kinda quiet in there for the past few minutes. Maybe they killed each other."

"What do you mean?" Allison asked.

The second man nudged the speaker in the ribs, and the man just shrugged in answer to Allison's question. Gambrell twisted the knob and went in, Allison following. Marty Goldman turned quickly to meet them. He was in his shirt sleeves, tie off, cuffs rolled up. In his right hand he held a long blackjack, with the strap looped around his wrist. Chris Herder was on the floor, cowering in a far corner. One hand was partially raised, either to ward off further blows or in supplication, and the other was holding his ribs. He seemed semistuporous. One eye had a large lump beside it, and blood from his broken nose had dried on his chin and shirt. Goldman also had small blood splatters on his arms and shirt. Gambrell looked from Herder to Goldman.

"What in the hell has been going on in here?"

Allison shook his head. "Marty, why in the world—"

"I haven't finished yet, Lieutenant," Goldman said, his face set, defiant. "So I'd appreciate it if both of you would just close that door on your way out."

Allison tried to move closer. Goldman backed away, raising the blackjack slightly. Allison stopped.

"Look, Marty," Allison said, "it's not worth it. He's just a small-time forger, and he probably can't tell you anything of value—"

"He's an agent, too," Goldman said adamantly. "Ask the lieutenant there. He had friends in the Bund."

"That only makes him a sympathizer, not an agent," Allison said. "And it certainly doesn't justify this kind of treatment."

Goldman snorted. "When are you going to turn in your Boy Scout suit, Greg! We're in a war! Nazis like this one are murdering hundreds, maybe even thousands of my people every day. If they were your people, you wouldn't be so goddamned squeamish!"

"Give me that blackjack, Mr. Goldman," Gambrell said. "There won't be any more—"

"This is a Federal matter!" Goldman snapped.

"And this is my jail!" Gambrell snapped back. "there won't by any beating of prisoners here—not even by Federal agents!"

"All right then, I'll take the prisoner out of your jail and—"

"You aren't taking him anywhere, Marty," Allison said.

"Do you plan to stop me?" Goldman asked, bringing the blackjack up.

"Yes."

"Then I suggest you make your try, Greg. I've still got work to do here."

"He'll have help," Gambrell said. "Reeves! Hardy! Get in here!"

The two detectives came into the room. Goldman came up on the balls of his feet, facing the men.

"Mr. Goldman is leaving now—without that blackjack you provided him with, Reeves," Gambrell said.

"I didn't—"

"Shut up," Gambrell said. "I'll deal with you later."

He looked at Goldman.

"All right, Mr. Goldman. We can do this any way you like. But I promise you that if you try to use that sap on any of us, you'll go out of here looking a lot worse than Herder over there."

Goldman set himself. Gambrell motioned to the two detectives and they started to move in. Allison quickly stepped between them and Goldman.

"Hold it, Lieutenant. Let me talk to Marty a moment." Gambrell shook his head.

"Don't we have enough trouble here without blowing the whole thing into a grand-jury investigation?" Allison asked.

"I don't have anything to hide," Gambrell said. "Your friend is the one—"

"Don't you? You allowed it to happen in your jail. And one of your men provided the blackjack."

Gambrell looked at Allison. "Just whose side are you on?"

"Wouldn't it be better if we could settle this quietly? We'd save everyone a lot of grief."

Gambrell finally nodded. "I'll give you five minutes. But we'll be right outside."

"Thank you," Allison said.

The men left. Allison turned to face Goldman. Goldman smiled sarcastically.

"Just can't quit being the Boy Scout, can you, Greg? Not even after three years in the CIC. Well, I suggest you just follow the rest of them out of here, because you aren't going to talk me out of this."

Allison studied Goldman's expression, his tone of voice. Perhaps he shouldn't be, but he was surprised at the intensity of Goldman's hatred.

"In that case, would you tell me why?"

"I've been telling you for weeks!" Goldman said. "The Nazis are slaughtering Jews by the thousands in—"

"This man isn't a Nazi."

"He's a collaborator! He helped them! And every time he helps one of them, a few more Jews die!"

Goldman stopped, almost panting. Allison remained still, studying him.

"There's something more, isn't there, Marty? Something you don't want to tell me. You were never like this. What happened?"

A small crack appeared in Goldman's hatred. He recovered quickly, but Allison had the clue he needed.

"No one feels that strongly about an entire group of people. You can only feel that way about individuals."

"The Jews do. We've been persecuted—"

"The Jews, yes, but you haven't, Marty. For you to feel this way, the Nazis had to do something to you personally. Who did they hurt? One of your family?"

Goldman stared at him. For a moment Allison thought that Goldman would attack him, then he looked away, avoiding Allison's eyes.

"I'm sorry, Marty, but I'm trying to understand. Maybe I can help."

"You can't," Goldman said shortly. "Just get out of here and—"

"I know your father came from Poland, Marty. Was it someone who still lives there? I didn't think you knew any of those relatives personally."

Goldman shuddered and looked quickly away, at the floor.

"My grandmother."

"What happened? Did they put her in a concentration—"

"She was executed." Goldman's tone was flat, emotionless. "And two of my uncles and their families."

"I'm sorry," Allison said. "I didn't—"

"At a place called Auschwitz in southern Poland. We ... We got word about two months ago. I didn't want to believe what was happening until then."

"Those reports sometimes get all fouled up. Maybe she—"

"She visited us several times in Chicago. She was ... We all wanted her to stay, apply for a permanent visa, but she wouldn't unless the rest of the family could come too, and the immigration quotas ..."

He couldn't go on. Allison let the silence grow. Finally, he walked over and put his hand on Goldman's shoulder. Goldman looked up. Tears were running down both cheeks. Allison found his handkerchief and handed it to him. In the corner, Herder stirred and moaned. Both men looked at him.

"It didn't help, did it?"

Goldman shook his head slowly.

"You could beat him to death, and it still wouldn't help. I won't tell you I know how you feel, but I do know that anything which hurts that deeply has to be worked out inside you. You can't take it out on anyone else."

Goldman wiped his eyes and took a deep breath. He seemed to be recovering from the hatred, the sickness, which had been building in him for the past two months. He looked at Herder again.

"I'm sorry about that, Greg. I know it's no excuse, but I didn't plan it. He called me a dirty Jew, said he was glad Hitler was ridding the world of them. It . . . Suddenly, all I could think of was my grandmother being stripped, humiliated, driven into a gas chamber by men like him—"

Allison put an arm around Goldman's shoulder.

"Why don't you go home, Marty? Forget this mess. Take some time off and visit your family. You've been carrying this around alone. Let them help you work it out."

Goldman looked up and laughed mirthlessly.

"Maybe you're right, Greg—Boy Scout philosophy and all."

Allison smiled. "Don't worry about this. I'll talk to the lieutenant."

"I'm not asking you to cover it up. I'll take whatever—"

"I know. Now give me that blackjack and get out of here."

Goldman hesitated, then handed him the blackjack. Allison helped him retrieve his hat, coat and tie from a chair and sent him out. Allison started to follow him, then Herder moaned again. Allison turned back to look at the man, see how badly he had been hurt. Goldman had done a good job on the face, but that would heal. Allison tried to pull the man's hand away from his ribs. Herder moaned and tried to back away.

"Don't. Please don't. I'll tell you anything you want to know. Just don't hurt me—"

The words were mumbled, run together but clearly understandable. Herder's eyes were shut tightly, afraid to see what might be coming next. Allison caught the arm again.

"Nobody's going to hit you. All I want is to—"

"I—I'll tell you. I'll tell you anything. Just please don't hurt me again."

Allison released the arm, glancing over his shoulder at the doorway. No one had entered the room. Gambrell must be talking to Goldman in the hallway. He looked back at Herder and pitched his voice low.

"You made some forged papers for the man who gave you the counterfeit money."

"Y-yes."

"What names did you put on those papers?"

Herder began to talk, and Allison quickly got out his pen and notebook.

30 STEFAN ROEBLING and Erika Huntington arrived in Santa Fe late on the afternoon of January 6. Low clouds covered the area, and the pass across the Sangre de Cristos had been full of fog, forcing them to drive very slowly and watch for the first flickering of oncoming headlights in the curves and dips. The mountains, the pines, the narrow roads reminded him of parts of Germany, but he could not relax, enjoy the remembrances. They were on the last leg of their journey, and the last two days, the six hundred miles from Oklahoma City to Santa Fe in the 1939 Ford Sedan, had drained him physically. He was not accustomed to driving such distances, at least not in the same country.

They had left Chicago separately, by plane and by train, rendezvousing at the Biltmore Hotel in Oklahoma City two days later. The ruse had worked. Neither had encountered any sign of the CIC along the way. On the third day in Oklahoma, the package of money from Sampson had arrived at the downtown post office. Erika had suggested they leave for Mexico immediately, but Roebling had been adamant about continuing the operation. When she could not convince him, she finally produced a slip of paper with a Santa Fe address on it.

"What's this?" Roebling had asked.

"The address of an agent named Michael," she had answered. "I made a call. He's found the installation for you."

The next morning he had purchased the Ford from a used-car lot in Oklahoma City, paying quite a bit more than the car was worth but getting an almost new set of tires in the bargain. Good tires were very hard to find, the salesman said, and the empty spaces to the west were bad areas to be stranded.

Through the salesman, Roebling also managed to contact a black marketeer and purchase a quantity of gasoline ration stamps to go with the car's "C"-class sticker. The stamps cost him more than the tires, including a commission for the salesman, but he couldn't afford to be frugal at this stage.

The next three days had been spent mostly in the car, covering a variety of roads and terrain. The first stretch, from Oklahoma City westward to the Texas Panhandle, had consisted primarily of concrete, built by the Works Progress Administration during the 1930s. The road had two lanes with small curbs sloping upward along the outer edges to narrow, poorly maintained shoulders of packed earth. He discovered quickly that those innocuous-looking little curbs could be very dangerous.

The Ford's steering was loose, the wheel having a good four inches of free play, and the ratios were much slower than those used on European cars. Consequently, he corrected the car's drifting too slowly and too carefully until he became accustomed to the swings. In the first fifty miles, they almost overturned twice. Each time, the car drifted two far to the right, the front tire found and quickly climbed the sloping curb, and they bounced dangerously along the potholed shoulder until he could get the car back under control.

After the second incident he had driven into a turnout and dirtied his clothes examining the front suspension. However, he could see nothing wrong and finally concluded that the Americans must be better drivers than the Europeans contended if they regularly drove such cars over such roads without decimating their entire population. He had gotten back into the car, assured a white-faced Erika that it wouldn't happen again and continued toward Texas.

Just before the Texas line, the land changed from rolling farmland to prairie, but the road surface remained concrete with the same curbed shoulders. He began to suspect that the salesman had taken advantage of his ignorance, his assumption that the road had remained in the condition described by Steinbeck in *The Grapes of Wrath,* to sell him the better set of tires. They passed through a series of small towns—Shamrock, McLean, Boydston, Groom, Conway—and finally pulled into Amarillo late in the afternoon. They stayed overnight at a small tourist court on the west side of Amarillo and were up at dawn to continue.

Shortly after crossing the New Mexico line, Roebling began to recant his thoughts about the car salesman. Many stretches of the road were little more than rutted gravel, with twisting climbs and occasional detours around construction crews. They passed through San Jon, Tucumcari and reached Santa Rosa in late afternoon. A short description by a service-station attendant of the road ahead convinced them to spend the night there.

The following morning found them climbing the five-mile-long hill just west of Santa Rosa. For once Roebling was glad that it was winter. In the long climb, the temperature gauge hovered dangerously close to the red line, and the Ford seemed to lose power as it climbed. At the top of the hill the land changed again, juniper and spruce beginning to appear, then pine and other evergreens. Finally, they stopped at a small gas station where U.S. 285 crossed U.S. 66, and Roebling consulted his map while the attendant filled the tank. Erika spent most of the time inside the station, next to a wood-burning stove, after one hasty trip to the unpainted outhouse.

On leaving the station, Roebling swung the car around and started up U.S. 285 for the last fifty-five desolate miles to Santa Fe. There was only one open gas station and no towns along the way, so they spent the time admiring the rolling pastures, the occasional herd of white-faced cattle, the distant blue-gray mountains. Finally, they reached

Santa Fe. Erika looked from side to side as they drove down a narrow brick street lined with close-packed adobe buildings and wrinkled her nose.

"It's a dirty little place, isn't it?"

"We're not here to sight-see," Roebling said tiredly.

"That's a comfort," Erika replied, her tone also revealing the strain of the past three days. "Why don't the people at least patch the places where the stucco has fallen off their houses?"

"It isn't stucco. It's adobe, a type of clay."

"Clay? These houses are made out of mud?"

"This area was settled by the Spanish," Roebling said.

"Yes, but that was three hundred years ago. They've had plenty of time to rebuild everything."

Roebling smiled. "You know the Spanish, Erika. They're large on tradition."

"Tradition, hell! They just look poor to me."

"Whatever you say."

Roebling pulled the car into a small gas station and had the attendant fill the tank. In the course of a short conversation he got a tourist map of the town and a pitch for the Isabel Tourist Court, which made Roebling think that the man probably got a small commission for every tourist he steered to the place.

Using the map, Roebling found the small house without much difficulty. He drove past and parked a half block away. Telling Erika to stay with the car, he walked back to the house. There wasn't any response to his knock, so he went around to the back. The windows were heavily curtained, blocking all view of the rooms inside, but the back door was unlocked. He took a quick look around, decided that he wasn't being watched and went inside.

He was in a small kitchen, one side containing a sink counter with cupboards above and below and the other side taken by a small gas range, an old-fashioned refrigerator with a round coil on top and a small pantry. The room was surprisingly clean, everything put away except for one coffee cup sitting under the cold-water tap in the sink.

He moved quietly across the room and stopped. To his left, at the end of the counter, the door to the adjoining room was closed. He tried the knob and opened it quietly. The room contained an old bed, a dusty bureau and several storage boxes. He closed the door and moved to the other doorway.

This door led into the front room, which had been turned into an artist's studio. The walls were cluttered with paintings, charcoal sketches, pastel portraits and a clutter of frames, easels, paints and brushes sitting on a variety of crates, small tables and patches of floor. He moved through the clutter to the last door.

That door led into the front bedroom—again a neat, well-kept room that belied the appearance of its neighbor and raised a suspicion that the person living here was a split personality. Roebling checked the room, then went through the bureau and small closet quickly. There were different sizes of underclothing in the drawers and an extra suit and shoes in the closet. Roebling took care not to disturb anything but did make a relatively thorough search. In fifteen minutes he was satisfied. He had not found the radio or any evidence that Michael was an agent.

Roebling walked back into the front room and stopped, listening to footsteps on the walk outside, then the scratching of a key in the lock. He retreated quickly into the bedroom, his right hand finding the .38 in the overcoat pocket.

The man closed the door and came into the room, peeling off a heavy woolen overcoat. He was of medium height, slim and fair, with blond curly hair and boyish features. As the man turned his back to add wood to the stove, Roebling opened the bedroom door and stepped into the room.

"Hello, Michael."

The man whirled, holding a stick of wood.

"Take it easy. I'm here to buy a painting."

Ernst Dahl, alias Talmadge Carver, alias Michael, watched him warily.

"What kind of painting?"

"A snow scene," Roebling answered. "Some cottonwoods. On a hill."

Carver relaxed somewhat but his eyes remained wary.

"Who are you?"

"Novalis."

"That doesn't mean anything to me."

"Then how about Martha?"

"Who's Martha?"

Roebling hesitated a moment, then crossed to the front door and waved to Erika. She started the Ford, drove it into the niche beside the small house and hurried inside, shivering.

"You certainly took long enough. I nearly froze out there. Hello, Tal."

"Hello, Erika."

Carver looked at Roebling sheepishly.

"Sorry. I should have accepted the recognition signal."

"Don't apologize for being cautious," Roebling said. "I'm surprised, however, that such a cautious man leaves his back door unlocked."

Carver smiled. "Believe it or not, that's deliberate."

Roebling lifted an eyebrow. "Why?"

"This is an artist's neighborhood. Everyone leaves their back door unlocked so people can drop over any time and borrow paint or coffee or whatever. If I didn't do the same, people would begin to wonder why."

"I see." Roebling paused, looking at Erika. "Maybe we had better find another place to—"

"Hey, no problem," Carver said. "I'll just pass the word that my sister and her husband are staying for a few days. No one will come in then without knocking. It's the custom."

Roebling looked at Erika again. She shrugged, warming her hands at the stove.

"It's still less dangerous than a hotel or tourist court."

Roebling finally nodded.

Carver smiled. "I'll clean up the spare bedroom. You can bring your things in and—"

"Later," Roebling said. "First, I'd like to hear what you've found out."

Carver paused to collect his thoughts. "Well, there's a large installation in the Jemez Mountains about forty miles to the northwest. It's on the site of a former boys school called Los Alamos—that's Spanish for 'The Cottonwoods.' The Army engineers are in charge of the post.

They've built a lot of individual laboratories on the mesas and in the canyons and brought in a lot of equipment."

"What kind of equipment?"

"Mostly machine tools, lathes, drills, presses, things like that. But recently, they've been bringing in some big scientific pieces too. And they've built quite a bit of housing for the civilian personnel who—"

"Civilians? What are they doing on an Army installation?"

"I don't know," Carver said. "But whole families have moved in. The wives come down to shop for groceries and clothes and things."

"You might work on some of those, Erika," Roebling said. "See if you can strike up a conversation, find out where they're from, what their husbands do."

"Most of them are from the northeastern part of the country," Carver said. "Even without the license tags on their cars, you can't miss those accents. The natives can't stand to listen to them."

"In that case, I'll be a friendly accent in a sea of foreigners," Erika said, smiling.

"I'd like to check out the area around the installation," Roebling said. "How close can I get in a car?"

"Not very close," Carver said. "There are only two roads into the site, and both are fenced before you get to where you can see any buildings. In fact, the fence circles the entire area and is patrolled day and night. You wouldn't have a prayer of slipping in there and out again without being detected."

"I was sent here to find out what's going on in there," Roebling reminded him. "So unless you know another way, I still want to—"

"Hey, no problem," Carver said, smiling. "Just take it easy for a couple of weeks, and I'll be able to paint you a picture of the whole camp, complete with nude cottonwoods and snow covered pines."

That night, as he lay in bed with Erika, Roebling asked her about Carver.

"What do you want to know?"

"Just how much of that was—I believe the American term is 'bullshit'—and how much was fact?"

"He's very good," Erika said. "His information has always been very accurate. Why?"

"Something about him bothers me. Also, he's only been here three weeks, but he already knows a great deal about a base which is supposed to be top secret."

Erika smiled. "He got lucky. He made a very good contact—an officer in the Base Provost Marshal's office."

"The Base Provost Marshal's . . . That's too dangerous! If he asks one wrong question—"

She kissed him lightly. "Don't worry about it, darling. There's no way this officer would ever turn Tal in."

He looked at her skeptically. "And why not?"

"Because." She kissed him again, this time with more interest. He pushed her away.

"Are you going to tell me or—"

"The officer is a homosexual."

"A homo . . ." He didn't finish. His mind was connecting the different sizes of underclothing in the bureau, the extra suit in the closet, Carver's slight femininity.

Erika laughed softly. "He likes you, darling. But I told him to forget it. You're mine."

"If he's a homosexual, how did he ever get into the Abwehr? Zeus would never permit—"

"Zeus doesn't know anything about it. Tal was an aspiring young actor until Ares discovered his sexual deviancy. Then Ares blackmailed him into joining the Abwehr, using his . . . 'talents' to extract information from other homosexuals. It wouldn't work in some countries, but in America it's a gold mine."

Roebling was silent, admitting all the potential uses for an agent of that type. Carver was probably right. They might not be needed at all here. But just the same, he intended to make his own investigation, to check Carver's information.

"Darling."

"What?"

She turned his head toward her and kissed him deeply.

31 GREG ALLISON sat at his desk in the Baltimore CIC headquarters, frowning at a page of doodles on an unlined pad. Two names—Prometheus and Novalis—were repeated over and over. Maybe the chief was right. Maybe he didn't know when to turn loose. Both Novalis and Erika Huntington were well out of the country by now. Allison should be satisfied with the knowledge that he had disrupted their operation and had exposed a very dangerous agent in Erika Huntington. The General Staff thought so. In fact, under the pile of papers on his desk was a letter of commendation signed by General Thomas McNarney, Deputy Chief of Staff, for his work on the case.

Allison snorted derisively. McNarney wasn't praising his work. He was simply playing politics, putting the best face on a fiasco, turning a loss into a gain for the Army. Colonel Kibler knew that he had blown it, although he would never tell Greg he felt that way. He didn't have to. With everything going for him, Allison had let Novalis sail into New York Harbor, take a train to Washington, kill Neil Davis, then wander through half the country without ever getting within sight of the man. He certainly didn't deserve a letter of commendation for that. Hell, he still didn't even know why Novalis had come into the country, what Prometheus was.

His recriminations were interrupted by a message-center clerk.

"Excuse me, sir. I have a TWX for you."

"Just leave it on the desk."

"Yes, sir."

The clerk put the envelope down quickly and made a hasty exit. Evidently, his moodiness was getting to be well known throughout the building. Allison picked up the envelope and stared at it. He already knew what was in it—another negative report for his files. After reaching a dead end on the names the Cleveland forger had given him, he had developed a list of priority targets based on what he knew and could suppose about Novalis. The list started with the B-29 plants in Seattle and Los Angeles, included a number of chemical plants in various parts of the country and ended with the submarine yard at Groton.

With Colonel Kibler's reluctant blessing, he had detachments in each area scour the surrounding towns for any sign of Novalis or Erika. In all cases, the reports had been negative. By the second and third sweeps, the reports had not only been negative but somewhat peevish about the time being spent on wild-goose chases. This would be the last report from the Seattle detachment.

Reluctantly, he tore open the envelope and scanned the message. It wasn't from the Seattle detachment. Halfway through, he skipped to the bottom, then started again, taking his feet off the desk and sitting up in the chair. Five minutes later he was bursting into the chief's office. Kibler looked up from a memorandum he was initialing, surprise and irritation in his expression.

"What's the—"

"Sir, I think I know what Prometheus is!"

"Oh? Well, that's good, but at this point, don't you think it's a little late for—"

"No, sir! In Greek mythology, Prometheus was the supreme trickster, right?"

"Yes, but—"

"He tricked Zeus into accepting bones and fat instead

of meat for his sacrifice. To retaliate, Zeus hid fire from man because Prometheus was also one of the fire gods. But Prometheus stole the fire from Zeus and returned it to earth again."

"For which Zeus had him chained and sent an eagle to eat his liver, which was immortal and kept replenishing itself," Kibler said. "We've been over this a hundred—"

"And Novalis was a German romantic poet, right? A man who wrote about nature?"

Kibler frowned. "Greg, if you have a point to make—"

"What if you reversed them? What if Novalis is really the name of the operation and Prometheus is the name of the agent?"

Kibler shook his head. "That doesn't make any more sense than the original—"

"Yes, sir, it does," Allison said. "The root word of Novalis is 'nova.' A nova is a star that suddenly grows very bright, then fades quickly, relatively speaking. That's analogous to an explosion. Prometheus was sent here to steal cosmic fire from us and return it to the Fatherland. The target for Prometheus or Novalis, or whoever he is, is the Manhattan Project!"

"The atomic bomb?" Kibler asked incredulously, then quickly lowered his voice, glancing at closed door.

"Are you serious, Greg?"

"Yes, sir," Allison said.

"But that's the best-kept secret of the war. The Germans don't even know it exists."

"Yes, sir, they do."

Kibler looked at him sharply. "Are you saying we have a leak? Is someone—"

"No, sir. But think about it a moment. They have an atomic-bomb project. We know that. And they know which scientists have escaped from Europe, come over here. Einstein, Fermi, Teller, Niels Bohr. They're the top nuclear physicists in the world. The Germans have to know we'd put them to work on a bomb."

Kibler relaxed a little. "They might guess," he admitted. "But there's no way they could know. Besides, I can't believe they'd send only one man to sabotage a project like—"

"Suppose he's only here to check out the project, assess its status and report back on whether—"

"No. No, I can't buy that," Kibler said, shaking his head. "Even given all the other arguments, I still don't believe the Abwehr would deliberately use a code name that might give away the whole operation. We'd never—"

"Wouldn't they?" Allison interrupted. "You remember Operation Pastorius, when the Abwehr landed eight agents by U-boat in June of last year to blow up the dryolite factory in Philadelphia? Well, Georg Dasch, the member who betrayed them to the FBI, stated that the operation was named for Franz Daniel Pastorius, one of the first Germans to immigrate to America. Pastorius laid out Germantown, Pennsylvania, and served as its first mayor. And we've seen the same kind of thing consistently in other code names. Whoever is in charge of the American desk for the Abwehr likes to play word games."

"And does he also like to sabotage his own operations?" Kibler asked. "How do you explain the counterfeit?"

"Maybe it was just a mistake. Everyone makes them sooner or later. Sir, I'd like you to ask General Groves for a full alert at Los Alamos. I want to fly out as soon as—"

"On the basis of your wild speculation that—"

"Yes, sir. And on this."

He pulled the message out of his pocket and handed it to the chief. Kibler read it quickly.

"He finally made a mistake," Allison said, smiling. "He used the driver's license that Herder made him as identification to buy a car in Oklahoma City. The salesman said that he asked about Route sixty-six west toward Albuquerque."

Kibler stared at the words on the paper. "It could be another trick. They still could have been heading for Mexico."

"Yes, sir," Allison said. "But can we afford to assume that they aren't trying for Los Alamos?"

Kibler looked up at him. "No. No, we can't."

32 DR. JULIUS ROBERT OPPENHEIMER, a lean man of six feet with inquisitive blue eyes, an aquiline nose and a prominent Adam's apple, moved quickly up the boardwalk to the military headquarters building at Los Alamos. The walk was alternately layered with mud and ice, which made very treacherous footing. Every few feet, a skid mark showed where an unwary soldier or civilian had slipped, some righting themselves before going down and some falling partially or completely off the walk into the snow. It would be worse in the spring, when the warming temperatures turned the bulldozed ground under the snow into a sea of mud. Oppenheimer negotiated the hazardous walk with a dancer's grace that belied his awkward appearance.

Los Alamos was gloomy and gray, a cold fog hugging the mountains above and filling the canyons below. Just over one year ago, in late 1942, there were trees where Oppenheimer now walked and a dozen boys—rich men's sons with asthma and other problems—played soccer in the snow. "Oppie"—as he had been nicknamed by the faculty and students at Holland's University of Leiden, where he had done postgraduate work after receiving his doctorate in theoretical physics from the University of Göttingen—

remembered watching part of that game from a car beside Brigadier General Leslie Richard Groves, the man he was now going to see. One month later, the Army had taken possession of the Los Alamos Ranch School, its lodge building, the log cabins used by the boys and 54,000 acres of poplars, pine and aspen surrounding it.

Within weeks the area was alive with activity. Construction crews worked around the clock, felling trees, bulldozing underbrush, erecting dormitories, mess halls, Quonset huts and various other temporary buildings to house the laboratory equipment and civilian and military personnel. An eight-foot diamond-link fence topped by three strands of barbed wire was built across the end of the mesa containing the primary access road, and grim-eyed military policemen manned the gates. Inside, everything was painted a dull, uniform green, excepting some later, sixteen-foot-square personnel hutments which were still covered with black tarpaper.

By the spring of 1943, the first scientists had arrived with their families to stand and stare at the unbelievably rude accommodations for which they had given up comfortable homes, friends, secure positions at universities and colleges across the country. In the Americans, the Kenneth Bainbridges and the Donald Hornigs, the reaction, after the initial shock, was one of acceptance, of accommodation, while they met the greater challenge. In others, like the Emilio Segrés, who were technically enemy aliens, the installation brought back memories of the concentration camps, the *stalags,* which could not be shrugged off so easily.

Both American and alien came throughout the spring, summer and fall of 1943. They arrived in Albuquerque by bumpy planes, in Santa Fe by tired old cars with frayed tires and in Lamy by crowded trains. In some ways, Lamy was the greatest surprise. The new arrivals stepped off a familiar, comfortable train onto a station platform which seemed in the middle of nowhere. Lamy, which consisted primarily of a depot and a small collection of adobe houses, was located on the eastern slope of the Sangre de Cristos mountains, across a pass from Santa Fe. Most of the new-

comers were surprised to discover that the Atchison, To-
peka and Santa Fe railroad, famed in a popular song, did
not even go to the city that contributed one third of its
name.

Following a bus trip across the pass, the first arrivals,
and the horde that followed, found themselves entering a
city that looked more like eighteenth-century Spain than
twentieth-century America. The streets were narrow,
winding and bricked in the downtown area. The buildings
were old, many showing their underlying adobe bricks
through holes in the façade. The churches were almost
uniformly Catholic, with steeples and bell towers and
heavy carved doors.

There were no neon lights, no trains or subways, no su-
permarkets, none of the everyday marks of civilization that
the immigrants from the Eastern population centers had
come to expect. There was only the harsh landscape outside the town and the seemingly inhospitable stares of the
natives within. To the Easterners, the natives were slow,
uneducated, uncaring peasants who deliberately misun-
derstood each question, each request for aid or comfort. To
the natives, the Easterners were rich, overbearing snobs
who expected money to buy them anything, including
friendship. The two groups detested each other almost on
sight.

The shock of entering the Royal City of the Holy Faith
of Saint Francis of Assisi was mitigated somewhat by a
gray-haired, energetic woman named Dorothy McKibbin,
who operated out of a small adobe dwelling at 109 East
Palace. The small sign on the front read U.S. ENG-RS, a
small grammatical mistake that added yet one more bad
impression to the rapidly growing list of the new arrivals.
However, Mrs. McKibbin soon convinced them that, despite the lazy courtyard setting, the situation was well in
hand. She heard their complaints, soothed their egos,
found their luggage and sent them on their way to the
"Hill" in a variety of motley cars and trucks scrounged
from used-car lots by the Army. Some were disconcerted to
find themselves riding with sacks of mail, pieces of furniture, laboratory equipment and other assorted odds and

ends needed by the new laboratory, but their worst jolt was yet to come.

The first leg of the trip was the easiest. The vehicles took the highway north out of Santa Fe for almost twenty miles to the tiny village of Pojaque, then turned westward on a two-lane graveled road that ran through cattle pastures and small farms, past the San Ildefonso Indian Pueblo, to the narrow poplar- and willow-lined banks of the Rio Grande River.

Across the river, the fun began. The road climbed steeply along the face of jutting cliffs, twisting and turning sharply without the comfort of guardrails, gas-pocket holes in the weathered lava face on one side, an almost sheer drop growing ever deeper on the other. For those whose fear was blunted by a sudden attack of sleepiness—caused by an unaccustomed lack of oxygen in the thinning air—chunks of pumice with which the Army Engineers had covered the road banged loudly against the fenders and underpans of the vehicles, often being thrown over the edge to disappear quietly into the emptiness below.

The ten-mile, 2,000-foot climb from the Rio Grande River to the Parajito Plateau took less than thirty minutes for the experienced drivers, but many first arrivals swore that it was a full eternity and that if they ever got down they were never coming back.

The Parajito Plateau, which had weathered over the eons into finger mesas separated by steep canyons, was the result of ancient eruptions by an immense volcano. The plateau lay just outside the eastern rim of that volcano, whose now extinct caldera, the Valle Grande, was the largest in the world. The newly formed Los Alamos Scientific Laboratory, code-named Site Y, sat well back on the plateau, almost totally hidden among the tall pines.

This was the country that Oppenheimer loved, that he had hunted from his nearby family ranch as a boy, that he had once called one of his two great loves, the other being physics. But Oppenheimer was not in such a reflective mood this gray winter day. He had just come from a meeting of the top scientists at the laboratory and was carrying a long list of needs, wants and complaints for General Groves. Groves was making one of his regular visits to the "Hill," and Oppenheimer planned to present the complaints in person. In the general's outer office, a WAAC corporal smiled, then asked him to wait. Oppenheimer sat down, fretting at the waste of time.

The meeting had been populated by a host of renowned scientists—Fermi, Teller, Lawrence, Szilard, Bethe, Segré, Bainbridge—and two recent arrivals, Niels Bohr, who had been recently smuggled out of Copenhagen, and Emil Julius Klaus Fuchs, a German expatriate who had been working with English scientists on the MAUD committee. Unlike the weekly colloquiums, this had been a special meeting. The colloquiums were designed to keep all of the top scientists abreast of each division's work, a cross-fertilization process that gave Groves nightmares about security problems. At Oak Ridge, where fissionable uranium-235 was being laboriously separated from the more common uranium-238, and in Hanford, Washington, where uranium piles were being used to generate the even more rare plutonium-239, the workers were rigidly compartmentalized, each knowing only what he needed to know to do his job. But Oppenheimer had insisted on the colloquium arrangement at Los Alamos, arguing that the best chance of completing the project successfully was to have all those top minds working together, knowing the other men's problems as well as their own.

The meeting Oppenheimer had just left had been called to discuss new equipment needs, but it had quickly degenerated into a forum for complaints—many inspired by wives—about the food, housing, overcrowding, Army mentality in general and especially the restrictive new security requirements. A scientist, a man who had been trained to believe that scientific knowledge belonged to the world, that personal glory, private interests, even national interests came second to the advancement of knowledge, Oppenheimer understood his colleagues' frustrations, just as he understood the need for secrecy, for producing the weapon that could end the war before the Germans could produce one. However, the understanding did not really help but simply added another dilemma to his tasks. Even more than Groves, Oppenheimer was the man in the middle, unable to appease or disregard either his civilian scientists or their military patrons.

The door to General Groves' office opened and Greg Allison appeared with the general.

"Doctor," Allison acknowledged.

"Mr. Allison," Oppenheimer responded.

"Hello, Oppie," Groves said. "Come in."

Allison left. Oppenheimer followed the general into the office, noting that the man had gained weight again.

General Leslie Groves was detested by most of the civilians on the Hill. He was not the recruiting-poster type, nor did he try to be. At five-eleven, with a head of thick, wavy hair, graying mustache, a paunch and a perennial double chin, Groves was one of those persons on whom a uniform, especially summer khakis, looked like last week's sheets. But the inability to wear a uniform well did not lessen Groves' military manner. He was a West Point man, a military engineer, the man who had, after reluctantly accepting the job of running the Manhattan Project—so named because it had originated in the Manhattan Engineering District of New York—pulled the whole conglomerate of civilians and soldiers together, welded them into a unit and made it work. Or at least he had made it work thus far. Despite his oversized ego, there were times when not even Groves believed that he could pull off the massive undertaking.

"General, I know you're busy, that you're only here for a few days before flying back to Washington and that you have many problems more important, but I think we should give the minor problems some attention before they also turn into major ones."

"Oh? What are these minor problems that threaten to overwhelm us?"

"My people are getting very upset over a number of things. I won't attempt to go through the entire list, but the most often recurring complaints center around the food, the—"

"They're eating a lot better than the men in the field—"

"—the overcrowding, the—"

"Some of my men are living in tents—"

"—the restrictive new security—"

"Look," Groves interrupted. "We've been over all these complaints a dozen times, Oppie. I know this isn't Harvard or Cambridge, but your people will simply have to live with a few inconveniences until—"

"I'm not reciting a list of petty gripes for you to brush away like so many flies," Oppenheimer said, his tone cutting through the general's litany. Oppenheimer was a man very much under control, but Groves's high-handed—some said Napoleonic—manner could irritate even Oppenheimer after a time.

"All right, Oppie. Let's hear it. But understand that it's your time as well as mine."

"I understand the physical rotation of the earth very well, General." Oppenheimer took a moment to reorder his thoughts. "I'll omit the more common complaints. I know that your men do their best to provide us with decent food, housing and transportation. Although I must tell you that your habit of inspecting the menus, then dictating memos telling the wives how lucky they are to be able to buy turkey and other common meats, do far more harm than good."

"They damned well are," Groves said.

Oppenheimer let the remark pass. "However, these new security regulations that the Provost Marshal, Colonel Williams, has instituted are especially disliked."

"They are absolutely—"

"It's bad enough that we can't have such simple conveniences as bank accounts in Santa Fe. It's even worse that we register all babies as having been born in P.O. Box 1663, Santa Fe. And it's bordering on absurdity that we have to use code phrases like 'urchin fashion' for 'uranium fission' and 'topic boat' for 'atomic bomb' inside a secure facility like this. But when the creeps start following men like Ken Bainbridge and Ernest Lawrence every time they leave the Hill and placing listening devices in family bedrooms, then

I think it's time someone should speak up. These men are simply not accustomed to working in such an environment. It could stifle their creativity."

"Creeps?" Groves asked, the hint of a smile touching the corners of his mouth.

Oppenheimer frowned. "I didn't intend to use that term. It's the nickname for your CIC people."

Groves allowed himself the smile. "Our GIs call your people 'long-hairs.' "

"I know," Oppenheimer said. "And we call your soldiers 'plumbers.' "

"I know that," Groves replied. "What do they call me?"

"Mostly G.G."

"And what do the initials stand for, besides the obvious?"

"A variety of things, depending on the mood and the linguistic ability of the man. I once even devised a phrase for you in Sanskrit."

"I won't ask for a translation. However, I don't think your people—or even you—realize how petty your problems are compared to mine. Would you like to hear?"

"Not especially."

"Let me tell you anyway. The President is worried that the Germans may be outstripping us in the race to build a 'topic boat.' He expresses his concern regularly to Secretary of War Stimson. The Secretary, in turn, relays the concern to me and asks for assurances that the project is on schedule."

"I know the pressures are—"

"I don't think you know the half, Doctor. Did you know that Secretary of the Treasury Morgenthau tried to have our special deposit of twenty million dollars canceled because no one would tell him how it was to be spent? Did you know that a nosy little Senator from Missouri—you know, the one heading the special Senate committee investigating national defense, Truman—wanted to inspect Hanford last summer? He'd heard complaints from some clown who said we were heating the water in the Columbia River too much, damaging fish reproduction or something."

"General, I—"

"Do you know that German intelligence may have knowledge of this installation and that an Abwehr agent may attempt to sabotage it?"

Oppenheimer's surprise was genuine. "No. How did they—"

"I don't know, but I'm damned well going to find out. Now do you understand why the security has been stepped up and why it will stay that way until this project is successfully completed?"

Oppenheimer was silent a moment. "I understand why you must be concerned with personnel off the installation, but I still must protest the listening devices in—"

"Wives go off the post too, Oppie. And I don't have to tell you how the wives would react if a CIC man followed them everywhere too. No, their ignorance is to their advantage. Otherwise, I may have to simply restrict everyone to the base for the duration. That's the only alternative to the current security measures."

Oppenheimer smiled. "If you tried that, General, your men would be in combat right here within a week."

"They're better trained and better armed than your civilians," Groves said, displaying the humorlessness for which he was also noted.

"I must get back to work," Oppenheimer said, rising. "I'm sure my people will understand after I tell them about—"

"You'll tell them nothing, Oppie. What I've told you— all of it—must not go beyond this room. If we have a man, or men, passing information to the enemy, then he mustn't be forewarned. Otherwise, our people would have a hell of a time catching him."

"General, I don't think anyone is deliberately passing information on the project to the enemy. Someone may have inadvertently said something, but—"

"I don't share your faith in human nature, Oppie, so let's do this my way."

Oppenheimer sighed. "You may know soldiers, General, but you know very little about scientists. After this is over, after you've plugged the leak, if there is one, then I expect a full explanation and an apology to all those who weren't involved. I'll call a meeting of the people and you can speak to them face to face. I don't think they'd appreciate another of your memoranda."

"Commanders never apologize to their troops, Oppie," Groves said. "And in case you've forgotten, you and all the others work for me."

33

STEFAN ROEBLING reached the small Spanish square in downtown Santa Fe and paused to pull his overcoat collar up around his face. In the center of the square was a bandstand surrounded by carefully spaced oaks, poplars and evergreens. The buildings around the square were old one- and two-story structures of brick and stone, some with refurbished exteriors to resemble adobe. The Spanish flavor of the plaza, the buildings, the small shops had been carefully maintained to give the impression that a viewer could be standing on a corner in old Madrid or Seville or Mexico City.

Across the square, running the length of the north side, was the Palace of the Governors. Built in 1610 by Don Pedro de Peralta, third Governor of "The Kingdom of New Mexico," its stucco walls enclosed almost one entire block and framed an inner courtyard large enough to accommodate a dozen of the small adobe houses like the one Tal Carver had rented. In the summer the shaded veranda would be packed solid with brightly dressed Indian women haggling with tourists over handmade silver and turquoise jewelry, and the plaza would be filled with artists sketching charcoal portraits for living expenses while they dreamed of becoming famous landscape painters.

Now the plaza was almost deserted, only a few hardy souls braving the cold and stillness of the growing darkness. Roebling turned eastward and hurried down the dimly lit street to the La Fonda Hotel. At the front door he paused to check the lobby, then walked through to the bar. The La Fonda was easily the best hotel in Santa Fe, and its bar was frequented by officers and scientists from Los Alamos.He had become a careful semiregular there, telling those who asked that he was a former defense plant engineer who had come to the mountains because of a minor tubercular condition. In the course of his visits to the bar, he had been able to pick up a fair amount of information on personnel now at Los Alamos, although he avoided direct questions about the people or the work being performed there.

The code names that the Americans were using for the scientists were easily translatable to anyone with his university background. The recent arrival of "Neal Brown," for example, could only mean that Niels Bohr had now joined the group. The "Mrs. Henry Farmer" with the Italian accent that Erika had met in a small market had to be Mrs. Enrico Fermi. As the list grew, a pattern began to emerge from the names—all were physicists. Combined with the information about the physical facilities that Tal Carver had gotten from Lieutenant Gordon Price, they now lacked only one essential piece of knowledge—the purpose of the project. Maybe he would get lucky tonight. One last piece of information, and they could all go home.

Tonight, the bar held only a few civilians. Roebling took a seat away from them and ordered Scotch. The bartender was new, an Anglo. He brought the drink, then lingered, leaning against the inner edge of the bar.

"Kinda slow tonight, isn't it?"

"It'll pick up," Roebling said. "It's early."

"Maybe," the bartender said. "You don't work up at Los Alamos, do you?"

Roebling sipped the Scotch, watching the man over the rim of the glass.

"No."

"Just wondering," the bartender said. "I hear they've called some kind of alert up there, won't let anyone off the base. I hope not. It'd sure hurt business here, ruin my chance for the good tips. The locals don't throw money around the way those people do."

"I haven't heard anything," Roebling said.

The bartender looked around the room, then leaned closer.

"Say, what do you think they're doing up there?"

"I wouldn't know."

"There're lots of stories. Did you hear the one about them making windshield wipers for submarines?"

He laughed at the joke and Roebling chuckled dutifully.

"That's pretty good, isn't it? But I heard a better one the other day. A guy swore on his solemn oath that he knew for a fact that they're building the front halves of horses. Only the front halves, mind you. Then they ship them to Washington, D.C., for final assembly. Get it?"

He laughed again, louder this time, and Roebling joined in politely.

"That's a good one, isn't it? We sure have plenty of horses asses in Washington now. They wouldn't need to build any of those."

"No."

The bartender quieted down, looking over his other customers again.

"Say, my name's Mike."

"Jackson," Roebling said. "Donald Jackson."

"Pleased to meet you, Mr. Jackson. I'm new here and I'm trying to get to know all the customers. What do you do?"

Roebling gave him a shortened version of his cover story.

"Bad lungs, huh? Sorry to hear that. How long have you been in town?"

"Not long."

"Well, I think you'll like it here. It's beautiful country. Of course, some people don't like it, but I think it has a lot of everything a man could want."

Roebling sipped the drink again. The bartender leaned over the bar.

"Say, could you do me a favor?"

"What?"

"My partner hasn't come on duty yet, and I need to use the john in the worst way. Could you kind of cover for me a minute? I don't mean run the bar, but if someone wants a drink while I'm gone, could you tell them where I went and that I'll be right back?"

"Sure."

"Thanks. I'm not supposed to leave, but this is getting to be an emergency. I'd hate to have someone complain and lose my job."

"Don't worry about it," Roebling said.

"Thanks. I'll only be a couple of minutes."

The man walked quickly around the end of the bar toward the restrooms. Roebling waited until he was out of sight, then rose and casually followed. When he reached the restroom door, he opened it carefully and slipped inside. The bartender was not at the row of urinals. Roebling looked around the end of the wall. The man was talking on the pay telephone, his back toward the door. Roebling backed out of the restroom quietly, walked quickly through the hotel and went out a back entrance.

Ten minutes later, Greg Allison was fuming at the bartender.

"Damnit, Arthur! You tipped him off!"

"No, I didn't, Mr. Allison." Special Agent Arthur Heston said. "There's no way he could have known I was—"

"Then why did he leave?"

"I don't know. I'm not even sure it was him. His hair was very light, almost blond, and he didn't have any limp that I could see. He didn't sound English either. In fact, I couldn't detect any regional accent. Maybe he was from California, like he said."

"He could have lightened his hair," Allison said harshly. "No, it was him. It had to be him! And you let him just walk right out of here!"

Heston looked at the other three agents for support. Their expressions were carefully neutral.

"All right, let's move," Allison said. "Donnelly, you and Carter take the northern area. Roades, you come with me. Check anyone on foot who comes even close to the description. And keep your radios open. If you spot any likely suspects, I want to know immediately."

"How do you know he's on foot?" Donnelly asked.

"I don't," Allison snapped. "But I don't think he would have driven into the hotel parking lot either. Check out the nearby parking lots first. If you see anyone driving out in a black Ford, stop him."

He looked back at Heston. "Call the office and get everyone out on this. And I mean everyone. I don't care if they're making love to their wives or someone else's. I want all of them on the street in ten minutes. Alert the Sante Fe police too. Got that?"

"Yes, sir."

"Then let's go!"

34 IT TOOK twenty minutes of steady walking for Stefan Roebling to reach Tal Carver's house. Several times he had stepped into alleys or entranceways as cars approached.

He had also seen three police cars, an unusual number for the area under the weather conditions and the time of night. Clearly, they were looking for him. He had been right in his assumption about the new bartender. He reached the house and checked the street both ways before entering.

Erika and Tal were playing cards on the small table in the kitchen. Both noticed the look on his face, but Erika was the first to ask.

"What's wrong?"

"I was spotted in the La Fonda. We've got to get out."

"Wouldn't it be better to hole up here?" Carver asked. "They can't make a house-to-house search of the whole city."

"The longer we wait, the more time they'll have to establish roadblocks, a dragnet. And if we stay here, sooner or later someone will mention your 'visiting relatives' to the wrong person and we'll all be taken."

"But—"

"He's right, Tal," Erika said. "This way you'll be clear—even if we don't make it."

Carver looked distressed. Erika put her hand on his arm and smiled at him. They had been acquaintances before but had become good friends in the past few weeks— which had surprised Roebling. He had not expected Erika to like a homosexual.

"What are you going to do?"

"Find a place in Albuquerque to stay until the search is called off, then try for Mexico. If we make Albuquerque, Erika will call you at four o'clock tomorrow and ask for Steve. You tell her that Steve went back to Chicago. If you say anything else, we'll know something's wrong and try for the border. If she doesn't make the call, then I suggest you get out immediately."

"I've got it. Steve went back to Chicago."

"Another thing. As soon as we leave, get off a message to Mexico City. Tell them everything we know about the installation."

"Right."

Roebling looked at Erika. "Ready?"

"I'm not packed."

"We don't have time. Tal can get rid of our things."

"Just a minute. I want my toothbrush."

Twenty minutes later they were approaching the edge of Sante Fe. They had passed several cars on the street, but none had turned around or tried to follow them. Roebling was beginning to breathe easier. In a few more minutes they would reach U.S. 285, be clear of the city.

"Why are we going this way?" Erika asked. "According to the map, U.S. eight-five is much shorter."

"It's also the main road to Albuquerque," Roebling said. "State Police units are probably watching it."

As they slowed for the last intersection before the highway, a car came out of the side street, ran the stop sign and skidded in front of them. Roebling pulled the wheel over, using all the brake he could without locking the wheels. The left front of the Ford hit the right door of the other car and bounced away in a shower of headlight glass. Both cars came to a stop quickly. Roebling shifted into reverse and backed clear of the other car. The other driver jumped out and ran toward them. Roebling stopped, digging into his overcoat pocket for the .38. The man ran up to Roebling's door.

"Is anybody hurt here?"

The voice was full of concern. Roebling glanced at Erika. She had been thrown forward but had caught herself. Roebling took his hand out of the overcoat and rolled the window down.

"No, we're fine."

"Thank God! I'm sorry. It was all my fault. My insurance will cover everything."

"Don't worry about it," Roebling said. "It's minor."

"I don't know. You might have some damage to your alignment. Why don't we check—"

"We're in a hurry," Roebling said. "It's an emergency. My wife's mother is dying and we have to get to—"

"Well, let me give you my card," the man said. "You can call me afterward, and we'll straighten everything out."

He reached inside his overcoat, putting his hand well down into the left side. Roebling jerked the wheel over and released the clutch. The rear wheels spun backward. The front end of the car swung around, knocking the man down. Erika braced one hand against the dash.

"Stefan! What are you doing?"

Roebling locked the brakes and shifted to low, using his right heel and toe to operate the brake and accelerator simultaneously. The moment he completed the shift, he was off the clutch again, the car suddenly lurching forward. The man was up on his knees, scrabbling toward his own car. The Ford's bumper caught him in the lower back and flung him forward, past the end of his car.

"My God, Stefan!"

Roebling locked the brakes again and shifted back to reverse, throwing an arm over the seat and looking back as the Ford again spun its tires changing directions. This time there were two bumps as the right wheels passed over the body. He stopped.

"I—I think I'm going to be sick."

"Not now!" Roebling ordered. "Slide under the wheel!"

He jumped out of the car, looking both directions as he ran to the body. Within a few minutes he had lifted it into the trunk of the other car and run back to Erika.

"Follow me"

Erika had her head on the steering wheel, taking deep breaths to hold down her heaving stomach.

"I—I'm not sure I can drive."

"Then take a look at this!"

Roebling tossed a CIC credentials case in her lap and ran back to the other car.

35 CAPTAIN KARL VON SCHROEDER rapped smartly on the heavy paneling of the door, then entered. Admiral Wilhelm Canaris was at the conference table, sorting through a stack of folders. On the table was an open briefcase with other folders already inside it.

"Preparing for your trip to Spain, Herr Admiral?"

"*Ja,* Karl. I must convince General Vigo and General Martinez to side with me, to deny the allegations against our Spanish operations. Otherwise—"

Canaris didn't finish. There was no need. Von Schroeder was well aware of the possible consequences to Canaris, to himself, if the steadily increasing criticism, the pressure, by the Foreign Ministry and the Sicherheitsdienst against the Abwehr was not blunted. Within the last week the Allies had exposed Abwehr operations in Argentina, where Agent Hans Harnisch had subverted the "neutral" government into joining the German cause in everything but name. As a result, the Argentine government had been forced to break off diplomatic relations with Germany on January 27, a move that cost Germany its last viable base in the Western Hemisphere and cost the Abwehr the invaluable services of one Rudolph Aguilar, the Argentine cultural attaché in the Washington Embassy.

Now Ambassador Hans Dieckhoff, who had taken over the Spanish post in November from Ambassador von Stohrer, a friend of Canaris, was sending in a steady stream of reports criticizing Abwehr operations in Spain. Dieckhoff's reports claimed Canaris' agents were "awkward bunglers" who were driving the Spaniards into the Allied camp. He had even insinuated that Canaris was playing a double role, telling the Führer that everything was fine while telling Generalissimo Franco that the war was lost and advising him to join the Allies. Unless the allegations could be countered by more favorable reports from the Spanish leaders, both Canaris and Von Schroeder knew that they would not survive.

"I regret disturbing you at this time, Herr Admiral, but I have something of extreme importance," Von Schroeder said.

Canaris looked up. "What is that, Karl?"

Von Schroeder held out a message. Canaris read it with growing interest.

"When was this received?"

"Yesterday. It was transmitted by an agent named Michael, but it came from Novalis and Martha."

"Have you had this analyzed by Professor Doktor Esau?"

"*Ja,* Herr Admiral. Doktor Esau believes that the location of the installation, the size and separation of the buildings and of course the names of the scientists working on the project can allow only one conclusion. It is an atom-bomb project."

"*Mein Gott!* How far along does the professor think they can be?"

"He cannot say," Von Schroeder answered. "However, with the scientists and the resources of the Allies, he is sure they are further along than we are."

"Professor Gerlach, Herr Reichsmarschall Göring's new Plenipotentiary of Nuclear Physics, is sure they are well behind us."

"*Ja,* Herr Admiral. But Professor Esau is not so afraid to disagree with Herr Göring's propaganda. I think I would agree with Professor Esau."

Canaris nodded. "What do you recommend?"

"We have three top agents in the immediate vicinity of

the project, Herr Admiral. I think we should take full advantage of the situation."

Canaris considered the suggestion. "Do you think they will have a chance?"

"All three have proven very versatile. And I do not think I need remind the admiral that a success such as this is badly needed at the moment. This alone could silence our critics for a very long time."

Canaris thought a moment more, then nodded. "Make the arrangements, Karl. But maintain utmost secrecy. Should they not succeed—"

Von Schroeder nodded. "I understand, Herr Admiral."

36 IT WAS two days before Special Agent Henry MacFarland's body was found in the trunk of the abandoned car. Greg Allison and Lloyd Cameron, commander of the Santa Fe CIC detachment, were called out to the abandoned logging road off the Las Vegas highway to identify the body before it was moved. A tall, slim Spanish-American, Sergeant Angel Castillo of the New Mexico State Police, met them at the site. An ambulance with two bored attendants waited nearby, and a nervous old man in a battered pickup truck was parked just beyond.

"The body's in here," Castillo said, opening the trunk of the Chevrolet. "Luckily, the weather's been cold. If this was summer, he'd be getting a little ripe by now."

Cameron flashed the sergeant a look, but Castillo ignored it. He had seen too many highway accidents in his fifteen years as a trooper to let one more body bother him. Allison prepared himself for the sight, then was surprised that there was no visible blood. Only the staring eyes, the tire smudges on the clothing indicated the massive damage that the body had suffered. Cameron inhaled jerkily and pulled his head out of the trunk quickly. Strangely, Allison felt somewhat detached. He had barely known MacFarland.

"Can either of you identify him?" Castillo asked, his pen poised over a small notebook.

Cameron nodded and walked away quickly. Allison spoke for both of them.

"His name is John MacFarland. He is . . . He was one of our people. Of course, I expect that to be kept confidential."

"No sweat," Castillo said, writing the name in his book.

"What does your preliminary investigation show, Sergeant?"

Castillo flipped back a page.

"The old man over there, Carlos Ramirez, found him about two hours ago. He comes up here twice a week to pick up slash from the old logging operations to burn in his stove at home. When he saw the car, he stopped, thinking someone might need help. He doesn't have a good reason for looking in the trunk, so he probably intended to steal the spare tire and sell it. At any rate, when he found the body, it scared him. He drove back to that gas station and told the man there. The man called Santa Fe, and they radioed me to investigate. The old man led me up here. I looked him over, but the only obvious thing is that he was run over somewhere else, then put in the trunk and driven up here."

"Do you have any idea where he was run over?"

"No. I was hoping you might be able to shed some light on that," Castillo said.

"He disappeared two nights ago in Santa Fe," Allison said. "This is his personal car, but he was working."

"On what?"

Allison hesitated only a moment. "He was looking for a man and a woman. You have their descriptions."

Castillo nodded, recognizing that any further questions along that line wouldn't be answered.

"Did you see any tire tracks, anything that might give us a lead?"

"No. You can see the ground's still frozen up here. So far, all I've got is a body and that dent in the right-hand door, if it wasn't already there."

"It wasn't," Allison said. "He was hit by a black Ford, a nineteen thirty-eight model.

"The one on my hot sheet?"

"The same," Allison said.

"You don't know that, Greg," Cameron said. He had recovered from the nausea and walked back over, but he carefully avoided looking in the trunk.

"Yes, I do," Allison said. "They made it out of town. They had to run over Mac to do it, but they made it."

"It could have been someone else. He could have—"

"You saw the black paint on the door. Mac obviously forced them to the curb, then got out to arrest them. They caught him in the open and ran over him."

"Mac wasn't that dumb," Cameron said. "He was a good man, Greg."

"Novalis is better," Allison said. "Mac shouldn't have tried to take him alone. This is the second man we've lost that way."

Cameron looked at Allison sharply. "I think we'd better discuss this later. Can we have MacFarland's personal effects, Sergeant?"

"They're in my car," Castillo said. "I'll get them."

He walked away. Cameron turned back to Allison.

"You need to watch what you say, Greg. None of the local police are cleared to—"

"Cleared?" Allison looked at Cameron incredulously. "You've got a man dead and two German agents running loose in the countryside, and you're worried about me using an enemy code name in front of—"

"I'm trying to follow procedure, damnit! And I'd advise you to do the same! We don't know the Germans did it. Mac could have stopped the wrong car. Or he could have had a simple accident and got out to inspect the damage. Most of the people up here don't like Anglos, Greg. Hell, he could have been run over by a scared teenager in a stolen car."

"Who then got out, stuffed the body into the trunk and drove both cars up here," Allison said sarcastically.

"He could have had friends with him. Anything could have happened. I admit that it looks like—"

Cameron stopped as Sergeant Castillo returned with the bag. Allison went through it quickly. MacFarland's credentials, wallet and gun were missing—the same items

Novalis had taken from Neal Davis. Allison asked Castillo about the items.

"That's it. I had it down as a robbery-murder until I discovered his shoulder holster. That's why I had headquarters call your office."

Cameron looked at Allison. Allison ignored him. They wound up their business quickly and let the ambulance take the body away. On the way back to Sante Fe, Cameron asked Allison what he intended to do.

"I'm going to Albuquerque. And I want all the men you can spare to help me."

"Why? If he's gone, you'd have a better chance of catching him at the border—"

"He's too smart to run straight to the border," Allison said. "He'll hole up in the nearest place where he can lose himself and wait until we begin to relax. But I plan to beat him at his own game this time. I'm going to comb him right out of his hole."

Cameron took his eyes off the road long enough to glance at Allison's expression.

"Are you sure you aren't outsmarting yourself? Even if he did do that to Mac, he could have simply doubled back to Santa Fe and holed up there again. You could be playing right into his hands by taking half my men on a wild-goose chase to Albuquerque."

Allison shook his head shortly. "He's gone. If he wasn't leaving, then he wouldn't have been out in the first place."

"But he can't have gotten what he came for yet. There wasn't time—especially with the tight security on the Hill. He—"

"He got it," Allison said. "I don't know how, but he got it, and he's headed back to Germany with it. But he won't get there. I swear that to you, Lloyd."

Cameron looked at him again. "Do you really believe that, Greg, or is it just part of the game?"

Allison frowned at him. "What game?"

"I don't know," Cameron said. "You tell me."

37 FOUR DAYS LATER, Stefan Roebling lay on a sagging bed in a one-room apartment in the southeast part of Albuquerque, away from the tourist cabins along Central Avenue. Across the room, Erika sat on a small stool in front of a cracked mirror, brushing her hair. She was clad only in panties and a brassiere, and the muscles in her back rippled slightly as she pulled the brush downward in long, steady strokes. He stretched lazily and rolled on his side, watching her.

It was crazy, but the last few days had been the happiest of his life. Surrounded by thousands of Americans, wanted by every police agency in the country, they had spent four glorious days ignoring everything but each other—loving, laughing, talking, loving again. He had come to know her as he had never known a woman before, and she had broken down his last barriers, become a part of him so deep, so vital that he could not imagine any further life without her.

They had become mates. Not lovers or spouses but mates in the primal, prehistoric sense. This must have been the way it was before marriage, before everything became so ritualized, so proscribed by society. Perhaps there was still an American Indian or an Australian aborigine or a member of an Amazon tribe who would still know how he felt, but he knew he could never explain it to any "modern" man.

She turned her head slightly and noticed him watching her.

"What are you thinking, Stefan?"

"You wouldn't believe it," Roebling said.

"Why not?"

"Because the Roeblings do not have such thoughts. And neither do the Huntingtons."

"I'm not a Huntington any longer, darling."

"Then what are you?"

"I'm a Roebling too."

"Oh?" He smiled. "I haven't married you yet, you know. I just might dump you once we're back home where the girls have more meat on their bones."

She didn't return his smile. "That wouldn't matter. I would still be a Roebling. I'll always be a Roebling."

He lost the smile slowly, realizing that she understood, that what had happened to him had also happened to her. Incredibly, he suddenly found himself wanting her again, the hunger rising as though he had not touched her, loved her, in a long, long time. She understood that too and came to him without being asked.

He took her in his arms and immediately felt a heightening of all his senses. Her touch sent electric currents all through him. Her perfume filled his nostrils. The taste of her was indescribable. It could not be. It was impossible, but each time with her was new. Hard mounds, soft hollows that his mind remembered but his fingers found fresh, exciting. He could not correlate his memories with his senses, and he no longer bothered to try.

They were almost lost in each other again when the tapping penetrated his consciousness. The alarms rang, but it took some time for Roebling to recover, to react. Erika reacted also but even more slowly than he. The figure at the door was Tal Carver. Roebling looked back at Erika, but she already had a wrap around her, the silver automatic in her hand. He put on his pants and unlocked the door.

Carver came into the room.

"I won't ask what you two were doing that took so long."

Roebling frowned and Carver's slight leer disappeared. "What's wrong?"

"I have instructions for you. I thought it wiser to drive down than to call your landlord."

Roebling nodded. "Has Mexico set up the contact point yet?"

"No."

"Then what's the message?"

Carver was looking at Erika. She lit a cigarette, ignoring him. Roebling caught an arm and turned him around. "I asked about the message."

"Don't be so cross," Carver said. "I didn't originate the order."

"What order, damnit?"

Carver flinched. "We've been ordered to destroy the installation."

"What?" Roebling's tone expressed his incredulity perfectly.

Carver shrugged. "That was my reaction, too. In fact, I was so stunned that I couldn't even acknowledge until they repeated it."

Roebling shook his head slowly. "No more. No more! We're going home! Heinie can go straight to hell! I'll stand court-martial before—"

"The order didn't come form Ares," Carver said. "Ares has been removed. The order came from Zeus."

"Canaris?"

Carver nodded. Roebling looked at Erika. She shook her head.

"It's a trick of the Americans. They want to draw us back, have us make an attempt so they can kill us."

Roebling looked at Carver.

"The code was correct in all respects," Carver said. "It couldn't have been the Americans."

"Don't do it, Stefan," Erika warned. "It's suicide! Don't even think about it!"

Roebling frowned. "What's the situation in Santa Fe?"

"Everything's back to normal. The alert has been canceled. My . . . friend visited me the other day and said the whole thing was just an exercise."

"What about the CIC office?"

"Less activity than usual. Most of the people seem to be gone."

"I don't like what you're thinking," Erika said.

"I'm thinking that I need to use Tal's radio," Roebling said. "Maybe there's an easy way to handle this."

"But it's too dangerous!"

Roebling smiled. "You heard Tal. Santa Fe is the only place they're not looking for us now." He looked back at Carver. "You said you drove down. In what?"

Carver smiled. "I have a car. I keep it in a rented garage in Santa Fe. I didn't want to look too prosperous to the other artists."

"Then we'll take it."

"Where's your car?"

"We had some trouble leaving Santa Fe. I dumped it three days ago."

Forty-three minutes after Roebling locked the door to the apartment, Greg Allison and five CIC agents kicked it in. Allison burst into the room, gun drawn, with the others just behind him. Within a minute they had determined that the room was completely empty. Allison jammed the pistol back into its holster and began slowly, calmly to recite his entire vocabulary of curse words.

38 MAJOR RICHARD OLIVER shifted his position in the armchair and glanced at his companions in the ready room. Billy Lee Holding, his wingman, was sprawled on the couch, his Texas-sized legs hanging well over the end. He was rereading an old issue of *Field & Stream,* reliving a bear hunt in Michigan that he had never taken but talked about all the time. Across the room, Benny Lefkowitz, a quiet, cynical man from Brooklyn, and Sandy Collins, a blond collegiate swimming champion from Southern California, were engaged in one of their marathon gin matches, confining their conversation to point totals and monies owed. As far as Oliver had been able to determine, the men had only one thing in common: Each was an experienced combat pilot. Lieutenants Holding and Collins had one tour of duty each, and Captain Lefkowitz had two tours, all flying the P-47 Thunderbolt fighter.

Oliver had three combat tours, all with the 56th Fighter Group of the Eighth Air Force—the famous Wolfpack— flying out of Halesworth, England. Holding and Collins had two kills each, Lefkowitz had four, and Oliver was an ace. He had been returned to the States, over his strong protests, after his fifth kill to receive the Distinguished Flying Cross and to be sent on a war-bond tour. In Los Angeles, he

had been taken off the tour without explanation and assigned to this small, mysterious fighter unit. Their job was
providing top cover, on call, for an even more mysterious
Army installation in the mountains to the north, but that
was all he knew.

Oliver went back to thumbing through the February 5
issue of *The Saturday Evening Post*. What had he done
wrong to be sent to such a godforsaken place as Albuquerque, New Mexico? He had been doing a good job on the
speaking tour, despite his dislike at being kept away from
combat while other pilots ran up their scores. It was important to him that he do well, be well thought of by the
generals. He wanted to stay in the Air Corps after the war,
wanted to make the service his career. So he needed those
kills to offset his ROTC commission. But no one would
ever tell him why he had been chosen for this duty—only
that it was very important and that they needed the best
men available.

His thoughts were interrupted by a sudden, urgent
honking of the klaxon horn. Immediately, the ready room
came to life. Holding came off the couch and jammed his
feet into fur-lined flying boots. Lefkowitz and Collins
dropped the cards and reached for their gear. Oliver
grabbed his flying jacket and ran for the door.

As he bounded down the stairs leading from the ready
room directly into the hangar, the ground crews were already opening the big hangar doors and turning over the
two lead Thunderbolts. The Pratt and Whitney radial on
Oliver's plane fired, belching blue and white smoke from its
exhausts, and came to life with a roar even as he covered
the short distance from the bottom of the stairs to its wing.
He went up on the wing and had one leg in the cockpit as
the crewman climbed out the other side. He stepped into
the leg straps of the parachute and sat down, the crewman
immediately leaning inside to help him.

Behind him the other pilots were going through the
same drill. The earphones in his leather helmet came to life
as he finished buckling in, and Oliver pressed the transmit
button on his control stick, his eyes scanning the instru-
ments.

"Red Flight rolling."

"Roger, Red Flight," a disembodied voice said in his earphones. "You are cleared for immediate takeoff."

Oliver glanced toward Holding's fighter and eased the throttle forward with his left hand. The dark-blue Thunderbolt with its plain Air Corps markings—no identifying unit insignia—began to roll. Holding kept pace, jockeying his fighter to stay to the right and slightly behind his element leader. Lefkowitz and Collins remained in the hangar. The procedure was that only the lead element of the four-plane flight would fly the intercept unless the tower ordered the full flight into the air. The second element, led by Lefkowitz, would remain at the ready, pilots staying in their planes so that they could be launched quickly if needed.

Oliver taxied quickly to the east end of the runway, making his engine check as he went. He turned the blunt-nosed fighter down the runway and immediately went to takeoff power. A quick glance to his right showed Holding in position, and Oliver shifted his eyes back to the airspeed indicator.

Since Kirtland Field was also used as the Albuquerque airport, both Oliver and Holding swept the sky in front as the two fighters built up speed. In previous scrambles the tower had done an excellent job of clearing traffic for the swift fighters, but both men held a fear that some civilian pilot might not get the word or might not be able to move his lumbering airliner out of their air space in time.

The air-speed indicator in Oliver's Thunderbolt rose steadily—eighty, ninety, one hundred miles per hour. At Halesworth he would be easing the stick back, feeling the heavy fighter break ground. At this altitude the Thunderbolt needed more speed, more runway to get off. Oliver watched the fence at the west end of the runway rush toward him.

In England the pilots who had flown the Spitfire—mostly members of the 4th Fighter Group whose nucleus had come from the Royal Air Force's three Eagle Squadrons—had taken an immediate dislike to the Thunderbolt, dubbing it the "seven-ton milk bottle." The lighter Spitfire had tremendous climbing and turning ability, whereas the Thunderbolt was capable of only a moderate rate of climb. But in other performance areas the Thunderbolt was clearly superior and had won a large following among American pilots who had not flown—and become wedded to—the Spitfire.

Oliver let the speed climb past one hundred ten miles per hour, then eased the stick back. The fighter lifted sluggishly into the thin air. Oliver moved the lever that raised the gear and banked to the right, climbing toward the mountains. The tower was on the air, directing him to assume a heading of 320 degrees. He lifted the flaps, adjusted the pitch on the big, four-bladed propeller and pulled the throttle back to climbing power. The air speed continued to move upward. Holding was in position off his right wing.

A second voice crackled in his earphones, fainter than the tower but clearly readable.

"Red Flight, this is Jemez One. Am at twelve thousand and proceeding toward target. Will notify if I spot him first. Over."

Jemez One was the call sign for the small spotter plane that flew daylight patrol over Los Alamos, watching for errant hunters and other intruders on the restricted reservation.

"Roger, Jemez One."

The tower started to transmit, then was interrupted by Colonel Foreman from his office on the base. Foreman was in command of all military flight operations at the base and monitored all Red Flight scrambles. He also had a transmitter linked to the tower antennas and was not shy about countermanding pilots' decisions, issuing orders and even correcting radio procedures. Unlike Oliver, Foreman took Red Flight scrambles very seriously.

"Jemez One, this is Red Base One. Return to patrol. Red Flight will handle intruder. Over."

There was a moment of silence. Oliver smiled behind his oxygen mask, imagining that the bored pilot in the spotter plane was calculating the odds of his survival if he ignored the order. The decision went to the colonel.

"Wilco, Red Base One. Am turning back. Out."

As soon as the tower was sure that Foreman did not intend further communications, it came back on the restricted channel with an adjusted course heading for Oliver. Oliver acknowledged, then added a question.

"Radar, what is the air speed of the intruder? Over."

The radar operator came on the line immediately. "Bogie is making approximately one-twenty knots on a bearing of ninety-three degrees true at fourteen thousand, Red Leader. He is now about eighty miles from the western boundary of restricted area. Estimate your intercept in approximately twenty minutes."

"Sounds like we've got one," Holding said in Oliver's earphones, echoing Oliver's own thoughts.

In addition to their familiarization flights, Foreman had scrambled Red Flight five times in the last two months, then critiqued each flight down to the last radio transmission, which he had recorded. Both Oliver and Holding had been running on only a half charge of adrenalin, each assuming that this was just another exercise. And perhaps it was. But if so, then Foreman had added several new elements, including a real live bogie for the radar operator. His information was too quick, too detailed to be simply part of a script. For a change, everyone's blood was flowing.

Oliver adjusted his fuel mixture again and watched the Thunderbolt climb through ten thousand at a steady one hundred sixty miles per hour, the regulation climbing speed. For once he wished for a higher rate of climb, although he knew that the distance would close quickly when he pushed over into level flight.

"Bogie had turned to a heading of eight-five degrees," the radar operator said. "Adjust your course to three-thirty-five degrees, Red Leader."

"Roger," Oliver replied, moving the stick slightly to the right. "Can you estimate type of target from signal? Over."

There was a short pause. "Signal is strong for the distance, Red Leader. He's bigger than you. I'd say multiengines. Over."

"Roger. How long to intercept? Over."

"Fifteen minutes if he doesn't change course again.

He'll pass north of the restricted area if he continues on present course."

"Roger."

The altimeter climbed through fourteen thousand. Oliver held the climb to the five hundred mark, then pushed over into level flight, readjusting the propeller pitch. The air speed built up quickly, rising to two hundred, two-fifty, then edging up toward three hundred miles per hour. The sky was marvelously blue, the thin air crystal clear. Below, the dark green of the coniferous forest was covered in the higher elevations by glaringly white, untracked snow. It was a damned shame that any country so beautiful from the air could be so ugly and inhospitable on the ground. Oliver dismissed the thought and concentrated on flying. The minutes ticked by.

"Red Leader, bogie has turned again and is now bearing one hundred ten degrees true. He seems to just be flying around, looking for a landmark. However, his new course will take him right over the restricted area."

"Probably a lost civilian," Oliver said, thinking aloud. "How long to intercept?"

"Come to course three-five-five degrees and you should have him in sight within three minutes."

Oliver reached forward and flipped on his gun and camera switches. Immediately, a red starburst appeared on the windshield in front of him.

"Is he still at fourteen thousand, Red Base?"

"He's down to thirteen-five, Red Leader, and still descending. Can you see him?"

Oliver scanned the area in front and below him. "Negative."

He held the new course for another minute by the panel clock, checking regularly. Red Flight was well to the northwest of the restricted air space now, but that distance would close quickly once they turned back to make the intercept. The radar operator spoke again.

"Two miles to intercept, Red Leader."

"Roger."

Oliver was beginning to sweat inside his flight suit, despite the temperature of the cockpit. The metallic taste of anticipation, of fear, was in his mouth. How could he have forgotten the fear so quickly? He had only remembered the rush of adrenalin, the buoyant high each pilot felt on engaging the enemy, the afterglow that remained after returning to base. He forced himself to remember where he was, in the middle of America chasing a lost civilian, not over occupied France preparing to duel with Focke-Wulf 190s.

"I've got him, ten o'clock low," Holding said, his voice ringing a little. Evidently, Holding was feeling the same adrenalin surge as Oliver. Oliver picked out the plane immediately. It was passing well below them.

"Got him, Red Two. Follow me."

Oliver pushed the fuel mixture into full rich, then went up and over in the best fighter tradition, although the twin-engined target below had no chance of outrunning the Thunderbolts. The heavy fighters picked up speed quickly in the dive—three-twenty-five, three-fifty—and Oliver brought the nose up, widening his reverse to kill off some speed and avoid overshooting the lumbering target.

He throttled back and moved in cautiously. Holding dropped back and held a position above and behind the target. Oliver came in high and crossed slowly from right to left, scanning the plane carefully. It was one of the old Douglas DC-2 models, the type that had been used as airliners and cargo planes in the Thirties before the DC-3 and its competitors had made them obsolete. It had a registration number but no other markings. He lost one hundred feet of altitude and swung in close. He could see the pilot in the left seat clearly. The man suddenly noticed the Thunderbolt and jerked his head around. Oliver swung the fighter away, unable to stay with the slower-moving plane without making wide S-turns.

"Red Base, this is Red Leader. Bogie is a DC-2 cargo plane, registration number N6301. I can see only one pilot. Other personnel unknown. Are you still not able to raise him?"

"Negative, Red Leader," the tower replied. "We've tried all frequencies."

Oliver swung back in toward the DC-2, pointing exaggeratedly at his earphones. The pilot caught on immediately and shook his head vigorously. His radio was dead. He pointed ahead of him, then shaded his eyes with his hand, indicating he was looking for a place to land. Oliver swung the fighter away again and made another wide turn to lose ground. Above and behind the DC-2, Holding was making the same turns lazily, covering his leader while waiting for orders. Oliver brought the Thunderbolt back alongside the DC-2.

He waved his right hand toward the pilot, indicating that he should turn right. The pilot watched his gestures uncomprehendingly as the Thunderbolt moved past. Oliver banked away to the left to come back for another pass. He was in the middle of his swing when his radio came to life.

"Red Leader, this is Red Base One. Report in."

"Red Base One, this is Red Leader. The radio on the bogie is out and the pilot is lost. I'm trying to turn him toward Red Base by hand signals. Over."

"Roger. Radar, how close are they to the restricted area?"

"Ten miles and closing, sir."

"Don't allow bogie into the restricted area, Red Leader. It could be a trick."

"Wilco," Oliver said, beginning another swing in toward the DC-2. He made another pass, waving more vigorously this time. Again the pilot didn't understand. His last glance showed the man holding up both hands and shaking his head. Evidently, he thought that Oliver was alone—playing some game to break the monotony of a training mission—and was proceeding on course until he could find a place to land. He couldn't know that a second Thunderbolt, with eight loaded fifty-caliber machine guns, was turning lazily behind him, waiting only for the word to drop him from the sky.

The radar operator's voice filled his ears. "Red Leader, you are now five miles from restricted area."

"Roger."

Oliver cut his turn short and shoved the throttle forward. Immediately, the fighter began to pick up speed.

He came back toward the DC-2 at a shallow angle, aiming his pass to cross in front of the bigger plane's nose. He thought of telling Holding his plan, but there was no need. Holding had a ringside seat for everything that was happening. The DC-2 pilot expected the fighter to turn away again and did not react until the last moment. The pass was closer than Oliver had intended, but the DC-2 banked sharply to the right just in time. At least he now had it turned in the right direction.

He was well past the cargo plane when he made the mistake. He turned to the right again to make a wide circle and come in behind the DC-2. He planned to take a position off its right wing, have Holding take a position off its left wing and escort it to the base between them.

But the pilot of the DC-2 was watching his every maneuver intently now. As Oliver began his right turn, the man banked away to the left, intending to put as much distance between himself and the obviously crazy fighter pilot as possible. The turn took him back to a course directly over the installation. Holding followed the DC-2, waiting for word from his leader.

The word came from radar. "Red Leader, bogie is two miles from restricted air space and closing."

Oliver started to tell the operator that he damned well knew where they were but was interrupted by Colonel Foreman.

"Red Leader, this is Red Base One. Do not, repeat, *do not* let bogie cross into restricted air space. Destroy at once. Understood?"

Oliver hesitated with his finger on the transmit button. The Thunderbolt was coming around in a climbing turn, the air speed registering just over two-twenty. The red gunsight ring on the front windshield was suddenly very visible. In another few moments he would be above and behind the DC-2, in position for an attack.

"Red Leader, do you hear me?" Colonel Foreman asked.

Oliver pressed the transmit button. "Roger, Red Base One."

In technical radio parlance, "Roger" meant "understood." The more correct term—the term Foreman expected—was "Wilco," which meant "understood and will comply." Oliver half expected a second transmission repeating the order, but the radio was silent.

The Thunderbolt's nose came around, and Holding's fighter was in front of him. Oliver banked slightly to the left to pass, ignoring Holding's look, and then swung wide to make his pass at the pilot's side of the DC-2. Even as the gunsight ring began to edge up toward the plane, Oliver was still searching for an option. He could apply a little left rudder, go for the left engine. But even if he didn't explode the wing tank, sending the man to an agonizing, conscious death, the crippled plane would be forced to hold its course, perhaps ultimately to crash into the center of the installation. No, he either had to kill him or let him go.

The sight ring touched the tail of the aircraft and began to inch up the fuselage. The range was closing fast. Oliver's mind automatically calculated the deflection shot, determining exactly when his forefinger should close on the red button so that the fifty-caliber shells—every fifth one a tracer—would meet the DC-2 at the nose, the cockpit, the left wing root. It was a simple physics problem, one he had successfully solved many times before on harder targets, a turning FW-190 or ME-109. This was too easy.

The distance between the planes was down to a thousand yards. At six hundred he should begin firing. Abruptly, Oliver chopped the throttle and kicked the nose of the Thunderbolt to the left. The heavy fighter skidded in the air, losing speed rapidly. Oliver straightened it and came in wide. The pilot in the DC-2 was watching the erratic maneuvers intently. Oliver edged in close, crowding him. The DC-2 turned away but not enough.

"Red Leader! What's happening up there?"

Oliver ignored the colonel. He rolled the Thunderbolt hard left to get more room to maneuver.

"Red Leader, you have just crossed into restricted air space," the radar operator said.

"Red Two!" Foreman barked. "Do you hear me?"

"Yes, sir," Holding said immediately, still turning lazily behind the DC-2.

"Tower! Record the time and date! Red Two! I *order* you to bring that plane down immediately!"

"Wilco, Red Base One."

"No!" Oliver shouted into his microphone, pulling up into a reverse to drop back toward Holding. "Colonel, it's only a lost civilian! He can't—"

"That's a *direct order,* Red Two!"

"Am beginning attack now," Holding replied, his tone even, cold.

"Red Two, hold your fire!" Oliver said, slamming his throttle to the stop, willing the fighter to move faster.

"Ignore that order, Red Two!" Foreman barked. "I have assumed full command and responsibility for your operation."

Oliver pulled the stick clear back into his stomach, fighting the G-forces of the turn that pushed him down into the seat, threatened to black him out as the blood rushed out of his head. As the nose came around, he could see immediately that he would be far too late to interpose his fighter between Holding and the DC-2. Holding was already diving on the unsuspecting plane. The DC-2 pilot was still watching him, totally unaware of the second Thunderbolt. Oliver screamed at him, at Holding, in frustration as Holding began firing. Oliver could clearly see the puffs of smoke from the guns, the empty shells falling out of the wing slots, the light streaks of the tracers crossing the rapidly narrowing distance between the two planes. The DC-2 shuddered under the sustained impact. Oliver found his transmit button again.

"God damn you, Holding! Stop firing! Stop it!"

Holding kept the red button on the front of his stick locked down. The DC-2 was falling off to the left, chunks of skin and other pieces of metal flying off into its wake. Oliver screamed again, but Holding followed it, pouring that continuous stream of tracers into the cockpit, the fuselage, the wing. Just as Oliver turned in behind them, a fuel tank exploded, tearing off a large part of the left wing, sending the DC-2 downward in an erratic, dying spiral. Holding followed in a wider, lazy spiral, his guns finally silent. Oliver veered away, automatically pulling back his throttle. He did not want to see the end.

"Red Base One, this is Red Two." Holding's voice was calm, detached. "Bogie has been destroyed. Estimate he will crash approximately one mile due west of installation. Over."

"Roger, Red Two. Good work. Mark the spot for Jemez One, then return to base. Out."

Foreman set the microphone on the radio table and turned back to his desk, ignoring Holding's acknowledgment. His initial assessment of Oliver—a feeling that Oliver's combat record had overridden—had just been confirmed. Even with his experience, Oliver had simply never realized, down in his guts, that his job was to kill people, not joust with other fighter pilots in sporting contests. As a consequence, Oliver was the wrong man to lead the Red Flight. He wasn't tough enough. Holding was the man—and to hell with rank. He would make him an acting captain tomorrow.

Foreman pressed an intercom button and ordered Oliver's file sent up. He would give Oliver his wish. He would transfer him back to England immediately for another combat tour. If Oliver was lucky, he might get another five kills and come home as a double ace—a genuine national hero—all without realizing that he had been in a war.

39 THE JEEP made its way slowly up the narrow, twisting road, following the fresh ruts in the deepening snow, slowing almost to a crawl in the sharp turns where the edge of the road had eroded away and the occupants could look down at the tops of sixty-foot pines. The mountains, the snow-laden trees were incredibly beautiful, silent except for the snarling engine.

The four people had left Los Alamos an hour earlier, driven down the mountain to State Highway 4, wound around the ends of the mesas, passed Bandelier National Monument with its ruined kivas and cave dwellings, then began the steep climb up over the edge of the volcanic rim. Above 9,000 feet, they crossed the pass and began the descent into the Valle Grande.

The road curved and suddenly the entire extinct caldera was spread out before them—176 square miles of shallow bowl rimmed by the cone of the great volcano, punctuated by small, pine-covered islands in a sea of white—pure, pristine, seemingly untouched by man or animal. The Jeep stopped and Greg Allison climbed out, feeling something like the first man to set foot in the caldera—proud, humbled, suddenly very conscious of his boot track in the glaringly white snow. He stood still, looking, listening to the silence, the absence of wind.

Sergeant Malcolm Lowrey, a thickset Military Police veteran with cold blue eyes, interrupted his thoughts.

"Kinda gets to you, don't it?"

Allison nodded.

"You oughta see it in the summer when everything's green and the grass is up to the cows' bellies. This's a ranch, you know. Over a hundred thousand acres. There's some buildings and corrals and such over on the west rim, but you can't hardly pick them out now."

Allison looked but couldn't see anything.

"That island out there. How far would you say it was?"

Allison gauged the distance. "Two miles. Maybe three."

Lowrey laughed softly. "It's about halfway to the other side, and the rim's twenty miles across."

"Are you sure?"

Lowrey's laugh was louder this time. "That's why they lose so many hunters out here. The air's too clear. It's damned hard to judge distances. You need to double or triple your first estimate."

Lowrey looked back at the other two MPs. "Sanger, bring Mr. Allison's snowshoes over here. Henson, move your butt! We ain't got all day!"

"Just how far is the wreck, Sergeant?" Allison asked.

"It's only a couple of miles up this side. Them Air Corps boys sure took their time about bringing it down. Another minute and it would have crashed right into the middle of the base."

After having gone less than a hundred yards, Allison was panting steadily, his lungs unaccustomed to the thin air. Despite the trail already having been broken by the earlier team that brought out the body, the going was heavy in the clumsy snowshoes. Long before they reached the site, Allison was regretting that he had insisted on seeing the wreck for himself.

Surprisingly, a fair amount of the fuselage was intact. The impact and explosion had buried or destroyed the front half, but the deep snow had extinguished the fire before it could gut the tail section. Pieces of the plane were scattered throughout the nearby trees, and Allison instructed the three MPs to make a wide circle, informing him if they found anything that might give a clue to the identity of the pilot or where he might have been going. Allison started with the remnants of the fuselage.

Three hours later he was stamping his feet, trying to bring some feeling back into his toes, ready to give up. Lowrey appeared out of the trees on the downslope and trudged wearily to him.

"There's some more pieces back down there, but they're just chunks of wing. Ain't even got any markings on them. You find anything?"

Allison shook his head.

"What say we call it a day?" Lowrey asked. "We've been over this whole area twice."

His tone indicated that he thought the whole trip was more than a little foolish anyway. The earlier investigation team had covered the ground very thoroughly. Allison nodded tiredly.

Lowrey called the other two men in. Private Sanger appeared a few minutes later from the trees on the right, but Private Henson didn't answer. Lowrey called again, then listened. There wasn't any answering shout.

"Damn!" Lowrey said, looking at Allison. "I warned him about wandering too far away. Twenty yards into those trees you can get turned around and totally lost."

"Surely he'd simply backtrack when he discovered he was going the wrong way."

"Maybe," Lowrey said. "But he's from the big city, New York. He may be too damned smart to think of anything that simple."

"Call him again."

Lowrey cupped his mouth with his hands and called one direction, then a second, then a third. He listened for a minute, then was preparing to call again when Henson came out of the trees behind him. Sanger said "Here he is!" and Lowrey turned, frowning. Henson trudged up to the group.

"Ain't you got enough sense to answer a call, Private?" Lowrey said.

"I was up a tree, Sarge. I had to get down first."

"Before you could yell? What in the hell were you doing up a tree?"

"Fishing this off a branch," Henson said, pulling a black object from under his field jacket.

Allison took it from him, turning it over in his hands.

"That's what's left of a camera, ain't it, sir?"

Allison nodded. The bellows and lenses were gone, but the back was mostly intact. It had been a very good camera, too, one of the types used by professionals.

"Where did you find this?"

"About fifty or sixty yards over that way. It was caught in the fork of a limb. I guess it fell out before the plane hit the ground. I looked around, but I couldn't find any other pieces. You want me to show you?"

Allison looked at Lowrey. Lowrey pointedly checked his watch. The sun was getting well down toward the western rim of the crater.

"No. We'd better start back."

"Ain't much to show for your coming all the way back from El Paso, is it?" Lowrey asked.

"No. But at least it's something," Allison said, hefting the damaged metal.

"Okay, Daniel Boone," Lowrey said to Henson. "You lead out."

It was after eleven when the knock came at the door. Three raps, a short silence, then another. Stefan Roebling relaxed somewhat but still checked the stoop through the window before unlocking the door. Tal Carver hurried inside, shivering.

"Man, it's cold out there!" He hurried over to the small heater in the tourist cabin, pulling his gloves off to warm his hands. Roebling put the pistol back in his pocket. Erika snapped off the small radio, stopping a weather report in mid-sentence.

"Well?"

"The plane was shot down. Joseph's dead."

"Are you sure?" Erika asked. "There wasn't anything on the news about it."

"And there won't be," Carver said. "The CIC has hushed the whole thing up."

"Have they identified Joseph yet?"

"No. All they know is that the plane is registered to the WestAir corporation in Salt Lake City. A CIC man is on his way up there now to check it out."

"Your lieutenant doesn't mind telling you everything he knows, does he?" Roebling said. "Are you sure he isn't getting suspicious about your questions?"

"I don't ask questions," Carver said. "I just listen. The more he tells me, the more fascinated I am by him, by what he's doing."

"It's the oldest and best trick in the world, darling," Erika said. "If you were a woman, you'd know all about it."

Roebling glanced at her, then at Carver.

"What now?" Carver asked. "We know the installation can't be bombed. Besides, we don't have a pilot any longer."

Roebling shook his head. "It's hard to believe the Americans would shoot down an unarmed civilian over their own country."

"But they did," Erika said. "And as far as I'm concerned, that ends it. I vote we go home before the CIC decides we've doubled back on them."

"I agree with Erika," Carver said. "Every day we stay here—"

"Not yet," Roebling said. "There may be another way."

"How?" Erika asked. "The installation's too spread out, too well guarded. We agreed that bombing would be the only—"

"Maybe we've been using the wrong perspective," Roebling said.

"What do you mean?"

He ignored the question. "Tal, when will Lieutenant Price visit you again?"

"We made a date for Saturday night, but—"

"That's too soon. Let's go over to your place. I want to use the radio again."

"Why?"

"To see what Zeus can supply us with and how soon."

40 THE WESTAIR "headquarters"—located in an old hangar on the back side of the Salt Lake City airfield—consisted of one cramped, dirty office which was littered with unfiled papers and greasy aircraft engine parts. The owner and manager was a small man with a big cigar and a cocksure, slightly belligerent manner. Grease stains on his hands, under his fingernails indicated that he also did a fair amount of his own mechanic work. Greg Allison showed the man his credentials, and the belligerence became tempered with caution.

"Are you Damon Haverford?"

"Could be. What do you want?"

"Some information."

"If that's all, then I'm him."

Allison moved a stack of papers and took a chair without an invitation. Haverford frowned slightly, but Allison ignored him. When in Rome . . .

"Do you own a DC-2, registration number N6301?"

"No."

"It's registered to your company."

"You asked if I owned it. I don't. The company does."

"Aren't you the company?"

"Only on the papers."

"I see. Do you know where this plane is now?"

"Why do you want to know?"

Allison paused, watching the man. "You keep an FAA log of your flights, I presume. Could I see it?"

Haverford quit chewing on his cigar, his caution temporarily overcoming his pleasure in playing the hard-nose. "You got the authority to look at my books?"

"No," Allison said. "But I can have the FAA here in a couple of hours. And if you force me to do that, I promise you that they'll also inspect every one of your aircraft from nose to tail and make sure that every nut is in place before you take one of them off the ground again. Now which way do you want to do this?"

Haverford tried to bluff it through with a hard stare, but Allison met his eyes evenly. Finally, Haverford dumped the cigar in an oversized ashtray already full of similar butts.

"I rented that plane three days ago. It's supposed to be hauling cargo from Albuquerque to Los Angeles."

"To whom?"

Haverford reluctantly dug into the desk drawer and came out with a rental contract. He had to hold it away from him a little to read it.

"Dockery. Daniel Dockery."

"I take it that you don't know this Dockery."

"It was business," Haverford said. "His license was okay. The multiengine ratings were up to date."

"What did he look like?"

Haverford shrugged. "Tall, kinda fair, normal-looking."

Allison extracted two pictures from his pocket. "How about this?"

Haverford held the first picture up and looked at it. "What is this? Some kind of drawing? I never saw a snapshot of a drawing before."

"Did the man look like that?"

"No. His face was a lot broader, you know, kinda square. The eyes were different too. Naw, this don't look nothing like him."

Allison handed him the other picture. "Have you ever seen her?"

Haverford studied the second picture, his expression changing slowly, the edges of his mouth curling upward.

"She's a helluva lot better to look at, I tell you. But I ain't seen her either. Wish I had."

"So do I," Allison said. "Could I see the rental contract?"

Part of the caution returned. "Why?"

"I want the information on Dockery."

"What'd he do?"

"Can I see it, please?"

Haverford handed it over reluctantly. While Allison copied down the San Francisco address, Haverford continued to ask questions.

"You never did tell me what this's all about. Has this guy been using my plane for something illegal?"

Allison handed the contract back.

"How were you paid?"

"Cash," Haverford said. "In advance. You don't think I'm gonna let some jackleg walk in here—"

"Did you have insurance on the plane, Mr. Haverford?"

"Insurance? Why would . . . Hey, wait a minute! If that bozo has damaged my plane, I'll—"

"Your plane crashed in the mountains north of Albuquerque three days ago, Mr. Haverford. As soon as we've finished with it, the Army will notify you when and where you can pick it up."

"Crashed! That sonofabitch! I'll kill him!"

"You won't have to," Allison said. "He's already dead. Good afternoon, Mr. Haverford."

Haverford came out of his chair. "Hey, wait! What's the Army doing with my plane? Why is—"

"The Army will contact you," Allison repeated. "Good day."

Outside, walking back across the tarmac, Allison felt a small sense of relief that the pilot had not been Novalis. Almost as soon as he had the feeling, the incongruity of the thought struck him. If anything, he should be wishing that it had been Novalis, that the man was dead and the chase was finished. At least then he would be sure that Novalis had not escaped the country with any information, however slight, that he had been able to pick up. This way he might never be sure.

41 THE PLANE WAS LATE. Stefan Roebling checked his watch, then looked toward the eastern horizon, shading his eyes. The sun was full up now, and cars would soon begin appearing on the narrow strip of U.S. 285 in front of him. He turned away, to where Tal Carver's Chevrolet was hidden behind the boarded-up gas station and grocery, silent victims of the Depression. The shadow of the building and the fogged-up windshield kept him from seeing Erika, but he knew she was there, in the front seat of the car.

He looked again toward the southwest, searching the sky for a glint of light, the faint sound of an engine. Still nothing. Damn them! Where were they? He walked a few steps back toward the car, his shoes crunching through the glaze of ice on the gravel driveway laid down by the now bankrupt proprietors.

Beyond the building, to the east and west and south, the gentle undulations of the open range land were covered with snow that reflected the brilliant rays of the morning sun. To the north the land sloped away sharply to a narrow valley, where an ice-covered stream glistened in the sun. Roebling's breath also glistened, forming tiny ice crystals that caught the sun momentarily before dispersing.

The sound of an engine reached him, then faded quickly. He stopped pacing and held his breath, scanning the southwestern sky. The sound came again on the light, northerly wind, faded, then came back stronger. It was an aircraft. He walked quickly back to the car and opened the door.

"Hand me that walkie-talkie."

Erika handed him the small radio, and he paused beside the car, scanning the sky. The sound was from the north, the wrong direction, and Roebling stayed close to the car, ready to duck inside. The glint of sun on metal just above the horizon confirmed that it was a plane. But what plane? The one he was waiting for should come from the southwest, from Mexico. He waited, shading his eyes. The engine sound grew, then the plane was fully visible, flying low, moving fast. A single-engined monoplane, high wing, civilian markings. Roebling held the radio up to his cheek and pushed the transmit button.

"Wanderer, this is Oasis. Do you hear me?"

Immediately, a voice came through the earpiece.

"I hear you, Oasis. What are the conditions?"

"Wind north-northwest about eight knots. Surface good but with patches of ice. Watch yourself."

"Right."

The plane roared overhead and made a wide, sweeping turn to the south, losing speed and altitude. Roebling moved out from behind the building to watch the landing. The plane completed its turn and settled gently toward the highway. It touched lightly, bounced once, then rolled toward him, its tail wheel slowly settling to the ground as it lost speed. When it reached the graveled driveway, the pilot pulled off the highway. Roebling waited while the pilot pivoted in the area and shut the engine down. By the time he got around the plane, two men had already climbed out of the cabin and were opening a storage compartment door in the fuselage. The pilot stayed inside the plane, watching the road in both directions.

Roebling smiled at the men and took a moment to shake their hands.

"Haupt, Borchers. It's good to see you again. Where're the others?"

"We are it," Borchers said. "There wasn't anyone else available."

"Why are you so late?"

The taller man, Herman Haupt, jerked his head toward the plane's cabin and snorted.

"Our stalwart pilot got lost. We flew all the way to Santa Fe before he knew where he was."

"Yes," Konrad Borchers said. "And that made him even more nervous than he was coming over the mountains at night. I don't like nervous pilots."

Roebling smiled again. "Afraid he'd set the plane down too hard for your cargo?"

"No. Too hard for me!" Borchers said.

"Hadn't we better get moving?" Haupt said.

Roebling nodded. "Put the suitcases in the trunk of the car and send the woman over here."

The two men took three suitcases out of the cargo hold and started toward the car. Roebling stepped to the front of the plane and opened the cabin door. Borchers was right. The pilot, a dark little man of uncertain ancestry, was nervous.

"You unloaded? I can go?"

"Wait a minute. I've got a passenger for you."

"I cannot stay. Someone may come along."

"This won't take long."

Roebling shut the door and walked to the tail of the aircraft. Erika was almost to the plane. He waited for her to come to him.

"You wanted me?"

"Erika, I want you to go back with the plane. You—"

"No."

"Let me finish. There's no need for you to stay, and it's much safer now than later, after we make the strike."

"I'm not going, Stefan. Only two men came in. The plan needs a minimum of three in addition to yourself."

"I'll use Carver."

"You can't," Erika said. "We both know that. Besides, Haupt has already told me that I'm to be on the team. They brought in clothes and—"

"They what?"

"Zeus ordered it."

"I don't give a damn about Zeus!" Roebling said roughly. "You're leaving now if I have to tie you—"

"No, I'm not! Not unless you leave with me."

"You know I can't do that."

"Then I'm not going either."

He reached for her, but she backed away. He started after her.

"Don't do this, Stefan! Don't try—"

He grabbed her before she could run. She tried to struggle, he quickly wrapped his arms around her, lifted her off the ground and began carrying her back to the plane.

"Don't be a fool, Stefan! Put me down!"

"You're going out with—"

"God damn you! Won't you ever learn? Zeus is no different from Ares. Ares tried to kill you and now Zeus has ordered you to commit suicide. And you're going to do it!"

He stopped.

"What are you talking about?"

She twisted in his arms. "Put me down!"

He finally set her on her feet but held onto her arms.

"If you're stalling for time, Erika, then—"

"Listen to me, Stefan. It's true! You aren't supposed to be here. I'm not supposed to be here. The Prometheus Operation was a fake!"

He studied her eyes, unbelieving. "The installation is real. The project is real. How can you say—"

"The Abwehr didn't know anything about an American atomic-bomb project until we told them. They simply used some information I picked up about a secret project in Manhattan to create a fake mission about a 'new weapon.' They didn't know it was true. You weren't supposed to uncover that installation back there. You weren't supposed to do anything except sit in a safe house in New York until I needed you!"

"You needed me? I don't—"

"You were never to meet me! You were to come to a drop in Washington and pick up plans for the American code machine after I had gotten them and photographed them. Then you were to be arrested with the plans so the

Americans would think they had recovered them before they could be transmitted. Your whole purpose was to cover me—to be a scapegoat for my operation!"

He stared at her, trying to deny the truth in her tone, her eyes.

"Ares used you then, and Zeus is using you now!" Erika said. "My God, why won't you believe me! The counterfeit was deliberate. The help to the CIC was deliberate. You don't even limp on the right leg!"

He could no longer disbelieve. Finally, everything fit— Jost's picking him for the job, North's consternation when he refused to follow orders, the way the CIC had been able to trail him. North. He had killed the wrong man. And now . . .

"You knew about the counterfeit?"

"No," she said. "I only knew that you'd be set up. I— I'm sorry."

He didn't reply. She tugged gently at his coat.

"You've done enough, Stefan. You can't stay now, let them use you again, kill you for nothing. Let's both get on that plane. We can go to Argentina, to Switzerland, wherever you wish. Let's—"

"It doesn't make any difference," Roebling said finally. "The Americans do have an atomic-bomb project, and—"

"The war's almost over, Stefan. The bomb will never be ready in time to—"

"Do you *know* that, Erika?" Roebling asked harshly. "Or are you lying to me again? I still have family living in Germany and so do you. Are you willing to take a chance on such a weapon being used on them?"

She lifted her chin. "You're a fool, Stefan, but—"

"I don't want to hear any more!" Roebling said angrily. "Go! Get on the plane and run away!"

She shook her head. "I am staying."

He took a deep breath, trying to control his temper.

"I order you to get on—"

"Stefan! Someone's coming!"

The guarded shout from Haupt distracted him. Erika tore loose from his grasp and started to run back toward the car. Roebling started after her just as the engine of the

plane began to turn over. He slipped on the icy gravel trying to stop, then got back to his feet. The engine caught
and the blast from the propeller almost blew him down
again. The pilot unlocked the brakes and the plane began
to move. Roebling chased it several yards before realizing
that he could not stop it. The plane turned onto the highway, headed south, and the pilot went to full power.

Roebling ran for the car. "Haupt! The radio! Get me the
radio!"

Haupt grabbed the walkie-talkie and ran toward him.
The two men reached each other and Roebling grabbed
the radio out of Haupt's hand.

"Wanderer! Do you hear me, Wanderer? Acknowledge!"

The engine noise was beginning to even out to a steady
drone, moving away faster and faster. Roebling pressed the
button again.

"Wanderer! Keep that plane in the area until the intruder is gone, then bring it back! Acknowledge!"

There was still no answer. Haupt tugged at Roebling's
sleeve.

"Let's get under cover until the car passes."

Roebling gave ground reluctantly, his eyes riveted on
the fast-moving plane. They reached the concealment of
the building just as an old pickup—its ranch name and
brand mostly obscured by dirt and time—topped the grade
and passed the front of the deserted station. Haupt pointed
down the road. The plane was a glint of light in the sun.
The pilot lifted off, but it staggered in the thin air and settled back on the roadway.

"He's not going to make it," Haupt said evenly, as if
commenting on the weather.

"What do you—"

"Watch."

Just as Haupt uttered the word, the plane dropped out
of sight into a low spot in the road. A second later, it
bounded crazily into the air, hung for a long second, then
stalled and fell almost straight down. Within another three
seconds, just before the sound of the impact reached them,
the plane exploded in a ball of fire. Billows of black smoke

quickly shut off the sight of the flames and started an upward spiral into the sky.

"There's a bad dip in the road down there," Haupt said in that same conversational tone. "We saw it coming in." He shook his head. "I'm glad I didn't know how scared Hernando was on the ride up here. Trying to take off downwind in this altitude with that load of gas. I'd probably have opted to walk in."

"You may get your chance to walk out," Roebling said angrily. "That was our ride."

He watched the smoke for another moment, then started for the car.

"Let's get the hell out of here."

42 ALMOST A WEEK LATER, Greg Allison strode into Captain Lloyd Cameron's office at the Santa Fe detachment of the CIC. Cameron was seated behind his desk, laboriously drafting a report in longhand on a ruled tablet. He glanced up and smiled.

"Greg! What happened to you? I thought you'd given up and gone back to Baltimore."

"I've been in San Francisco chasing a shadow," Allison said.

"The pilot of that plane? What did you find?"

"He didn't exist. At least not under that name."

"The license was a fake?"

"No. The license was real. It was issued to a man calling himself Daniel Dockery who took all the tests and demonstrated his competence. But Dockery wasn't real. Or if he was, he's the first man to die twice."

"What do you mean?"

"I mean Daniel James Dockery was born in nineteen-twelve, died in nineteen-fourteen and then applied for a copy of his birth certificate in nineteen-forty-two. He has an apartment in San Francisco, but as far as we could tell, he has no family, no friends, not even a job."

"Another agent?"

"Probably," Allison said.

Cameron tapped the pencil eraser on the pad. "Then I'd say that confirms it."

"Confirms what?"

"Novalis and the woman have made their escape from the country without getting anything of value. The Abwehr had another agent attempt to fly over the installation and take aerial photographs to find out what's there."

Allison frowned. "Has anything happened here?"

Cameron shook his head. "Quiet as a church mouse. The Hill's been back to normal for three weeks now, and we haven't had a single incident."

Allison found a cigarette and lit it, still frowning. Cameron leaned back in his chair.

"What's the problem? I thought you'd be pleased. Colonel Williams is. Even General Groves wasn't too unhappy. All in all, everyone thinks we did a pretty good job of—"

"We didn't get Novalis," Allison said.

"No, but we stopped them from getting any information about—"

"Did we?" Allison asked.

"Of course we did. The fact that they sent another agent to overfly the installation proves that—"

"It doesn't prove anything," Allison said. "We don't even know that Dockery was a German agent. He could have been a smuggler, anything."

Cameron's eyebrows went up. "You're now saying that he wasn't an agent? I thought you ... Just what is the matter with you, Greg? You're unhappy when no one else sees as many German agents as you do, then you're unhappy when they do."

Allison rubbed his eyes. "I'm sorry, Lloyd. I'm beat. I guess I'm also so damned frustrated that I can't admit they're gone. I've been chasing Novalis all over the country now for two months, and to think that he just slipped over the border ..." Allison looked up. "Have you heard anything from the Mexican authorities?"

Cameron shook his head. "Not a word. But then I didn't expect to. Did you?"

"No. It's too easy to bribe people down there."

Allison rubbed his eyes again. When he opened them, the secretary had slipped into the room and was handing Cameron a piece of paper. As Allison watched, Cameron scanned it quickly and initialed it.

"What's that?"

"Just an interview with the rancher who saw the plane crash," Cameron said.

"Someone saw it?"

"Not the DC-2. This was a light-plane crash just off U.S. 285 south of Lamy."

"When?"

"Almost a week ago. We didn't know anything about it until a piece appeared in the paper, but I had Carter check it out with the State Police."

"And?"

Cameron looked at the report. "There isn't much to tell. This plane had landed on the highway. Probably some kind of engine trouble. It was taking off again just as this rancher came along. He said it tried to go straight up, then turned over and crashed. Sounds like the pilot didn't get the trouble fixed after all."

"Have they identified the pilot?"

"No. They couldn't even identify the plane. Everything was too badly torn up and burned."

Allison straightened in his chair. "Have the police checked all the nearby air fields?"

"As far away as Phoenix and Denver. No one has reported missing any planes. He was probably one of those air gypsies who still wander through occasionally, never filing any flight plans. We may never know who it was."

"It couldn't have been Novalis?"

Cameron shook his head again. "No. Carter asked the coroner that. The man wasn't that large, even before he burned."

Allison puffed on the cigarette, thinking. "Doesn't that strike you as odd, Lloyd?"

"What?"

"Two air crashes within a week in a remote area like this and neither of the pilots can be identifed."

"Maybe, but there's nothing to indicate that it isn't just coincidence."

"Is it? What if it isn't?"

"I don't follow you, Greg. What are you trying to say?"

"What if Novalis and Erika Huntington didn't slip into Mexico? What if they doubled back to Santa Fe after giving us the slip in Albuquerque? What if they arranged for a friend to get aerial photographs of the base and, when that failed, had a plane fly in some equipment or maybe friends from Mexico?"

Cameron laughed shortly. "That's a lot of 'what ifs,' Greg. I don't think anyone would believe that—"

"I do," Allison said, surprised that the statement was true.

Cameron lost his grin. "You can't be serious."

"Why not? We can't afford to—"

"Why won't you let go of this, Greg? This isn't the movies. In real life not everything ends up tied together in a neat package. Sometimes you have to settle for a draw."

"I want your men again, Lloyd," Allison said, ignoring Cameron's comments.

"Why?"

"I want to check every hotel and every tourist court in Santa Fe. They're here and I intend to—"

"Not again! Look, Greg, we have other things to do, other investigations going on that—"

"Damnit, Lloyd! Don't you understand that—"

"I understand perfectly!" Cameron snapped back. "You can't stand to think that this German agent—*your* German agent—has dusted you off. He didn't play fair! He skipped out and left you hanging, having neither won nor lost, and you can't accept that."

"That has nothing to do with it, Lloyd. I know that—"

"No! No, you don't *know* anything, Greg! If you did, I'd be the first to put every man we've got into another sweep of this town, but it's a waste of time!"

"Is it?" Allison asked. "Then you tell me where they are. We know they've left Albuquerque, but they haven't crossed the border, legally or illegally, that anyone knows. Also, they haven't bought or stolen another car, and no one has seen them at any airfield or bus or train station. That means they've gone to ground again, somewhere that we aren't looking for them. Here!"

Cameron shook his head. "They could be anywhere. South America. Even Germany by now."

"Now who's guessing?" Allison asked.

Cameron frowned. "I never said I can prove—"

"There's one point you're overlooking, Lloyd."

"What's that?"

"If I'm wrong, all we lose is a little more time and sleep. If you're wrong, we could lose a great deal more."

Cameron inhaled deeply, his jaw muscles clenching momentarily. Allison watched him. Cameron finally nodded.

"All right, Greg. You've got three men. That's all I can spare for—"

"Six," Allison argued.

"Three men," Cameron repeated. "And only for three days. If you don't turn up something by then, I'm taking them *back!"*

43 FIRST LIEUTENANT GORDON PRICE turned the corner and walked quickly down the narrow street toward Tal Carver's house. The darkness, the cold wind laden with tiny snowflakes could not slow his steps, dampen the warm feeling inside him. Finally he had found someone who understood, who really cared about him as a person, who did not think of him as a possession to be flaunted, an All-American football machine or a faceless body to be trained and outfitted and pushed into a pre-formed slot.

Tal cared. He really cared—unlike Gordon's father, who had left his family when Gordon was three, and Gordon's mother, who had spent twenty years smothering Gordon with her hatred for his father. Gordon's relationship with Tal had grown so quickly, so easily since that chance meeting on the plaza that at times it was almost frightening. And yet it was right. Tal had helped him accept his needs, his desires in a way that his prior companions had not been able to do.

Price smiled to himself. One chance meeting that had changed his life. The quiet Sunday afernoon in Santa Fe. The small Spanish square. The lone artist sketching the Palace of the Governors. Price had stopped to watch and, for once, the uniform had not been a barrier to conversation. Each had quickly recognized the empathy, the commonality between them. Tal had invited him to the little house toward which he was heading now and he had hesitantly accepted. He had first thought the house ugly, dirty, but now he saw it as beautiful. Behind its thick adobe walls their love, their life together were safe.

Price stopped at the doorway, looked both ways, then inserted his key into the lock. He stepped inside and shut the door quickly. Across the room Tal was seated on a stool, working on a large canvas—an autumn scene along the Rio Grande with splashes of aspens in yellows and golds. Tal looked around and smiled.

"You're late."

"I'm sorry," Price said, slipping out of his coat and taking off his cap. He crossed the room quickly, and Carver lifted his face. Price kissed him lightly on the lips and ruffled his hair.

"Miss me?"

"Yes. Are you hungry?"

"Starved. Have you eaten?"

"I was waiting for you. What would you like?"

Price shrugged. "Whatever you have—unless you'd rather go out."

Carver shook his head. "I've been simmering some spaghetti sauce all afternoon. It won't take long to cook the spaghetti if that's all right with you."

"Sounds good."

Carver wiped the paint off his brushes and stood them on end in an old coffee mug.

"You sit down and take it easy. I picked up a bottle of Chianti this afternoon, and I'll make some garlic bread if you'd like."

"That's fine."

Carver had just started toward the kitchen when the knock came on the door. Price stopped, halfway to the chair.

Carver smiled. "Don't worry. It's probably just one of the neighbors wanting to borrow something."

Price watched uneasily as Tal crossed the room and

opened the door. Two men in overcoats, their hats pulled down against the wind, pushed Carver aside and stepped into the house. Carver looked at Price, his expression a mixture of surprise and fear. Price stood motionless as the taller of the two men, a lean man with black hair and blue eyes, came across the room and held out a credentials case.

"Special Agent Reynolds, FBI." He motioned toward the other man. "This is Special Agent Harris. You're Lieutenant Gordon Price?"

Price thought of denying it, then nodded slowly. His throat was too constricted to trust his voice. Reynolds looked at Carver.

"Both of you sit down. We want to talk to you."

"About what?" Carver asked, his voice sounding strained.

"Just sit down," Harris said gruffly.

Price lowered himself into the chair, unable to take his eyes off Reynolds. Carver quickly moved over and sat down on the chair arm beside him. Reynolds took a small notebook from an inside pocket and flipped through a few pages. Harris was watching both of them with a stony expression.

"Now then," Reynolds said, looking up. "I'll come directly to the point. We know all about both of you and your 'relationship.' We've had both of you under surveillance for some time, so it will be pointless to waste time trying to deny anything. We even have infrared pictures of you performing—shall we say—'unnatural sex acts' on each other."

"Oh my God!" Price said hoarsely, his fingers digging into the chair arms. Carver grabbed his arm and held on tight, his face mirroring Price's own horror. Price looked at his hands. He wanted to run, to burst out of this confined space and run and run and run until he was far away from this house, this city, this world. But he couldn't move. He could barely breathe.

"What . . . What are you going to do with us?"

Reynolds' expression was cold. "Nothing will be done with *Mister* Carver. He's committed no Federal crime. But you're a different matter, Lieutenant. You're a member of the armed forces of the United States. And working for the Provost Marshal's office, as you do, you must know the regulations covering homosexual activities."

Price lowered his head into his hands, wishing Carver would move away, quit holding onto him.

"Yes."

"Good," Reynolds said. "Then I can make this as short as possible. Harris, take Carver into the bedroom and close the door."

Carver tried to hang onto Price, but Harris pried his hands loose and led him away. Price looked at the distraught face, the pleading eyes, before Harris pushed Carver into the bedroom and closed the door.

"What . . . What is he going to do to Tal?"

"Nothing except make sure that he doesn't overhear the rest of our conversation," Reynolds said.

"Why?"

"Because I have a proposition for you, Lieutenant, and I don't want your friend to hear it."

Price almost giggled. The idea of the disapproving FBI agent propositioning him was too incongruous. He took a deep breath, smothering the urge. The fear was making him a little giddy.

"Did you hear me, Lieutenant? I've been instructed to offer you a proposition. If you take it, then you'll be given another chance. If not—"

Reynolds let the rest of the sentence hang in the air. Price let out part of the breath he had been holding.

"What . . . What proposition?"

"There have been some security leaks from this installation recently," Reynolds said. "Mr. Hoover believes that the CIC protection of this base isn't adequate, but he has been unable to convince Secretary Stimson of that fact so far. So we want you to help us stage an illegal entry into Los Alamos, as a demonstration of the inadequacy of your security measures."

"I can't . . ."

"You don't have a choice," Reynolds said evenly. "Either you cooperate, or we turn our information on you over to Colonel Williams."

Price flinched. "You—"

"And if you're thinking that you might be given a general discharge and a quiet ride home, forget it. You know how important the installation is, and you know what happens to people who threaten its security."

Price knew. There had been two cases of soldiers talking too freely about their work since he had been at Los Alamos. Both times the offender had been visited in the middle of the night by two large MPs. Each man was roused quietly, his clothes were packed, and he was well on his way to a remote, primitive atoll in the South Pacific before his barracks mates discovered the rolled-up mattress the next morning.

Price shuddered. "I—I agree."

"Good," Reynolds said. He described the plan quickly, then checked Price on several parts.

"You understand exactly what we want you to do?"

"Yes."

Reynolds studied him a moment. "If anyone is forewarned about this test, if anything goes wrong, then we'll assume you were the source and act accordingly. Is that clear?"

"Yes, sir."

This time Reynolds nodded. "Okay. Go back to the Hill and stay there. If we need anything further, we'll contact you."

Price rose quickly, then hesitated. "What about Tal? You won't—"

"We won't hurt him," Reynolds said. "But we will keep an eye on him until you've done your part of the job."

"And afterwards?"

"We'll let him go."

"You promise?"

"Just make sure you don't make any mistakes, and he'll be fine. Otherwise . . ."

Price nodded quickly. "I'll do what you want. Just don't hurt him. Okay?"

"We won't harm a hair on his head," Reynolds said.

Price quickly put on his coat and cap. Reynolds opened the door for him, watched him walk quickly away, then closed the door and called across the room.

"It's okay. He's gone."

The bedroom door opened immediately and the two other men came into the living room.

"I must congratulate you, Stefan," Herman Haupt said, smiling. "You should have gone on the stage."

"Thank you, Herman," Roebling said. "For a time I wasn't sure whether he would accept our story."

"You needn't have worried," Carver said softly, almost sadly.

"Oh? Why not?" Haupt asked.

Carver looked directly at the man, then turned away.

44 THE OLD CHEVROLET topped the last rise and Stefan Roebling braked to a halt. Immediately, Herman Haupt and Karl Borchers grabbed their packs and were out of the car, running across the road. Roebling followed their progress until they disappeared into the trees, then checked his watch. Beside him, Erika Huntington watched the road behind them. Roebling shifted to low gear and the car began to move. They rounded a short curve, and the fence, the double gates, the Military Police guardhouse were less than a quarter mile away.

Roebling slowed the car as they neared the gate. Two uniformed MPs, their webbed belts and holstered .45s worn outside their field jackets, came out of the gatehouse and waited. Both men's breaths were visible clouds in the cold air. Two other MPs remained inside the wooden frame building, watching.

Roebling stopped the car in response to an upheld hand. The first MP, a corporal carrying a clipboard, walked around to Roebling's window. The second, a PFC, came to the right side and peered in at Erika. Roebling rolled his window down and showed the corporal his forged Army Air Corps identification card.

"Captain Costain and Lieutenant Nash from Kirtland Field. We should have approved entry."

The corporal checked both identity cards against the day list on his clipboard, nodding as he found the names.

"Would you mind stepping out of the car, please?"

"Why?"

The corporal looked apologetic. "Orders, sir. We have to search your vehicle and each of you."

"Search us?" Roebling asked, his tone carrying irritation. "I wasn't informed that personnel searches were standard procedure—"

"They are for this base, sir. Now if you'll please step out of the car."

Erika looked at Roebling. Roebling hesitated a moment, then opened his door. Erika followed suit.

"Open your coats, please."

Roebling did. The corporal began patting him down.

"You realize, of course, that you'll have to make an exception for Lieutenant Nash."

The corporal hesitated, then looked toward the gatehouse. The sergeant first-class inside caught the look and came out. He was a large man, about thirty-five, with the noncommittal expression of a career soldier. Roebling could easily picture him in a Wehrmacht uniform without changing the expression at all. The corporal introduced him as Sergeant Mosler, then quickly explained the problem. Mosler looked at Erika.

"You'll have to make an exception, Sergeant," Roebling repeated. "I won't allow any of your men to search the lieutenant."

Mosler wasn't intimidated. "My orders are to search all visitors, Captain. Otherwise, they are not to be admitted."

Roebling started to protest further, but Erika interrupted.

"I think I can solve the problem, Sergeant."

She quickly unbuttoned her coat and slipped out of it, handing it and her purse to the PFC standing near her. Underneath, she was wearing a nurse's uniform which fit considerably tighter than regulation. Erika raised her arms and pivoted slowly. The MPs watched in open admiration.

"Will that do, Sergeant?"

Mosler cleared his throat and nodded. "All right. Check the car."

The other MPs reluctantly turned away from Erika. Roebling watched as they looked through the car's interior, under the hood and fenders, then in the trunk. As they started to open the two olive drab boxes with the white stenciling on the sides, Roebling spoke up.

"Be careful with those field kits."

"Yes, sir," the corporal said.

Sergeant Mosler walked over to look in the trunk. The corporal opened the first box carefully and looked inside.

"Just what are in all these different bottles and things, sir."

"Can't you read the stenciling, Corporal?" Roebling asked, his tone carrying a growing irritation. "Those are water-testing kits. We need those chemicals to check for bacteria in the water supplies here."

"Have we got some bad water up here, Captain?" the PFC asked.

Roebling frowned at him. "I didn't say that, Private. And I don't want you spreading any such rumor around. This is just a precautionary check. Is that clear?"

"Yes, sir."

"Are we going to be here all day?" Roebling asked, looking back at Sergeant Mosler.

The corporal also looked at Mosler. Mosler finally nodded. The corporal closed the lid on the second case and backed out from under the trunk lid. Roebling closed the trunk.

"Can we go now, Sergeant?"

Mosler met his gaze levelly.

"Give them their badges, Casey."

The corporal quickly handed out the visitors' badges.

"Wear those at all times," Mosler said. "I'll have PFC Hawkins guide you into the Provost Marshal's office in the Jeep."

"Fine."

They got back into the car while Hawkins coaxed the cold Jeep into life. The corporal unlocked the gate and opened one side enough to let both vehicles through, then pulled it shut behind them. Roebling accelerated carefully, keeping pace with the Jeep. Erika looked at him, smiling in relief.

"So far, so good."

He managed a smile for her but didn't answer.

"Oh look!"

They were emerging from a grove of trees onto an open mesa running all the way back to the ridge formed by the rim of the volcanic crater. To the right of the road was a small airstrip, just one runway extending from almost the tip of the mesa back to a stand of trees. Beyond the airstrip was the sharp drop of a tree-lined canyon, its far side rising steeply to another finger mesa, dark with snow-laden evergreens.

"It's beautiful," Erika said. "It looks like Bavaria."

"Except for this," Roebling said, looking to the left. They were passing a large wooden building about one hundred yards away, across a shallow ravine. The ugly olive-drab paint could not begin to match the richness of the trees against which it sat.

"What is that, a power plant?" Erika asked.

"I don't know," Roebling said. "It wasn't on Carver's map. Price must never have mentioned it."

They fell silent again, both imprinting the building, the terrain, the distances on their memories. Roebling took a moment to glance at Erika. She had overcome her initial reaction to the beauty of the landscape and was concentrating on landmarks. He felt a pang of regret that he had let her talk him into coming. Carver had volunteered—reluctantly—to be one of the entrants through the fence, but none of them had seriously considered him. His talents—valuable as they had been to the mission—did not include the training nor the temperament for the job.

They reached the end of the airstrip and the road curved slightly to the left. Ahead, buildings appeared, new structures, some painted, some still raw wood or tarpaper-covered, set on space obviously stolen from trees in the very recent past. Roebling could see vehicles, people moving quickly, purposefully. The place was alive with activity.

The road forked and the guide Jeep stayed to the left. As they passed the fork, the side road ran straight up the hill toward the snow-covered rim of the crater. On either side of that road stood a series of long structures, some re-sembling barracks and others more obviously warehouses and shops.

The road they were on continued southwest for a short distance, then also turned west. The guide Jeep slowed, and Roebling kept pace. This was the main street of the installation. More warehouses lined the street, inter-spersed with other facilities, including a few Army squad tents still pitched in one area. Roebling's Army back-ground allowed him to pick out certain landmarks—a mess hall there, machine shop here, motor pool farther up. None of the buildings had signs—only letter and number desig-nations.

About halfway up the street, the guide Jeep slowed and turned into a snow-packed parking lot. Roebling followed and parked beside the Jeep. PFC Hawkins waited for them on the steps and led them inside the building. They en-tered an anteroom equipped with a stove, several wooden benches for visitors and a high counter that divided the room almost in half. The layout was not unlike that of most police stations Roebling had been inside, including a radio room and operator immediately adjacent to the ser-geant's desk behind the counter.

Behind the counter, Sergeant Malcom Lowrey—in woolen winter uniform, the black MP armband covering a portion of his six stripes—listened to Hawkins' story, then looked over Roebling and Erika. Three other enlisted men behind the counter also looked at them curiously. Every-one wore clearance badges. Roebling handed the sergeant his forged orders. Lowrey read them carefully.

"I was told to see Lieutenant Price, Sergeant. Is he here?"

Lowrey nodded. "Yes, sir. I'll get him. In the meantime, would both of you please sign the visitors' log there?"

Just down the hall, Greg Allison sat across the desk from Colonel Albert Williams, the Base Provost Mar-shal. Williams was a big man, well over six feet, with the shoulders and arms of a heavyweight prizefighter—which he could have been. But he had preferred the Army. It suited his sense of order. He liked everything and everyone to be properly marked, displayed and in its place. Consequently, Allison's civilian suit and casual manner offended him slightly, although he had long since objectively accepted the need for such personnel. Still, that didn't mean that he had to like them.

"Captain Cameron is in charge of the Santa Fe detachment, Captain Allison. If he feels his men are needed for other assignments, then I won't override his decision."

"But, sir," Allison protested, "we have two German agents, maybe more, in Santa Fe right now for the express purpose of—"

"You have some proof of that, Captain?"

"I've already given you all the facts about—"

"Those were speculations, not fact."

"All right, sir, they're speculations. But that doesn't mean they aren't true. We simply can't afford to ignore the possibility—the probability that the project could be in imminent danger of sabotage by these people."

"We're not ignoring anything, Captain," Williams said. "But I'm afraid your estimate of the 'probabilities' of such an attempt are substantially higher than anyone else's. I've spoken to Captain Cameron about this matter, and I must say that I think he's given you far more cooperation than anyone could expect. Frankly, I wouldn't have let you disrupt my organization nearly to the extent that he has. Thus, I suggest that you leave a full report of your activities and suspicions with Captain Cameron and return to Baltimore. I assure you that we can adequately handle the security of this installation."

"I didn't mean to imply otherwise, sir. It's just that I know this agent very well, and I believe that he won't quit until he's made an attempt to destroy or seriously damage the work that's being performed here."

"On what do you base that assumption, Captain?"

"It's not easy to explain, sir."

"Try," Williams said, his tone making it an order.

"Well, first, he's had too many chances to quit. We were lucky to break his cover early. He was almost arrested in

Washington and had to kill one of our agents to escape."

"I know all that."

"Now in such circumstances, a normal agent would have been concerned primarily with getting out of the country. Instead, this man eluded all pursuit and made his way to Chicago. He was also almost arrested there, but he again escaped. We had him pinned down in Chicago for a time, but he figured out how we were trailing him and decoyed us to Detroit."

"Get on with it, Captain."

"Yes, sir. After Chicago, he passed up another chance to flee the country and came here, still attempting to accomplish his mission."

"You're saying he's a fanatic."

"No, sir. Fanatics don't reason—at least not nearly that well. We'd have caught a fanatic long before now."

"Then just what in hell are you saying, Captain?"

Allison took a deep breath. "I guess I'm saying that I believe this man is very intelligent, very well trained and very dedicated."

"Dedicated? What kind of an assessment is that? You sound as if you admire the man."

"I think 'admire' is too strong a word, Colonel, but I have developed a kind of respect for him. You know, the way one soldier respects another, even though they're in different—"

"I think I've heard enough, Captain," Williams said. "Your request is denied. I suggest you catch the next flight back to Baltimore."

"But, sir—"

"That's all, Captain! I don't think you understand what this is all about. This isn't some kind of game, some sport where the winners and losers shake hands after it's over, then go out together for beer. We made that mistake after the first war, and we won't make it again. When we get the Huns whipped this time, we'll keep our foot in the middle of their goddamned necks for the next fifty years. And the damned Japs too!"

Allison bit his lip. Williams was the third person to accuse him of playing games. He thought of trying Colonel

Kibler again, but the chief had already turned him down, leaving it to the judgment of the men at the site. Kibler had lost faith in him too. Why not? He was beginning to lose faith in himself. Maybe they were all right. Maybe *he* was the one who . . .

"Is there anything else, Captain?"

"No, sir. Thank you for seeing me."

45   HAD HE NOT STOPPED to thank Sergeant Lowrey for his help, Greg Allison would have been out the door and on his way to the front gate when the report came over the radio. The spotter plane, Jemez One, reported movement inside the fence, in Los Alamos Canyon below Omega Site. Allison was immediately alert.

"That could be them, Sergeant."

Lowrey was skeptical. "We get quite a few of those reports, Captain. It's mostly deer. Hell, sometimes the pilots get so bored they'll report anything just to break up—"

"Base, this is Jemez One. Confirm two intruders moving up the canyon toward Omega Site. Over."

"Roger, Jemez One," Corporal Roth, the radio operator, said.

Allison looked at Lowrey. Lowrey nodded.

"Okay, Roth. Order Alert Condition Two and—"

"Make that Condition One, Corporal," Allison interjected. "We can't assume that—"

"Ignore that order!" Colonel Williams barked, coming down the hallway.

Allison looked around. "But, sir—"

"We're not going to upset the civilians for two lost hunters, Captain."

"Sir, we don't know—"

"I'll handle this, Captain," Williams said. "Corporal Roth, broadcast Alert Condition Two and give the intruders' location. Sergeant Lowrey, get your teams on these people. I want men above and below them in the canyon in five minutes."

"Yes, sir," Lowrey said, picking up the telephone.

Allison started for the door.

"Where're you going, Captain?" Williams asked.

"To Omega Site, Colonel."

Williams started to call him back, then decided to let him go.

Stefan Roebling braked the Chevrolet cautiously, watching the Jeep in front of him. Since leaving the Provost Marshal's office, they had driven west, topped a rise with a small power house and frozen cooling pond, then passed a series of barracks-style apartment buildings. According to Carver's information, the top scientists lived here. The buildings were named "Bathtub Row" because their inhabitants were among the few lucky enough to have one of those prized conveniences. Black coal smoke had been visible from the fireplace chimneys as they passed.

The road had continued on through a thick stand of pine, then reached an intersection. To their left, next to the canyon drop-off, sat a small wooden building clearly marked. It was a hospital. To the right, the road ran northward along the outer base of the crater rim, an area mostly covered by trees but showing the effects of clearing, of new construction. All through the area Roebling had seen new buildings rising and more areas being cleared. The activity was constant.

Hawkins' Jeep turned left, passed the hospital, then turned right, beginning a descent into the canyon. Roebling followed at a safe distance, focusing his attention on the narrow roadway. The packed snow was slick and dangerous in spots. They descended sharply along the face of the canyon wall, reached the canyon floor and passed a turn-off leading down the canyon, toward Omega Site. According to Roebling's watch, Haupt and Borchers should be getting close to that site by now. It had been a gamble, splitting the team, but it doubled their chances of seriously damaging the project. If either one of them succeeded . . .

"Watch it, Stefan," Erika said.

Roebling looked up quickly. The road curved sharply back to the left in the narrow canyon floor, reversing itself for the climb out onto the adjacent mesa. But the Jeep was not gaining speed for the climb. In fact, the brake lights showed it was stopping. Roebling eased the car to a halt.

"What do you think?" Erika asked.

"I don't know," Roebling answered.

Erika quickly opened her coat and pulled the bottom of the uniform up almost to her waist. Taped to the inside of her right thigh, above the stocking top, was the small automatic. She grimaced as she ripped the tape loose. PFC Hawkins stepped out of the Jeep and began walking back toward the car.

"Keep that out of sight," Roebling said. "He may just want to caution us about the road ahead."

Roebling opened his door and stepped out. Hawkins stopped in front of him.

"What's the problem?"

"We've had an alert, sir," Hawkins said. "There are intruders on the base. The air cover spotted them in this canyon."

"Then I suggest we keep moving, get on over to—"

"No, sir, we can't do that," Hawkins said. "We'll have to go back to the Provost Marshal's office until—"

"That's nonsense, Private!" Roebling said angrily. "We're almost there! Now get back in that Jeep and drive on!"

"No, sir," Hawkins said adamantly. "We have strict orders for this kind of thing. You'll have to back down to the Omega Site turn-off and—"

The sharp bark of the automatic seemed unnaturally loud in the stillness. A puff of dust, of cloth fibers, seemed to leap from Hawkins' field jacket as the bullet struck his chest. He staggered backward in surprise, then fell heavily.

Roebling went after him. By the time he knelt over the body, the eyes were already glazing. Roebling lifted him quickly, grunting at the strain on the bad leg, and started for the Jeep.

Greg Allison came into the canyon too fast and locked up the brakes trying to make the turn into the Omega Site road. The Plymouth skidded sideways and came to a halt with its nose almost against a tree. It took a moment of rocking the car back and forth before the back tires caught and the nose came around. He was almost back to the road to Omega Site when he noticed the fresh tire tracks going into the stub road leading up the canyon. He stopped, checking the area. A Jeep was parked just beyond some trees. He could see part of the vehicle but no signs of life. He looked down the canyon toward Omega Site. There was no traffic as far as he could see. Cursing himself for wasting time, Allison set the handbrake on the Plymouth and jumped out, leaving the motor idling.

He approached the Jeep cautiously, .38 in hand, watching the vehicle, the surrounding trees. PFC Hawkins' body was in the back, jammed down in between the seat backs and the radio. It took only a moment to determine that he was dead. Allison pulled the body to one side, uncovering the transmitter microphone. He picked it up and tried to contact the base. No one answered. He tried again, checking the frequency knob. Again, no answer. The switches were on. He pulled the body farther to the side and looked down under the brace on which the radio was mounted. The power wires had been ripped loose. Allison let the body fall back and ran for the Plymouth.

In the car, he spun the rear wheels heading into the Omega Site road, then just as suddenly locked them up again. It didn't make sense. Why would they try to hit Omega Site from two directions? And if the first two intruders were decoys, then what other site would the other intruders be after? Omega Site held the reactor. What other target would as seriously damage the project as . . . He froze in horror. My God, this was Friday! He slammed the car into reverse and began backing around again.

46 THE TECHNICAL AREA HEADQUARTERS was yet another of the two-story wooden buildings, constructed like a barracks but containing offices for the director, administrative personnel and a conference room for the colloquia. There were a number of mud-splattered cars in the graveled parking lot as Allison slid the Plymouth to a halt in front of the walk. He killed the engine and took the keys but left the driver's door hanging open as he ran up the slippery wooden walk toward the door.

Just inside the door was a small reception area with an MP corporal behind a desk. Allison flipped out his credentials.

"Has anyone you don't know entered this area in the last thirty minutes?"

The corporal looked puzzled. "What do you mean, sir?"

"Visitors, damnit!" Allison snapped, grabbing up the log book. He read down the names and times quickly.

"Do you know this Captain Costain?"

"No, sir, but he—"

"What about this Lieutenant Nash? Do you know him?"

"It's a her—I mean she's a nurse. She—"

"A woman? What does she look like?"

The corporal shrugged. "Well, sir, she's about five-four, maybe one-fifteen, very pretty with black hair and blue eyes—"

"Where are they now?" Allison demanded.

"Somewhere inside. They're checking our water supply for—"

"Get on that phone!" Allison ordered. "Tell Colonel Williams that Novalis and Erika Huntington are in the Tech Area Headquarters, then follow me."

The man looked puzzled. "Who did you say—"

"Forget the names! Just say two German agents!"

"German—"

"Make the call, Corporal!"

"Yes, sir!"

Allison drew his .38 and started down the hall, forcing himself not to run, checking each office cautiously as he passed. They could be anywhere, but he was betting that Novalis had only one target in mind. The conference room. It was now almost four o'clock, and each Friday at three-thirty the director held a colloquium of all the top scientists at the laboratory. The very thought tightened the muscles in Allison's chest, restricted his breathing.

In one room just down the hall and around the corner were Robert Oppenheimer, Enrico Fermi, Edward Teller, Hans Bethe, Niels Bohr, Leo Szilard—perhaps even Albert Einstein, who was an occasional visitor. Two hand grenades. One ball of plastic explosive the size of a man's fist. Novalis wasn't trying to damage the project, to delay it. He intended to destroy it totally by killing the only people who could build such a weapon.

Allison reached the corner of the hallway and stopped, flattening himself against the wall. Footsteps were coming up behind him. He looked around quickly, saw the now white-faced corporal and motioned him against the wall beside him.

"I called—"

Allison cut him off, holding a finger to his lips for silence. The corporal nodded and drew his .45. Allison took as deep a breath as his constricted muscles would allow, then looked around the edge of the wall cautiously.

Around the corner, the hall opened into a small bay containing a secretary's desk, chairs for visitors and two closed doors. The door behind the secretary was marked "Director" and the other door—the one in the far wall—led into the conference room. There were three people in the bay. Dr. Oppenheimer's secretary stood beside her desk, chatting with a nurse whose long black hair came below the shoulders of the white uniform. The third person—a man in an Army overcoat—was bending over an open field kit near the water cooler on the far wall. As Allison watched, he glanced over his shoulder at the two women, then reached into the bottom of the kit and lifted out a gray object. Allison stepped out from behind the wall, leveling the .38.

"Hold it right there!"

All three people looked at him. Allison recognized Erika Huntington immediately and felt a surge of triumph. Finally. Finally! The man rose slowly, a molded ball of plastic explosive in his right hand, the silver pencil detonator already embedded in the ball. He fit most of the descriptions that Allison had seen, but they had not caught the essence of the man. Allison smiled at him, feeling magnanimous, even kindly toward him.

"It was a good try, Novalis."

The man's expression didn't change.

"Captain Allison!"

Oppenheimer's secretary had recovered from her initial shock and was angry. She started toward him.

"What do you mean coming in here with a gun! Dr. Oppenheimer will be furious—"

"Don't get into the line of—"

He was too late. Erika ducked behind her, drawing the automatic. Allison dodged back, running into the MP as Erika brought the gun up. The secretary stopped and looked back—directly into the muzzle of the automatic. The shock hit her again and she backed away on rubbery legs, still blocking Allison's line of fire. Novalis was moving.

"Out the back! Let's go!"

They ran down the hall. Allison pushed the secretary to one side roughly.

"Go out the front, Corporal! Cut them off!"

The MP ran back up the hall. Allison ran after Novalis and Erika. As he reached the back door he slowed, then changed his mind and burst through it. The walk in front of him was empty. He swung around. Novalis and Erika were nearing the corner of the bulding to his left, trying to run in the knee-deep snow.

"Halt or I'll fire!"

Erika threw up her arm and the automatic cracked. Allison reacted automatically, firing the .38 three times before he could stop himself. Novalis grabbed his right thigh and went down on one knee. Erika tried to fire again, but he caught her arm.

"No! Help me!"

She pulled him around the corner of the building as Allison began running toward them. He slowed as he neared the corner, expecting to see a hand, the pistol at any moment.

"The window! Throw it through the window!"

Allison put on a burst of speed, suddenly realizing that they were on the side of the building with the conference room. He cleared the corner and slid to a halt. Novalis was down in the snow just beyond the corner, one hand still holding his wounded leg. Erika had struggled another thirty feet and was nearing the conference-room windows.

"Hold it, Mrs. Huntington!"

She looked back, the automatic in her right hand and the ball of plastic explosive in her left. Just at that moment the first window of the conference room was raised, and a man stuck his head out. Allison recognized the lean face, the aquiline nose immediately.

"What in the hell is going on out here? Don't you people know we're having a—"

"Get back!" Allison shouted. "For God's sake, shut that—"

The crack of the automatic and the blow to his side were almost instantaneous. He staggered a step, then caught himself, fighting for balance. He couldn't breathe. He could only watch, almost uncomprehendingly, as Erika dropped the automatic and shifted the plastic explosive to her right hand. Dr. Robert Oppenheimer finally realized the danger and ducked back inside, jerking on the window. It stuck and Oppenheimer's attempts to close it became frantic. Allison managed to inhale shallowly and raise his arm, only to discover that the .38 was no longer in his hand. He looked down and saw the gleam of metal in the snow near his foot, but it seemed a hundred miles away. He looked up as Erika drew back her arm to throw the explosive.

He tried to yell at her, distract her, but only managed a hoarse croak. It was a nightmare, played in slow motion on a stark background—the glaringly white snow, the olive-drab paint on the building, the pale, pale blue of the winter sky. Erika's hand started forward. Then, suddenly, some unseen force, some vicious fist, smashed into her chest, lifting her off her feet and turning her around in the air. Allison watched the gray ball escape her fingers and make a short arc before disappearing into the snow. He involuntarily shut his eyes, expecting a huge blast, oblivion.

When he opened them again, Erika was lying perfectly still, face down, her white uniform blending into the snow. The corporal was wading toward them through the snow from the other end of the building, his .45 now trained toward Novalis. Novalis was still holding his leg, his head hanging, his eyes averted from Erika's body. Allison felt his careful balance begin to waver. His body was not functioning very well. He couldn't focus his eyes, maintain his concentration. Someone was at the window again, talking to the corporal or to him—he could not tell. He decided that he'd better get off his feet, but he was no longer sure which way was down. He tried to bend his locked knees, to kneel down, but he suddenly tipped forward and the soft snow rushed up to meet him.

47 IT WAS FOUR DAYS before Greg Allison persuaded the doctors at the Los Alamos hospital to allow him into a wheelchair and let an aide push him down the hall to Stefan Roebling's heavily guarded room. He finally argued successfully that if he was strong enough to dictate an hour-long report to a stenographer, to survive three visits by Colonel Williams and two by General Groves, then he was certainly up to a fifty-foot trip down the hall. Major Gilbert, the surgeon who repaired the damage to his side, laughed at the comparison but ultimately agreed, warning him that he would put a strict time limit on the meeting.

There were two MPs outside Roebling's room and another inside. Allison finally persuaded them to leave him alone with Roebling, promising to yell if Roebling tried to get his handcuffed arm free of the bed frame and leap out the window. When they were alone, Allison leaned back in the wheelchair, taking deep breaths to clear a slight dizziness, inspecting the face of the man lying on the bed. Roebling's expression was carefully neutral.

"They tell me you won't say anything, won't talk to anyone," Allison said.

"I gave them my name, rank and serial number, Captain Allison. Would you like me to repeat them for you?"

Allison shook his head. "How's your leg?"

Roebling hesitated, then shrugged. "No bones were broken. How badly were you hit?"

"The bullet missed the kidney. The doctors say I'll be good as new in a month or so."

"Then you're lucky. Erika is . . . Erika was a very good shot."

"I know."

Both men were silent a moment. Roebling was looking at the sheet covering his legs, but his eyes were far away.

Allison cleared his throat. "Did they tell you that the two men in the canyon were killed?"

Roebling looked up.

"They refused to surrender," Allison explained.

Roebling nodded. "They would. They were good men."

"There's something else you should know," Allison said. "Whatever you may tell us will no longer hurt any of your comrades. Admiral Canaris has been removed from command of the Abwehr, and the agency has been put under the SD. A number of the top Abwehr people fled to Switzerland and traded information to our OSS for asylum."

Roebling lifted an eyebrow, then allowed himself a small smile.

"A good try, Captain, but it won't work. I don't believe you."

"It's true," Allison said. "The admiral was blamed for the collapse of Abwehr operations in Argentina and Spain. He was also accused of collaborating with dissidents who want to overthrow Hitler and negotiate an end to the war."

Allison detected a slight change in the smile, a lessening of the skepticism.

"Even if all you say is true, Captain, I still won't tell you anything."

Allison shrugged. "I'm not asking for any military information. I just want to know more about you personally."

Roebling's smile returned fully. "Don't tell me that you're already writing your memoirs, Captain."

Allison smiled in return. "It wouldn't do any good if I was. This will all be classified for a very long time to come."

"Then why do you ask?"

"You led me a very long chase, Captain. In fact, you almost brought off your mission. You were a very worthy opponent."

"Worthy opponent?"

Allison shrugged again. "Perhaps that was a poor choice of words, but I came to feel that we almost were playing some kind of chess. I had the home field and all the resources of the Army, and you had just six people, but you still almost beat me."

Roebling laughed scornfully, then suddenly stopped, his eyes filling with caution.

"Another good try, Captain. I almost told you whether you had now accounted for all the remaining Abwehr agents in the country."

"It wasn't a trick," Allison said. "We've already picked up the ones still alive. Lieutenant Price was very willing to tell us about Tal Carver after your attempt on the colloquium. And Carver told us about Rodolfo Aguilar in the Argentine Embassy. And Dockery and Owen are dead. We even know about North, thanks to your Captain von Schroeder. By the way, you might be interested to know that Major Jost was executed a few weeks ago for trying to sabotage your operation."

Roebling was silent.

"So you can see that the Abwehr doesn't have anyone left in America, except for a couple of double agents who happen to be working for the FBI."

Roebling slowly shook his head. "Why would you tell me all this?"

"To convince you that—"

"You really do believe that this was some kind of game, don't you, Captain?"

"I didn't say—"

"Yes, you did!" Roebling said, his sudden anger surprising Allison. "We played a game, move and counter-move, and now it's over, so you want me to understand just how completely you've won! Well, it wasn't a game, Captain. There was too much at stake for me to consider it a game. I lost—more than I would ever put into any game. So why don't you go away! Leave me alone!"

Roebling turned away, looking out the window. Allison made an effort to control his own anger, breathing deeply.

"If you're worried about being executed as a spy—"

"Worried!" Roebling looked back, laughing harshly. "Captain, right now I'd almost welcome a firing squad!"

"Well, you won't get one," Allison snapped.

"Of course not," Roebling said. "You Americans have to keep up your pretensions. There'll be the trial first, with some defense attorney pretending to defend me vigorously, then they strap me into an electric chair and—"

"You won't be executed," Allison stated flatly.

Roebling laughed again, an ugly, sarcastic sound. "I'm not a fool, Captain. And you aren't being kind by trying to—"

"You have too much information about this facility, this project, that the government can't afford to have made public in a trial."

"Then there'll be no trial," Roebling said. "You will simply execute me."

"That's unconstitutional—even in wartime," Allison said.

Roebling's expression changed, becoming less sarcastic, less antagonistic, tempered with a slight incredulity.

"Then what will you do with me? Put me in one of your maximum-security prisons to rot until—"

"We can't. You might tell the guards something they aren't cleared to hear."

"Then what other alternative is there?"

"You're going to be sent to the same place that military personnel here are sent when they don't keep their mouths shut. You're going to spend the rest of the war on an American-held atoll somewhere in the South Pacific."

"Are you serious?" Roebling asked incredulously.

"Everyone who knows about this project is either dead

or in American hands, Captain. So General Groves has decided that the best thing to do with you is put you completely out of touch with anyone until the war is over. I expect you'll have a few friends to keep you company—Captain von Schroeder, Tal Carver, even ex-Lieutenant Price. From what I hear, there are plenty of Americans there to guard you."

Roebling's skepticism faded for a few moments, then reappeared slightly.

"So we have a reprieve—but only until the war is over. Then—"

"I don't think any of you will ever be tried, Captain. By that time you'll have been in custody a year, maybe two, without even a hearing. That would severely prejudice the prosecution of your case. And no one will care by then anyway. I expect that you'll be held a while longer—until things settle down—then allowed to return to Germany or wherever."

Roebling was silent for a time, the skepticism gone, replaced by something quiet, sad.

"I apologize for my earlier remarks, Captain Allison. Perhaps you are right. Perhaps this is all just a game of some sort, and we Europeans have forgotten how to play it. We take it too seriously."

It was Allison's turn to think, to study the other man.

"You surprise me, Captain. I thought you no longer cared whether you lived or died."

"I don't," Roebling said. "I was thinking of someone else."

"Mrs. Huntington?"

Roebling nodded. "Ironic, isn't it? All I had to do was give up, turn myself in, and you'd sentence both of us to a South Seas island for the rest of the war. Now . . ."

He didn't finish. Allison watched him, letting the silence grow, holding back the smile. Finally, he spoke.

"She isn't dead, Captain."

Roebling's head jerked up.

"If that is some type of cruel joke—"

"She's upstairs in intensive care," Allison said. "It was touch-and-go for a couple of days, but Major Gilbert is a topnotch surgeon. He took out her right lung and repaired a large number of damaged blood vessels. Those forty-fives really hit a person hard, but she's pretty much out of the woods now. I expect she'll be joining you on that island in about a month or so."

Roebling closed his eyes, as if offering a prayer of thanks. When he opened them he was smiling.

"Thank you, Captain Allison. I wish I had a better way to say it, but thank you for telling me."

"You're welcome."

An MP stuck his head in the door.

"The doctor says time's up, Captain."

"All right," Allison said. He looked back at Roebling. "I'll try to see you again before you go."

Roebling nodded. "I'd like that."

The MP came in and turned Allison's wheelchair around, heading for the door.

"Captain Allison."

Allison stopped the chair by dropping one hand on a wheel.

"What?"

"Are you a career soldier?"

The question surprised him.

"No. I mean, I didn't go through West Point. But I haven't thought beyond the end of the war."

"Then I advise you to get out as soon as the war is over. Go back to whatever you were in civilian life or start all over, but get out of the CIC."

The thought of his father's law office in Chicago seemed especially distasteful at the moment. He was surprised that Roebling—of all people—would even suggest such a thing. Roebling read the expression on his face.

"You aren't going to take my advice, are you?"

"I'll think about it," Allison said. "If you'll tell me why you suggested it."

"It's simple. I've come to like you."

"I'm afraid I don't understand."

"Don't you? It can't remain a game forever—not for anyone."